BETWEEN DARK AND LIGHT

AN ALLISON HART NOVEL
BOOK 3

ROBIN MAHLE

HARP House Publishing, LLC.

Published by HARP House Publishing
May 2020 (1st edition)

1

The demise of yet another once-gleaming retail beacon was relegated by the local news broadcast to the ticker at the bottom of the screen. Reminiscent of the NASA missions of the 1970s, Americans just didn't care anymore. Nevertheless, the imminent closure of the East Citrus Park Mall in Tampa meant bargains galore for Tabitha Barnes, a wife and mother who counted every penny.

The need for a new set of crisp white sheets was what drew her to the giant red tag, going out of business sale at the mall's flagship department store. At those prices, Tabitha considered a new blanket too. However, five-year-old Hayden Barnes, Tabitha's son, had something else in mind. The impatient boy was eager to leave and relentlessly tugged on his mother while she studied the bargain sheets. "Are we done yet? I'm tired of standing here."

"We're almost finished." Tabitha reached for the sheets and the nearby coordinating blanket. "Okay. Let's go to the checkout counter." She hurried through the aisle while the boy spiraled into a near meltdown, nearly running into a man who stood nearby. "Oh, I'm so sorry. Excuse me."

"That's okay, ma'am." He smiled politely.

Embarrassed, Tabitha turned to her son. "Hayden, please behave. You made me run into that nice man."

The register was in sight and as Tabitha approached, she was fourth in line. Not ideal, but what was a few more minutes of waiting? Anyone with a cranky kindergartener could present plenty of evidence to the contrary.

Hayden clawed at Tabitha's arm. "I want to go now."

"I know you do, sweetheart. Just a few more minutes, okay? I have to pay for this stuff."

He groaned and flailed like a puppet whose strings had knotted. But as luck would have it, something of interest captured his attention. Boxes of superhero action figures were displayed on a nearby shelf. The man his mother had bumped into now held one of them in his hand. He looked at Hayden, presenting to him one of the chisel-jawed savers of the planet.

Hayden shook his head with disapproval.

The man picked up a different one and with his eyebrows raised in silent request, he appeared to wait for the boy's nod.

Hayden looked at his mother as she stepped a few inches closer to the register with her back to him. He walked toward the man and pointed to the shelf. "This one. He's the best."

"He is, huh?" The man nodded. "You probably know more about these things than I do. What's your name?"

"Hayden. Is that for your son?"

The man chuckled. "I don't have a son, but I have a nephew and his birthday is coming up. I think he's about your age."

"I'm five," Hayden proudly held his fingers in the air.

"You know what? I'm going to get this one. And as a thank you for helping me make the right choice," the man shoved his hand in his pants pocket and retrieved a coin. "Have you ever seen one of these?"

Hayden peered at his hand. "It's a nickel."

"Ah, but not just any nickel. This one is very special." The man turned it over. "It has a buffalo on it. They don't make these anymore. Would you like it?"

Hayden glanced back to his mother who had reached the cashier.

Tabitha placed the sheets and blanket on the checkout counter. "Hi, how are you?"

"Doing all right and you?" The woman scanned the items.

"Good, thanks. I almost didn't make it in here today, but I knew I wanted to get in on the deals before it was too late."

"Well, you snuck in under the wire. Store closes next week." The cashier bagged the items. "That'll be $53.25, please."

"That is a bargain. Makes the trip worth it." Tabitha inserted her card into the reader.

"Thank you so much, ma'am." The woman handed her the receipt. "Enjoy your day."

"You too, thanks." Tabitha turned around and the smile she wore faded. "Hayden?" Her eyes darted around the counter between the other people in line. "Hayden? Where are you?" She turned to the woman behind her. "Did you see a little boy around here?"

"I just got in line, I'm sorry," she replied.

Tabitha's heart jumped into her throat. "Hayden?" Her voice grew louder, and customers turned in her direction. She walked toward the aisles and down each one calling his name, her heart racing faster as each moment passed.

Other shoppers came to her aid and called out for the boy too. One of them approached the cashier. "Can you call security, please? It looks like a boy is missing."

Tabitha made her way to the escalators. "Hayden?" she screamed. "Hayden Barnes." She looked downstairs at the faces peering up at her. She could see them covering their mouths, their faces wearing the fear she wore, probably thanking God they weren't in her shoes.

Her hands trembled and she dropped the plastic bag that hung from her wrist. A dizzying, sinking feeling washed over her and her knees weakened. Tears streamed down her cheeks and her mouth turned dry. "Somebody took my son." She gripped the railing near the escalator, and at the top of her lungs, she screamed, "Somebody took my son!"

ONE YEAR LATER

THE CHECKOUT LINE WAS THREE DEEP WHEN ALLISON HART stepped behind those waiting. She placed her sunglasses on her head and smoothed out her fitted button-down blouse. In her hand was a box of allergy tablets. She waited inside the independently run pharmacy owned by Arlene and Jeffrey Godwin. The quaint drug store had withstood competition from the likes of Walmart, Walgreens, and many others because the people who shopped there appreciated the personal service.

The purchase was a means to get to the register and size up the 27-year-old woman who stood behind it. Sure, it was smack-dab in the middle of springtime in Tampa and allergy season was in full swing, but Allison never suffered from hay fever or other such maladies. Instead, she stood in the line because Arlene and Jeffrey suspected the cashier was stealing from the store and hired ACL Investigative Services to find out.

"Good afternoon." The cashier wore her hair in a short brown bob and donned a pleasant smile while taking the box of tablets and scanning in the barcode. "Will that be all for you?"

Allison brushed away strands of blonde hair that had fallen from her bun and returned the cordial greeting with a smile of her own. "Yes, thank you. You know, it's refreshing to see a successful independent store like this. There are so few anymore."

"I agree. I'm lucky to work here. The owners are very generous to the employees. Here's your receipt, ma'am."

"Thank you." Allison took the receipt and kept her eyes on the woman. "It would be a shame to see this place go out of business. The owners work so hard."

The woman's smile faltered. "Have a nice day."

"You, too." Allison walked out of the store and returned to her car. She slipped inside her trusted old blue Honda Civic and dropped the bag onto her passenger seat. With her phone in her hand, Allison made the call. "Charlie, I'm in the parking lot. They're closing in half an hour. I'm going to wait until I see her come out."

"The owners talked to the bank. I'm heading over there now. We'll meet up when it's done," Charlie replied.

"Yep. See you soon."

"Hey, Alli? What if she suspects something's up?" Charlie asked.

"As long as the bank teller doesn't act like something's wrong, things should go smoothly. You'll be in the back with the branch manager. Nothing will appear out of the ordinary. Don't worry. This will be smooth like butter."

"Butter clogs your arteries," Charlie quipped.

"Stop worrying. I'll see you later." Allison ended the call and waited for the store to close. The sun had dipped below the tree line and the parking lot was almost empty. She had parked near the far end of the lot next to a furniture store.

Bayshore Pharmacy was anchored at the corner of the small strip mall located on the south end of the city. Arlene and Jeffrey had knocked on the door of ACL Investigative Services two weeks ago, distraught by the idea one of their employees was embezzling. They had asked the partners, Allison, Charlie, and Lucy to look into the matter, not wanting to go to the police until they were certain of their accusations. And maybe not even then.

The team started digging and now they were ready to prove to the owners that they had a thief in their ranks.

As the skies dimmed and the streetlamps flickered on, the cashier named Joslyn emerged from the store and locked its doors. Allison studied her while remaining hunkered down in her car.

Joslyn pulled out of the parking lot and turned onto the road. Allison already knew the destination—Union Key Bank. Today was Friday and the weekly cash deposit was made every Friday at 7 pm sharp. Most folks used electronic forms of payment so whatever cash was brought in was placed in the safe until the end of the week.

Allison turned the key in her ignition and inched toward the road before turning on her headlights. According to the owners, Joslyn was responsible for making the weekly deposits and had done so for the past six months. Only in the last two months did they notice something was amiss with the receipts. Arlene and Jeffrey conveyed Joslyn's weekly routine. She would go inside and hand over the blue envelope to the cashier. A receipt would be handed back and Joslyn would leave.

So where was the disconnect? It had taken some time, but Allison and Charlie got to know Joslyn and her routines. They uncovered her inner circle through social media and soon realized she had a friend who worked at Union Key Bank.

Joslyn arrived, right on time, and stepped out of her car. In her hands was the blue canvas envelope. Allison parked nearby and retrieved her phone to send the text to Charlie. *"She's here. Get ready."*

———

Joslyn walked inside and approached the merchant teller.

"Hi there, what can I help you with today?" The teller wore a wide smile and smoothed down his blue tie.

"Hi, Mario," Joslyn began. "How are you today?"

"Doing well, thanks. Glad it's Friday. Are you making a deposit?"

She lowered her gaze and peered at the envelope. "Yep. Here you go." She placed it on the counter.

"One moment and I'll get you your receipt." Mario unzipped the envelope and began counting the money and matching it up against the deposit slip. The cash was short by $200 from what was written on the slip. "So, the grand total is $4,322?"

"You got it. I believe that's what I wrote on the deposit slip," Joslyn replied.

"I'll just give this a second count." He laid out the bills in front of her and counted aloud. When he reached the end, the $200 shortage became clear. "$4,322, right?"

Joslyn looked at him with growing concern and discomfort. "That's right. That's what I have written down. Is there something wrong, Mario?"

"No. Not at all."

Joslyn spotted the look in his eyes, then noticed the bank manager hurrying toward her.

The manager's hand gripped her arm. "You're making the deposit for Bayshore Pharmacy?"

"Yes, I am." Her voice cracked. "Let go of me. What are you doing?"

"Ma'am, why don't you follow me? There's no need to make a scene." The manager held her gaze.

Joslyn wriggled from the manager's grip and ran to the door.

"Grab her!" He yelled.

A security guard who stood on the other side of the bank rushed toward her, but she'd already reached the glass doors. Joslyn ran through, looking over her shoulder as the guard drew closer.

His gun at the ready, he yelled, "Stop!"

Allison stood outside the doors, positioning herself in Joslyn's path when the two collided. They fell to the ground and Allison wrestled the woman's arms. "You really want a bullet in your back? Is 200 bucks a week worth your life?"

The guard straddled the two of them and pulled Allison away before yanking the woman to her feet.

Allison dusted off her clothes and straightened the now-cockeyed bun on top of her head.

Charlie ran outside, her stout features making for a slower stride. All the while, her black spikey hair, capable of withstanding 20-mile-an-hour winds, hadn't budged. "Alli, are you okay?"

"Fine." She blew away the hair that had fallen on her face. "I'm fine."

———

THE OFFICE OF ACL INVESTIGATIVE SERVICES WAS OPEN FOR business thanks to Lucy's early arrival. Lucy Boyce, the 20-year-old daughter of Allison's all-too-brief mentor, Tommy Boyce, knew her way around the industry and had helped form the partnership.

When Allison and Charlie entered, a fresh pot of coffee awaited them.

"Ah, coffee." Allison dropped her bag on her desk and headed straight for the pot. "Anyone else care for a cup?"

"Yes, please," Charlie began. "I'm still two cups short of my daily quota."

"I'm okay for right now, Allison, thanks," Lucy added.

"What time did you get in?" Allison asked.

"About 7:30. No big deal. It's nice to get a few things done before the phones start ringing."

"You mean before Alli and I start yakking? These phones don't exactly ring off the hook. Not yet." Charlie sat down at her desk. "Arlene and Jeffrey are coming in around 10 to close out the case file and settle the bill."

"I'll print up the final statement." Lucy turned to her computer. "It seemed like an easy, open-and-shut case, huh?"

Allison walked back to her desk. "I think the owners were disappointed more than anything, thinking one of their employees could do something like that. For us? No crooked politicians, no dangerous gangs. Yeah, it was a cakewalk compared to that. I wouldn't mind more cases like that one."

"What did the lady have to say for herself?" Lucy added.

"We didn't stick around for her statement," Charlie began, "but I cozied up to one of the detectives and asked how it went down."

"How it went down?" Allison eyed her. "Been watching cop shows again?"

"As I was saying," Charlie winked back, "the detective said she'd been skimming at her other jobs too. The owners never checked her references when she was hired on, but if they had, they might've thought twice. No one could prove anything until we came along."

"Maybe we'll get a five-star review on Yelp." Allison sipped on her coffee. "Do we have anything on the docket for today?"

Lucy pulled up the schedule. "Apart from closing out this case, we don't have any other meetings today."

Allison nodded. "Then I guess Charlie should call that detective she buddied up to and ask him to throw us a bone."

———

HER SURGERY WAS SCHEDULED FOR 7 AM, LESS THAN AN HOUR away. Tabitha Barnes secured the hospital gown and slid under the covers of the bed. She looked at her soon-to-be ex-husband, Erik. "Well, it's almost time. Thank you for driving me here this morning. Mom's still kind of sick and she didn't want to take a chance giving me anything while I'm recovering."

"It's fine, Tabby. I don't mind. I'm glad I could help. This is a simple, routine procedure. You'll be in and out and I'll take you home later today."

She tucked her short brown hair behind her ears. "I know. I'm not worried. I've been through worse."

Erik nodded. "We both have, and we've survived. This will be a walk in the park."

The doctor knocked on the door and gently pushed it open. "Okay, Tabitha. We're ready for you." He looked at Erik. "We'll take good care of her. When she's in recovery, a nurse will come to get you."

"Thanks, Doc." Erik turned to Tabitha a final time. "You'll do great. See you on the other side."

The orderlies wheeled her out of the room and through the halls of the hospital. The lights in the ceiling stung her eyes.

"Okay, Mrs. Barnes. Here we are." A nurse pushed the button that opened the doors to the operating room.

Tabitha was wheeled to the center and lifted onto a table. A large spotlight hovered over her, though it was turned off. Doctors and nurses entered the room. One of the nurses placed a warm, heavy blanket over her. "Thank you."

"It gets pretty cold in here." The nurse patted her legs.

Another doctor sat down and slid in his chair to her head. "Tabitha, I'm Dr. Jimenez, the anesthesiologist. I'm going to start your IV."

Tabitha lay on the table amid the organized chaos as the staff prepared for surgery. Instruments were wheeled in on carts. Machines that monitored her vitals were turned on.

"How you doing, Tabitha?" Dr. Jimenez asked.

"Fine."

"Good. I'm going to place this mask over your face now and I want you to count backward from 100 for me."

She nodded while he placed the mask over her mouth. "100, 99, 98." Her eyes closed.

———

TABITHA WALKED ALONE IN A MALL PARKING LOT. THE clouds were dark and raced across the sky. On examining her body, only a thin hospital gown covered her, and her feet were bare. She shivered and wrapped her arms around her midsection. The place was deserted. No cars anywhere. As she looked back at the buildings of the mall, they appeared shuttered. Plywood on the glass doors. Graffiti on the block walls.

"Hello?" Tabitha took careful steps. Glass from broken bottles lay all around her. "Is anyone here?" Her skin raised with goosebumps as a light wind blew through the thin gown.

"Mommy?"

She whipped around. "Hayden? Hayden, is that you?" Tabitha

hurried to the boy who stood only feet away. Glass sliced her feet, but she continued with barely a flinch. "Baby, what are you doing here? How are you here?"

"Mommy, I'm okay." The boy of only five grinned.

Tears streamed down Tabitha's cheeks. She took Hayden by the arms and pulled him close in a tight embrace. "Oh, baby. I've missed you so much. I've never stopped thinking about you. Not once."

"Why didn't you come find me?" His deep blue eyes pierced right through her, burrowing into her heart.

"We tried. Daddy and I tried. The police. We all tried. But you're here now. We can go home now."

Hayden opened the palm of his hand and held it out.

"What is that? What are you holding, sweetheart?" Tabitha peered at it. "I don't understand. Where did you get this?"

"He gave it to me."

She wore confusion on her face. "Who gave it to you? Hayden, who gave this to you?" She picked up the coin from his palm.

"The man with no hair." Hayden turned back as if something had caught his attention. When he returned to Tabitha, he continued. "I have to go now, Mommy."

Panic infused in her tone, and she trembled wildly. "No. No, you can't leave. We're going home now, Hayden. It's time for Mommy to take you home." She tugged on his arm, but he wouldn't budge.

"I can't go home, Mommy."

———

"Tabitha? It's time to wake up. Can you hear me?"

Her eyes fluttered and her brain felt enshrouded in wool.

"There you are," the doctor smiled. "The surgery went well.

We removed your gallbladder. Tabitha, do you know where you are?"

Her eyes opened into slits and she tried to focus on the doctor, but his face was blurred. "In the hospital."

"That's right. You're in the recovery room. The nurse has gone to find your husband."

Focus returned to her and so had something else. A sudden, terrible urge to break down into tears overcame her.

"Hey, hey now. It's all right. It's just the anesthesia wearing off. You're okay." The doctor patted her hand and turned to see Erik walk in with the nurse.

"Why is she crying?" Erik rushed to her side. "Tabby? Tabby, are you okay?"

"Some people come out of sedation in odd ways. There's nothing to be worried about. She'll settle down in a few minutes," the doctor said.

Erik took hold of her hand. "Tabby, it's me. It's Erik. You're okay. You just came out of surgery. The doctor says you're doing great."

"He was there, Erik. I held him in my arms. He was there." She turned away and continued to sob.

"Who was there? It was just the medication. It was a dream," he said.

"He was there. I swear to you, Hayden was there." She covered her face with her hands.

"I'm sorry, who is Hayden?" the doctor asked.

Erik peered at him. "He's our son. He went missing a year ago."

2

It had been financial touch-and-go since ACL Investigative Services opened its doors, but creative budgeting had helped the team stay afloat. There was no mistaking, however, that no one was getting rich. The important thing Allison tried to remember was that she was doing something for herself, not for some bloated bureaucratic agency. Her partners, Charlie and Lucy had stood beside her and nothing could replace the loyalty and faith in their friendship.

As they worked at their desks, the door handle turned and caught Allison's attention. She looked at Lucy. "Are we expecting anyone?"

Lucy tightened her long ponytail, brushing down the soft dark locks. "No." When the woman entered, she stood to greet her. "Good afternoon. How can I help you?"

"Is this the private investigating firm?" Tabitha Barnes closed the door and took cautious steps inward.

"Yes, it is." Allison approached the woman with an

outstretched hand. "I'm Allison Hart, the 'A' in ACL. That's Lucy and that's Charlie Wells. What can we do for you, Ms?"

"Barnes. My name is Tabitha Barnes."

"Well, Ms. Barnes, please have a seat and you can tell me what it is you need." Allison led her to the guest chair opposite her desk. "Would you like a cup of coffee or some water?"

"I'll take water, please. Thanks."

Lucy pushed away from her desk and opened the bar fridge under the credenza to retrieve a bottle. She handed it to Tabitha.

"Thank you."

"Of course." Lucy returned to her desk but not without a glance at Charlie, who had so far remained silent.

Allison wore a tender smile and folded her hands in her lap while waiting for Tabitha to begin.

"I guess I should start off by saying that a year ago, actually, 11 months and 12 days ago, my son went missing."

"I'm so sorry." Allison's eyes revealed her compassion.

"Yes, well, we went through the whole police and citizen searches, the canvassing of, well, a lot of the area. My husband and I, I should say my soon-to-be ex-husband and I worked with a detective with the Tampa Police. He and his team did everything they could, but they exhausted their leads and the case has just withered away."

Charlie approached and stood behind Allison's desk. "Ms. Barnes, it sounds as though the police put a lot of effort into finding your son."

She nodded. "I believe they did, and I suppose this gets me to why I'm here. I had surgery about ten days ago. Nothing major, just a routine operation. It all went well. But something happened to me while I was under."

Allison interrupted. "Like a reaction?"

"No. No, nothing like that." Tabitha wiped away a stray tear.

"While I was under, I saw my son. He stood alone in an empty mall parking lot. He disappeared from a mall. I got to hold him again." She choked back her emotions. "I asked him why he was there, and he showed me something. In his hand was a coin and he said a bald man gave it to him. When I tried to get him to explain, he said he had to go. Then he just disappeared." She cleared her throat of the building sentiment. "When the doctor woke me up, it all came flooding back to me—what I had seen. I sobbed and tried to explain it to Erik, my husband. The doctor dismissed it as a reaction, for lack of a better term, to the anesthesia. He said some people have hallucinations when they're under."

"What do you think it was?" Allison asked.

"I think my son was trying to tell me something. I know how this must sound. I promise you, I'm not crazy."

"We don't think you're crazy, Ms. Barnes," Charlie said. "I can't imagine what you have been going through this past year. I have two boys myself."

"Are you here asking for our help with finding your son?" Allison asked.

"I've never given up hope that Hayden would be found, but that hope has faded with each passing day, month, and now almost year. I know that if I go to the police and tell them what I've told you, they'll shoo me away, dismissing the whole thing, just as my doctor did. Just as my husband did." Her eyes closed slowly and upon reopening them again, she continued. "I try to stay grounded, Ms. Hart, but when I saw him—it felt so real. His embrace was warm and gentle. He smelled just as I remembered." Her chin quivered. "What I'm saying is that maybe there was a reason why Hayden came to me while I was in that state. A reason he showed me that coin and told me about the bald man. I'm here to ask for your help in finding this man. Whoever he is, he took my son. I'll be honest with you, I don't know if Hayden is still alive. But I have every intention of finding the one who took him."

Allison glanced at Charlie and Lucy, both of whom had reddened eyes. It was impossible not to feel Tabitha's pain. What concerned Allison, however, was offering this woman hope that she and her partners had the ability to find her son when the police had not. "Can I ask you, Ms. Barnes..."

"Please, you can call me Tabitha."

"Tabitha, the bald man—do you think you might know him?"

"I don't think so. Certainly, no one comes to mind. You see, I lost Hayden at that mall; the one from this supposed hallucination. It's closed down now. Last year, many of the stores were closing and had deals and I thought, why not do some shopping before they're all gone?" She scoffed. "If I hadn't gone that day..."

"You can't do that to yourself, Tabitha," Charlie said.

"That's what my therapist always says." A modest smile appeared for just a moment. "I came here because I know the police—they all have good hearts—and I know how hard their jobs are. I also know that what I'm telling you would be dismissed or buried. The visions of a woman grieving for her missing son. All I am asking is that you see it as I do—a sign." She studied the three women who appeared concerned. "I can pay you."

"Tabitha, it isn't about the money. Don't get me wrong, we only survive if we earn a living, but I just don't know if this is something..."

"Do you have kids, Allison?"

"I do. They're grown now."

"Lucky you. Please, I need help. I can't give up. You have to understand."

Allison surrendered. "Okay. We will do what we can with the information you have. We'll need you to sign a contract showing that you have designated us to work on your behalf. The police won't tell us anything without that."

"Of course." Her eyes appeared to glimmer with hope. "Thank you, Allison. Charlie. I just need someone to believe in me."

———

DETECTIVE SHANE "SULLY" SULLIVAN WATCHED THE officers and staff traverse the stationhouse as he appeared to mull over Allison's story. His deep-set brown eyes peered up at her, the lines on his face hardly noticeable for a man of forty. "This is crazy." He turned to Charlie who stood next to her as they hovered around his desk. "Charlie, you know I'm right. I mean, come on."

Charlie shrugged.

"That's all you've got?" he asked her. "It's not like you to let slide any opportunity to hit me with a comeback. You two are serious about this."

"You didn't see her, Sully. Alli's right," Charlie began. "We have to do what we can for this woman."

Allison held Shane's gaze. "She gave us the name of the detective who was working the case. Tabitha gave us all her contact information regarding the police. Will you consider making an introduction for us? I know most of the detectives here think we're a couple of rubes, and that's why I'm asking you to give this detective a heads up. Tell him what we're about; what we've done, then introduce us," Allison said. "We can go on our own, if necessary, but we could use a little talking up."

"None of these guys—the ones who know you—think you two are rubes. You've both done incredible work in the short time that ACL has been operating. It isn't that. It's the fact that the victim's family member is sidestepping law enforcement. That's going to be the rub."

"I understand that," Allison continued. "She doesn't believe there is another choice. Please, Shane."

Resigned, he began, "I'll call you when the meeting's been set up."

"Thank you. Can it happen today? We need the files as soon as possible," Allison added.

"I'll do my best."

"Thank you, Shane. In the meantime, I think Charlie and I will take a drive to the shuttered mall where it happened and have a look around."

"What mall?" Shane asked.

"East Citrus Park."

"I thought that place closed down a few years ago," he continued.

"Sounds like it was only last year. They had a big going-out-of-business sale and our client went there with her son to cash in on the deals, and then he disappeared," Allison replied. "We'll have a look around and give you time to ease us into an intro with Detective Freddy Bryant. He's the lead investigator. Thanks again, Shane."

———

ALLISON ROLLED TO A STOP IN THE MIDDLE OF THE PARKING lot in front of what was the East Citrus Park Mall's main entrance. She cut the engine and peered through the windshield. The shrubbery was overgrown. Weeds pushed through the cracked asphalt. The entrance was sealed with steel rolling doors.

"Place looks like a ghost town." Charlie surveyed the grounds. "I used to come here with my friends in high school. We'd hang out, eat at the Orange Julius, and walk around like we owned the place."

"That's all a teenager could do back in those days. It's a piece of Americana and it's just gone," Allison replied.

"Tabitha said she was at Penney's when it happened. We should drive around and find where that was," Charlie added.

"Sure." Allison started the car again and pulled onto the loop road around the mall. "I think that was it up there. You can still see the darker paint where the sign was mounted on the wall."

"Do you think the parking lot in her dream meant something?" Charlie asked. "Tabitha said she last saw her son inside, but in her vision, or whatever we're calling it, he was out here somewhere."

"Charlie, I don't know if what Tabitha saw means anything, if I'm being honest."

"You don't believe her?"

"It's not that I don't believe her. I'm sure her vision felt all too real. But what if her doctor was right? It was a side-effect of the anesthesia. I've come out of surgery feeling funny."

"Alli, we agreed to take this on. You have to believe her or we're doing her a disservice." Charlie opened her car door. "Let's just have a look around, okay?" She stepped outside.

Allison joined her, knowing Charlie was right, as usual. If she couldn't believe in her client, then why take the case at all? "Now that we're out here, I guess we should split up and look around."

"Look for what?" Charlie asked.

"I don't know. Maybe if we see it, we'll know. I'll start over here. We'll give it half an hour and hope something catches our eyes." Allison headed north while Charlie headed south. It had been a year since the boy had been seen. If there was any shred of evidence here, it would surely be gone by now. Storms, wind, rain, even people, although, the mall had been closed for some time.

Allison kept her eyes on the cracked and crumbling asphalt as she walked to the loop road and turned back down again. "The coin?" she muttered.

Tabitha offered no description of the coin her son held in the palm of his hand. It could've been anything. How many coins could there be in one parking lot, anyway? Turned out—a lot. Allison picked up every one she came across regardless if it was covered in muck, or oil, or hardly resembled a coin at all. She started back in the direction of the car and spotted Charlie heading the same way. Allison held out the bottom of her grey floral blouse and let the coins hang inside as though resting in a hammock.

Charlie cocked her head, adjusting the black-rimmed glasses on her nose. "What are you holding?"

"Coins." Allison jiggled them in her shirt. "I thought if this has to do with a coin, then I'm picking up all of them."

"I wish you would've said something to me." Charlie raised a 7-11 foam cup. "I put mine in here." The money rattled inside. "We really do think alike, don't we?"

Allison grinned. "I guess we do. Anything stand out to you?"

"No, but I must've picked up 10 bucks. You?"

Allison slipped behind the wheel onto her grey cloth seats and tipped her shirt into the center console cup holder. After Charlie stepped in, she continued. "There's probably 10 bucks in there too. I don't know if it'll help but right now, we have nothing to lose."

———

The second floor of the downtown Tampa police station was where the Major Crimes division resided. This was also where Detective Shane Sullivan had his sights set on and had been promised the next job opening. Right now, however, he was leading Allison and Charlie to Detective Freddy Bryant's office for the introduction he had promised them.

Shane wrapped his knuckles on the open office door. "Detective Bryant, I brought the partners of ACL Investigative Services, as we discussed."

Bryant peered at the two of them with what Charlie would later describe as smoldering brown eyes. "I've seen you two around here before. Sully, you and these ladies worked the Southside Runners investigation a few months ago."

"We did," Allison replied. "Now we've been hired by Tabitha Barnes to…"

"Help her find her son who's been missing for almost a year?" Bryant interrupted. "I pray to God you didn't fill her head with hope about finding that boy. If you think my team and I haven't been looking, then you're sadly mistaken."

"That's not what this is about at all," Allison pressed on.

"Come in then. No point in you standing in my doorway. I got it from here, Sully. Thanks."

Shane glanced at Allison who lent a subtle nod. "Okay then. I'll leave you guys to it."

After he left, Allison began, "Tabitha came to us early this morning. I'll be the first to admit that I was hesitant about accepting this case. Not only has it been a year, but the circumstances that prompted her visit were—well, they were difficult to swallow."

"Come sit down, please, and shed some light for me." Detective Bryant wore a Van Dyke beard woven with steely gray streaks on a sharp jawline. From his seated position, he appeared slightly thick around the middle, but otherwise fit for a man in his early 50s.

Allison sized him up. "She came to us after undergoing a routine operation during which she experienced what her doctor called a hallucination. Tabitha referred to it as a vision of her son, and he held in his hand a coin."

"What kind of coin?" He pressed on.

"I don't know. My hope is she'll be able to call on her memory for that detail. She also said her son mentioned a bald man had taken him."

"This came from a dream while she was under anesthesia?" Bryant wore a look of incredulity.

"Yes," Charlie jumped in, "She doesn't know anyone matching that description. She did, however, fill us in on where the abduction took place."

"The old East Citrus Park mall," he replied.

Charlie nodded. "I think it's clear, Detective Bryant, that Tabitha is desperate, as I would be if I were in her shoes. My partner and I aren't here to tell you how to do your job. All we can do is look into the new information she's given us. And we're asking for you to do the same."

Allison felt a welling of pride for Charlie. Her partner was always good for a witty comeback or observational humor, but there was a tender side to her. This case had already had an impact and they'd only just begun.

Detective Bryant pulled up close to his desk and leaned over. "Look, I understand where you're coming from. It's a gut-wrenching case, believe me, I know. But I am terrified of giving Tabitha and Erik false hope. They've been through enough."

"They have," Allison added. "Tabitha doesn't think anyone will believe what she saw. Her doctor and her husband dismissed it as a side effect of the anesthesia. Somebody's got to believe her and that has to be us."

He nodded. "Fair enough. I can't stop her from seeking your help. I have the affidavit giving you permission to review the files. I'll have copies of them sent to your office first thing in the morning. Will that be soon enough?"

The women traded glances before Allison answered, "It's soon enough. Thank you, Detective Bryant."

3

Two mason jars filled with coins sat on Allison's desk. It seemed like a ridiculous idea now, picking up each one she and Charlie spotted in the mall parking lot. What had they hoped to accomplish? The coins hadn't been cleaned or touched in any way except when they were picked up off the ground. It was a desperate move that meant they had no clear direction in which to take this investigation and that was what scared Allison the most. They had no idea what any of it meant, so for now, those coins would sit there on the corner of her desk.

Shane opened the door of the office with a box in his hand. "Good morning." He continued inside and set down the box on top of the credenza. "Hey, Lucy."

"Hi, Sully. What's that?"

Allison stood from her desk and approached. "Please tell me those are the Hayden Barnes files."

"Why else would I be here?" he replied.

"Oh, I could think of another reason." Charlie nudged Allison, though she dismissed the notion. "I thought Bryant was going to drop them off himself."

"I mentioned I'd be in the neighborhood and that I'd save him the trip," Shane replied.

"Thanks for that." Allison eyed Charlie who raised her brow in return. "Anyway, this will tell us where Bryant left off."

"He didn't really leave off anywhere," Shane added. "It was a matter of leads drying up, is all."

"I didn't mean to suggest he gave up." Allison thumbed through the box of files. "I just mean, I wanted to see how…"

"I know." Shane placed his hand on her shoulder. "Listen, if there's anything I can do, you just let me know, okay? I hope you guys do find something that will resurrect this case."

Allison nodded. "We do too. Thanks again and I'll talk to you later."

"You got it. See ya, Charlie. Lucy. Catch up with you guys soon." Shane walked to the door and turned as though he wanted to speak. Instead, he smiled politely and showed himself out.

"Let's see what we have in here." Allison grabbed the box and moved it to the folding table against the front wall.

Lucy pulled back her long dark hair and twisted it into a bun before securing it with a hair tie. "Where do you want me to start?" She headed to the table where Allison and Charlie emptied the box's contents.

"I want to see the list of suspects or persons of interest, and the interviews that were conducted," Allison began. "Photos of the scene, too."

"That will help us piece this together now that we've been out there. Who knows? We might be able to make some sense out of those coins on Alli's desk," Charlie added.

"It'll take some time to parse the information. Hope you two didn't have anything else planned for today," Allison said.

Charlie scanned the room as though looking for something and with a wry smile, added, "I'm sorry, did we have another case to work on?"

"No need to point out the obvious." Allison returned to her desk. "I already know how much we need this case, so how about we get down to business?" She opened the files and started with the witness statements. Several rested in her pile alone and as she read each one, whatever hope she had of finding something relevant began to fade. "I don't see reference to anyone having seen Hayden at all. Almost as if he disappeared into thin air. Certainly nothing that points to a bald man." She looked at her partners. "Have either of you come across reports from the mall's security footage?"

"I thought I saw something about it. Hang on." Lucy thumbed through the files on her desk. "Here it is." She walked to Allison and stood over her shoulder as they both reviewed the information.

"None of it captured Hayden inside the mall and there were no cameras in the parking lot." Allison sighed. "I thought these places always had cameras in the lots?"

"Not everywhere, apparently," Lucy added. "The only way the suspect could've taken the boy without being spotted on the mall's security was if he was taken from an exit inside the store itself."

"Meaning he didn't go through the mall," Allison added. "Which would make sense. Why expose yourself by traipsing around with a kid who wasn't yours? No. Whoever it was had been intent on getting in and out fast." She looked at Lucy. "What about the possibility that the abductor knew where cameras were installed and was careful to avoid them?"

"Someone who worked at the mall." Lucy nodded. "I can look through the POI names again and see if any of them worked there. But I have to think those people would've been vetted."

"Lucy's right," Charlie said. "Bryant knows what he's doing, Alli. I don't know if we'll somehow magically make a connection based on this same information that they couldn't."

"I'm not looking for holes in his investigative work," Allison began. "But you're forgetting something. All of this was looked at without consideration for a bald guy. Tabitha had never mentioned that before."

Charlie peered at the jars of coins on Allison's desk. "So, we're looking for a coin and a bald man. Sounds like the title of a dime novel."

———

THE STACK OF FILES INSIDE ALLISON'S CARRIER BAG WEIGHED heavily on her shoulders as she returned home. The house was empty with Nolan away, practicing with his team. She missed him terribly and empty nester syndrome had set in. It hadn't been the same with Micah. Of course, there was also the strain they suffered, and had only recently begun to rebuild the bridge between them. Micah was away at school and Nolan was beginning his life doing what he loved. These were things Allison had already experienced. She had built a life, a family. Now that family was leaving her. However, this job was her opportunity to build a new life. A life of her own.

She set down the files on the kitchen counter and opened the fridge to grab some leftover chicken salad. It was 8 o'clock in the evening and while the team had scrutinized much of the case file documents, she wanted to pay particular attention to these files. They focused on the events after Hayden's disappearance. The brief media attention it received. The following up on tips that had been collected by those claiming they'd seen him. All of this had piled on and had led up to a breakdown suffered by Tabitha, which drove the current divorce proceedings between her and her husband, Erik. That part wasn't relevant to the case, but it did speak to the domino effect.

She opened the file labeled "Forensics - crime scene photos." The inside of the store, the outside, the parking lot adjacent to it. It was impossible to know exactly where the boy had been taken and so it appeared that they captured anything and everything in the immediate area.

Allison pulled a photo of the interior of the store. It revealed that most of the shelves and racks had been picked clean. But, more importantly, she didn't spot anything significant. Much as Detective Bryant hadn't either.

Without so much as a warning, loneliness swept over her. Maybe it was the thought of losing one of her own children or it was the fact that she was alone. Probably a combination of the two.

Charlie was always one Allison could call on in times like these. But she had children, two teenage boys, who had practices and games and all the rest. Allison didn't have a large circle of friends. It was different when the kids were young. Leo's job at the school left them with plenty of opportunities to socialize with other parents, but that was gone too.

There was someone else she could call, though her intentions could be easily misconstrued. Shane Sullivan had been a good friend, even more so over these past several months since she dove head-first into this business. He had feelings for her and had alluded to them more than once in his own, nonchalant manner. While the age disparity wasn't significant—he was 8 years younger —it bothered Allison. Right now, though, she needed a friend not only for the company but to join in her search for new information about a little boy who had been missing for a year. Someone who would become just as invested as she had.

With the phone in her hand, she made the call. "Hey, it's

Allison." She smiled. "Good thanks. Hey, I don't suppose you're busy right now, are you?" She nodded. "You mind coming over and helping me look through some of these files? I could use a second pair of eyes. Great. Okay, I'll see you soon. No, I've eaten, but feel free to grab something for yourself if you're hungry. I don't have much here. Okay, bye."

————

Shane stood beneath the amber glow of the front porch light when Allison opened her door. "Thanks for coming. I see you brought food." He wore dark jeans and an untucked white Oxford shirt with rolled-up sleeves. It was clear that he had changed from when she saw him earlier this morning. He'd even re-styled his hair and she smelled the fresh scent of his musky cologne.

"I brought enough for the both of us if you're interested." He held up the fast food bag. "Who doesn't love French fries, right?"

"I can't argue with that. Come in. I'm set up in the kitchen." She closed the door behind him.

"Wow, you weren't kidding. You've been busy." Shane set down the food on the table as he peered at the files spread out on her kitchen island. "This wasn't everything, was it? I thought I had more than this."

"Oh, no. Charlie and Lucy both took home armfuls. We needed to be completely up to speed on the status of this case before making a decision on how to move forward."

"Sounds like a good plan. I see you're drinking wine."

"Just the one glass. I still need to stay sharp. There's beer in the fridge."

"Don't mind if I do." Shane pulled out a bottle of Corona and popped the cap. "Photos, huh?"

"Yep." Allison sat down on a stool and continued to pore over them. "I've been staring at these for a while."

Shane pulled out food from the bag. "Anything?"

"Nothing out of the ordinary." She unleashed a heavy sigh. "I hope we're doing the right thing, here, Shane."

He swallowed down a bite of the burger. "What do you mean?"

"I mean this. All this. Detective Bryant was right to question our motive. Look, we need the case, we need the money, but I don't want to put this poor woman through anything more than she's already suffered."

"She came to you, Allison. She needs your help." He sat down next to her. "You'll figure this out. There was something I wanted to talk to you about, too, if you don't mind me changing the subject."

"Right now, I welcome a change," she replied.

"You know I've been keeping a low profile. Not telling anyone what I suspect regarding the Martin Hernandez shootout. Well, except for Detective Baylor."

"Ah, our crooked FBI agent, Dave Reddick. Did something happen?" Allison asked.

"Baylor and I have been meeting on a regular basis, just to keep each other in the loop if either of us gets a hit. We met last night. He said Agent Reddick was about to be promoted. Senior Supervisor or something like that, I don't know. I don't keep up on the FBI's organizational charts. Point being, he's moving up the ladder."

"And when that happens, he makes a few more friends, things get murkier," she replied. "Possibly more dangerous."

"Yeah. I wanted to get your thoughts. Do you think it's time to cut bait?"

Allison cast down her gaze. "It's hard for me to offer my

opinion since I walked away from it. When all this happened with Logan Carr, it was pretty scary for us. Then to find out Agent Reddick was likely being paid off by someone inside the Southside Runners and then he killed Hernandez. Well, it wasn't a road I wanted to travel."

"That was because you're not law enforcement. It shouldn't fall on your shoulders," he replied.

She peered up at him again. "I don't know Shane. I mean, look, the proof you have against Reddick is thin."

"Paper thin, which is why we've held off."

"Exactly. You're next in line for a Major Crimes post. Jumping on this now, without solid evidence, could put that in jeopardy. I don't even want to think about the other reason it presents a problem for you," Allison replied.

Shane rolled the bottle of beer between the palms of his hands. "Then there's Baylor. It could get ugly for him too." He turned his gaze to Allison. "I don't know what I thought you could say that would make this easier. Like somehow you had the ability to cut through the bullshit and figure this out, you know?"

"I wish I could do that for you, Shane. I really do." Allison pushed around the photos on the countertop as though they were pieces of a puzzle. She stopped for a moment and peered at one of them before picking it up.

"What's that?" Shane asked.

"The parking lot outside the store where Hayden Barnes was last seen. Charlie and I drove down there before our meeting with Detective Bryant."

"Something's caught your eye. What is it?" He leaned closer.

Allison examined the image with a furrowed brow. "When Charlie and I went there, we just sort of meandered around and I started collecting the coins that I spotted."

"Why?" Shane asked.

"Because Tabitha Barnes mentioned that in her vision, her son held out a coin. She didn't say what that coin was, so I thought, hell, I'll just pick up coins and see if they mean anything." She pushed the photo nearer to him. "Take a look here. This tree planted in the center of these two parking spots."

"I'm looking at it."

With her index finger, Allison pointed to the tree trunk where a coin lay. "This picture was taken within hours of the abduction. See that quarter there? It's a little hard to decipher because the focus is on the tire tracks next to it but look closely."

"Okay, it's a quarter. Sorry, I'm a little slow. What are you getting at?"

"Here's what I think. There would be countless coins in and around that parking lot. Some, like this one, they might've captured in the crime scene photos. What do you suppose the odds are one of the coins I picked up would match one of these coins in the photos?"

Shane pulled back and snorted. "Odds of that happening are probably greater than winning the lottery."

"Probably. But what if Tabitha could tell us what kind of coin she saw? Don't you think that could lead somewhere?"

"Where, exactly?"

Allison pulled upright and shook her head. "I don't know yet. Maybe it'll come to me when I ask her."

———

THE KNOCK ON TABITHA BARNES' DOOR CAPTURED HER attention. She pushed off the sofa, mindful of the slight twinge that lingered where the keyhole incision had been made during her surgery. The knock sounded again.

"I'm coming. Hold on." She shuffled to the door and opened it.

"Erik? What are you doing..." Before she could finish, he pushed inside. "What's wrong?"

"How could you do this?" he asked.

"Do what?"

"How could you hire some private investigator to look into Hayden's disappearance?" Erik walked into the living room. "I mean, what were you thinking?"

"What choice did I have?" She followed him. "What I saw when I was under, it was real, Erik. You didn't believe me. The doctor didn't believe me. There wasn't a chance in hell that Detective Bryant would've believed me either. So what was I supposed to do? Ignore my son?"

"It was a dream, a hallucination." His arms flailed and his cheeks reddened. "My God, Hayden has been missing for a year. A year!"

"You think I don't know that? You think I wouldn't do anything in this God-forsaken world to get him back? *That's* why I'm doing this. *That's* why I hired a private investigator. What are you doing for Hayden, Erik?"

"That's not fair." He paced a small circle in the middle of the living room. "I did everything in my power, and it didn't bring him back."

"I can't give up. I'm sorry. He's my son."

Erik approached her and gently took her by the shoulders. "He's *our* son. Now you've got people digging up the past, rehashing the pain. Christ, I can't go through that again. Honestly, I don't know how you can either. Look at what it did to us the first time."

"I wasn't the one who left. You did," she replied.

"Because it was too much. Because I couldn't stomach watching you cry for hours on end or finding you in the middle of the night in Hayden's room, sleeping on the floor. You stopped talking to me. I stopped being your husband. I was just another person who stood in the way of you finding our son."

"This doesn't have to involve you, Erik. They don't need anything from you. I told them what I saw and they're working on it."

"On what? What are they working on exactly? These people want your money, Tabby, nothing more. Don't you see that?"

"No, I don't. And if you had been there when I met with them, you wouldn't think so either. Two of the women are mothers. They understand. They want to help me figure out what my vision meant. What if it opens up a new lead? How could I possibly ignore that opportunity?" She wiped away the tears that had spilled down her cheeks. "I don't need you to help pay for it. I don't need you to do anything. This is something I have to see to the end, and I won't apologize for it."

"I miss him too, Tabby. God knows how much," Erik began. "I don't want you to think that after a year, he's going to suddenly resurface. That's all I'm saying. We've lost our son. We've lost each other. It's time to accept that."

She regarded him. "You can accept it. I won't."

4

A long the front wall of ACL's office, two folding tables used to organize case files now had over 100 coins lined out on top of them. Lucy had arranged them ahead of the arrival of their client, Tabitha Barnes.

Allison peered at the table. "This looks good, Lucy. Thank you. I don't suppose anything stood out to you."

"Well, this one's different." Lucy pointed to a nickel coin. "I don't think I've ever seen one like that in real life."

Allison slipped on her reading glasses and leaned closer. "The markings are rubbed almost completely off, but..." She picked it up and examined it. "It's a buffalo nickel."

"Oh, wow. They're like super old, right?" Lucy replied.

"They're pretty old. Some of them are worth a lot of money, I think." She set it down again. "Interesting."

The office door opened, and Charlie walked inside. "Look who I found in the parking lot." She held the door for Tabitha.

"Good morning," Allison said. "It looks like you're walking around a little better."

"I am, thank you. The pain is better and I'm almost back to normal."

"Glad to hear it. Can I get you a coffee?"

"Sure." Tabitha walked over to the table. "What's all this?"

Charlie followed her. "Lucy set this up this morning. None of us is sure if this will mean anything to you, but we had to try. When Allison and I checked out the mall, we roamed around the parking lot in front of JC Penney's, picking up any coin we spotted in the unlikely event that one of these might strike a chord for you."

Allison approached with the cup in her hand. "Here you are."

"Thank you." Tabitha took a sip before continuing. "Well, gee, I don't know. After we talked last night, I scoured my brain for reminders of what that coin was Hayden held in his hand. It wasn't something I had my focus on, you know?"

"We get it," Lucy began. "That's why we did this. To see if anything might jog your memory."

"I was reviewing the case files last night with a detective friend of mine and we studied the parking lot pictures. Particularly ones with coins in them." Allison started back to her desk to retrieve the photos. "I know it seems strange, but I thought, why not see if any of them match what Charlie and I found?" She returned to the tables and set down the pictures. "I haven't done a side-by-side comparison yet, but let's give this a try."

They studied the pictures against the coins on the table. After several minutes of silence, it was Allison who finally spoke. "I don't see any matches. Do you guys?"

"It's damn hard to tell given some of the coins we picked up are practically rubbed raw. Then you have dirt and grime sticking to them," Charlie said.

"Maybe we should clean them," Lucy added. "That might help."

"What would help is if Tabitha recalled anything." Allison peered at her. "Do any of these ring a bell for you at all?"

With a shake of her head, Tabitha sighed. "I'm sorry. They're all just coins."

Allison placed her hand on Tabitha's shoulder. "Don't be sorry. It was a long shot."

Tabitha picked up one of the coins. "What's this one here?"

"A buffalo nickel," Allison added. "They're getting pretty rare these days. I doubt I've seen one in ten years. And that one's in pretty bad shape."

She nodded. "Yeah, I guess it is." Tabitha turned away. "I feel like I'm wasting your time."

"We don't feel that way," Charlie replied. "This is a process. I'm sure Detective Bryant has already relayed that to you."

"Oh yes. He made that quite clear." She turned back. "If I could just remember more details from the dream. Now that it's been more than two weeks, the images are fading even faster. I'm struggling to see his face anymore or feel the warmth of his hug."

"Hey, it's okay," Allison said. "We aren't giving up. You shouldn't either. We'll press on and when something does click, it'll be worth the push."

"Unless there was something else you needed from me, I should probably go," Tabitha said.

"I think we're good for now. Detective Bryant, while reluctant, has been cooperative. But if anything pops up, just give either one of us a call."

"Thank you, Allison." Tabitha turned to Charlie. "You too and Lucy, you went through all this trouble."

"It was no trouble. We want to help you," Lucy replied.

Tabitha started toward the door and opened it but stopped in her tracks. "Hang on." She swung back and walked to the table again.

"What is it?" Charlie asked with a dash of hope on her tongue.

Tabitha lightly touched the coins with her fingertips. "I—I don't know what this is, but I remember something." Her fingers landed on the buffalo nickel.

"You've seen it before?" Allison began. "Maybe on the day Hayden went missing?"

Tabitha pursed her lips and shook her head. "I don't know. Maybe." She looked at them with pleading eyes and held the coin between her index finger and thumb. "This means something."

Allison nodded. "Then we'll work on what that something is."

Tabitha smiled warmly. "Thank you. Thank you all for what you're doing." She walked through the door.

After the door closed, Charlie turned to Allison. "We'll work on it how?"

"She only referenced that coin after we brought it to her attention, Allison," Lucy added.

"I picked up on that. I'm not sure how we'll work on it, but we better put our heads together and figure it out."

———

CHARLIE STEPPED BEHIND THE WHEEL OF HER WHITE CHEVY SUV with Allison waiting in the passenger seat. As she closed the door, Charlie began. "What did Detective Bryant say when you told him about the coin?"

"All I heard was a big sigh on the other end of the line," Allison replied. "If Tabitha thinks it could be important, then we can't afford to ignore it. All we can do is bring it to his attention and see if he can run the marker through the database."

"Marker?" Charlie asked.

"It's like a clue or an M.O. or something like that. Something specific to a case. At least, that was what Shane called it."

"You told him about this already?" Charlie pulled out of the parking lot.

"Last night. I mentioned he and I were going over the case files. It sort of came up—markers."

"I see. And with Nolan away for spring training and Micah at school, did the young detective stay over?" Charlie eyed her with a raised brow.

"Stop it. And if you must know, he did not stay. It's not like that between us. Why do you keep insisting that it is?"

"Oh, I don't know. Maybe because any opportunity Shane gets to see you or work with you in some way, he jumps on it. And by that, I mean, the case. Not you."

"Oh good. I wasn't sure." Allison pursed her lips. "Maybe Detective Bryant will see it as a marker."

"Maybe." Charlie continued the drive to the downtown stationhouse when Allison's phone buzzed in the center console. "Who is that?"

"It's a text from Shane..."

"His ears must've been burning," Charlie countered. "What does he want?"

"He's asking us to stop by before we see Bryant." She looked at Charlie. "I know what you're going to say and don't. He wants to see us about the case."

"I wasn't going to say anything." Charlie kept her eyes on the road but smirked in response. "We're here anyway. Might as well find out what Sully wants this time."

Allison joined her as they walked across the street. The high-rise glass-covered building was on the opposite side with an adjacent parking structure, but Charlie had been lucky enough to find a metered spot along the street.

Charlie walked inside first and made a beeline for the information desk. "Hey there, Felix."

"Charlie Wells. What brings you by?" Felix worked most days and had become chummy with the women of ACL.

"We have an appointment with Detective Bryant, but we'd like to stop in to see Sully first if he's around," she replied.

"Is he expecting you two?" Felix eyed Allison as she approached.

"He sure is." Charlie leaned in. "But if you ask me, I'm pretty sure he's more interested in seeing this one back here than he is in me." She tossed a nod to Allison.

"Oh. Well, then, go on back." Felix wore a thick mustache that made his grin look menacing, though he had been the kindest officer in the entire station.

Charlie and Allison walked to Shane's desk inside the bullpen and he stood on their approach. "Good. You're here. Come take a look at this." He returned to his seat and punched in commands on the keyboard before turning the monitor toward them. "I wanted to run a couple of searches before you met with Bryant. Do with this what you will."

"What are we looking at, Shane?" Allison asked.

"I ran a search for recent missing children cases. Particularly kids who match Hayden Barnes' description."

Allison showed renewed interest. "And?"

"There have been 3 in the past year, but that's throughout the entire state, not just here in Tampa."

"What does that mean?" Charlie pressed on.

"I think you should check with Bryant to see if there are any similarities to these cases."

"Why wouldn't he have done that himself already?" Allison asked.

"He might have, but I'm just saying, it's worth asking him about. I assume he gets alerts through the database but just ask. See what he says."

Allison nodded. "We'll ask him. Thanks, Shane."

"No need to thank me. Anyway, go. I don't want to make you late."

Allison and Charlie started upstairs. Allison lagged behind for a moment and when the two reached the landing, she began, "Wait."

Charlie turned around.

"What do you think about what Shane said?" Allison asked.

"It's worth a mention."

"Yeah. I think so too. I'm concerned that Bryant might think we're going to Shane for help instead of him."

"Alli, men pissing around each other is nothing new. If he gets ticked off about it, so be it. We're doing our jobs." Charlie made her way to Bryant's office. "Good morning, Detective."

Bryant peered up. "Charlie, come on in." He spotted Allison behind her. "Good morning, Allison. Please, let's sit down and catch up."

He seemed especially pleasant this morning, which sparked concern for Allison. "Thanks for seeing us. I know how busy you are."

"Not at all. Do me a favor and close the door behind you." Bryant laced together his fingers and rested his hands on his desk. "I got an interesting call from Erik Barnes earlier. He mentioned that he wasn't on board with what you both are doing for his ex-wife. He thinks you're taking advantage of her."

"Apart from the fact that's not true," Allison began. "I don't see how it's relevant to what we're doing. Tabitha is our client. Not Erik."

"That may be true, but he's considering filing a complaint against your firm. They are technically still married, and he is the father of the victim," Bryant replied.

"By the look on your face, you agree with him," Allison added.

"As I've stated before, I think you are offering hope to a woman who has suffered for a year. Look, I'm not saying you're intentionally misleading Tabitha Barnes, but I am of the belief that your involvement will do nothing to forward the investigation into her son's disappearance." Bryant used his index finger and thumb to stroke his beard.

Allison inhaled a long breath. "Then I guess you don't want to hear something that might open a door to a lead for you."

He scoffed. "A lead? And what might that be?"

"If we're only wasting everyone's time and money, then we certainly don't want to waste yours." Charlie shifted in her seat as though preparing to leave.

Bryant eyed her. "Who brought you this supposed lead?"

"Tabitha," Allison answered. "But Charlie's right. We have no desire to waste anyone's time. Thank you." She followed Charlie's lead by gathering her things.

"Hang on." The detective surrendered. "Just tell me what you have."

Allison looked at Charlie who nodded for her to continue. "Tabitha came to our office earlier this morning. I should go back a step and tell you that Charlie and I made a trip to the mall where the abduction took place. We, of course, couldn't get inside since it had closed down, so we searched the parking lot for any clue that might remain."

"A clue in the parking lot? The boy was last seen inside the JC Penney's," Bryant said.

"Do you want to hear about this lead or not?" Charlie asked.

He nodded. "Go on."

"Charlie and I had a walk around there," Allison continued. "We realized exactly what you're saying now, that the odds of finding anything there after this long were slim."

"I had better odds of becoming a Sports Illustrated swimsuit model than we did of finding anything relevant," Charlie added.

Allison shot her a glance. "So you see, we were realistic in our expectations. But to make a long story short, because Tabitha had mentioned in her vision that her son held out a coin, we decided to collect whatever coins we found in the area. I'm not sure why, call it a hunch."

"I follow you," Bryant added.

"When Tabitha came in this morning," Allison continued. "Our other partner, Lucy, had arranged the coins, which turned out to be around one hundred in total, and Tabitha looked at them to see if any might spark a memory."

"And?" He appeared to grow impatient.

Allison opened her laptop bag and retrieved a Ziplock. "She thought this one might mean something."

"She thought? She wasn't sure?" Bryant asked.

"No. Not really. But it does seem odd that this was there." Allison set it on his desk. "It's an old buffalo nickel."

Bryant picked it up with his large hands and studied it through the plastic bag. He nodded. "This is interesting." He set it back down on his desk. "But I'm not sure it's relevant."

"That's why we're here, Detective," Charlie said. "Buffalo nickels aren't that common anymore. I realize that one is weathered and worn, but Tabitha saw a coin in her son's hand. She thinks it could have been one similar to that one there."

"But she isn't sure," he reiterated.

"As I said, she isn't sure," Allison replied. "But what if something like this coin was found near or around the other three missing children cases in the state that most closely resemble Hayden Barnes' investigation?"

"How do you know about those?" Bryant asked.

"Sully, downstairs. He ran a search through the missing

children's database. Came up with three similar cases," Allison replied. "We didn't ask him to. We weren't trying to sidestep you. He did it because he's a friend who's trying to help."

Bryant appeared to mull over the comment. "Here's what I think. I think Sully should keep his nose out of this. I'll talk to him about that. Good intentions or not, we don't need more fingers in this pie. Then, I'll look into your so-called lead. If it falls flat, I think you both ought to relieve yourselves of this investigation and let Tabitha and Erik Barnes get on with their lives. If you do that, I'll convince Erik to forget about filing a complaint against your firm. Can we agree to that?"

Charlie scoffed before looking at Allison for a reply. When she cast down her gaze, the answer was clear. "You want to go along with this?"

"It's a reasonable request, Charlie. This is all we have to go on and frankly, Detective Bryant is right. If it amounts to nothing, we can't justify continuing on. It'll be a dead end." She turned back to the detective. "But if it turns out to be valid, then you agree to stop fighting us and start helping us."

Bryant nodded. "While I haven't exactly been fighting you on this, I will be open to moving forward."

"Thank you," Allison replied. "Now let's take a look at those other investigations."

5

The sunrise over the lake was the singular reason Gary Lucado had purchased the cabin in Land O'Lakes. That was about four years ago and was the only possession he retained after his unpleasant divorce. There wasn't much in the way of furnishings, but the sofa was comfortable, and the television worked. The 53-year-old made the trip from Kissimmee on most weekends and especially when the weather turned nice, which it had now.

Early morning was the best time for fishing, and he placed his favorite fishing hat on his head and grabbed his tackle box. Around the back of the home was his own private dock, though it had seen better days. Something to add to his "to-do" list.

With a camping chair slung over his shoulder, Gary reached the end of the dock and prepared to drop a line. A sip of his coffee from the travel mug, and with the line baited, Gary cast his rod and slumped down in the chair. The tall, but full-sized man fit into the chair, though it had been a tight squeeze.

"Hey."

Gary swung around. "Andrew? What are you doing here?"

"I didn't mean to startle you. I just got off work and decided to come up. I didn't know you'd be here." Andrew pushed his hand through his dark blonde, wavy hair.

"It was going to be a nice weekend, so I thought, why not? Are you staying?" He asked with some concern.

"No. No, I forgot something from the last time I was here. I figured traffic would be light, so I'd just come and grab it. I hope you don't mind." The young man with an athletic build shoved his hands into the pockets of his torn black skinny jeans.

"Not at all. Hey, if you got time, grab another pole from the garage and sit with me."

"Thanks, but I need to be getting back. I saw you out here and wanted to let you know I was going in."

"Your dad must've given you the key, huh?" Gary asked.

"I hope that's okay."

"Course it is." Gary turned back to the lake. "Just don't snag my beer, kid."

"I won't. Thanks, Gary. Oh, and I'm glad to see you're wearing a hat. Last time we fished, your head got fried."

"I learned my lesson." Gary tapped on the hat. "Gotta watch the old bald head."

———

SHANE SULLIVAN HAD WORKED ON THE FIRST FLOOR OF THE Tampa police station for the past few years. A detective in the Investigations and Support unit, he was now biding his time to move upstairs to the Major Crimes Bureau. Once a spot opened up, at least according to his lieutenant, it was his.

When he caught sight of Detective Bryant marching toward him with a scowl on his face, Shane figured the meeting with

Allison and Charlie hadn't gone over well, and his assistance hadn't been appreciated. Although, a little forewarning might have been nice on their part. They must've slipped out when he was in Evidence on another investigation.

Shane displayed a closed-lip grin. "Detective Bryant. Good morning."

"Sully, can I have a word?" Bryant replied.

"You got it." Shane remained at his desk.

"Upstairs. Now." Bryant turned around and started up the staircase without turning back.

Shane hustled to catch up to him. "What's going on?" When Bryant didn't answer, he pressed on. "Does this have anything to do with your meeting with the partners at ACL?"

He stopped cold. "What do you think?" Bryant started ahead. "We're going to my office. We'll talk there."

Shane didn't say another word until they reached Bryant's office where he promptly shut the door the moment Shane walked inside. "Did I do something to piss you off?"

Bryant returned to his desk and dropped onto his chair. "What the hell are you doing, Sully, huh?"

Shane continued inside and sat down. "I'm not sure I follow."

"Do you really think I didn't follow up on those other investigations involving the missing kids around the state? Do you think I don't know how to do my job?"

As though a light bulb went off, Shane nodded. "Ahh. This is about ACL. Well, now that I know what it is you're pissed about, I can address your concerns."

Bryant was older than Shane by ten-plus years. The fifty-something veteran detective had worked in Major Crimes for the past seven years. Kidnapping was the majority of his cases, and of those, he'd been a big player in solving 80 percent of them. He eyed Shane with noted irritation. "Telling those P.I.s about the other cases did nothing but egg them on. They actually think there could be a connection. Do you see what you did?"

"I offered them a workable path to move forward. I'm not sure I see the problem." Shane leaned back in the chair, cool as ever.

"I know you want to make a move up here. I know you're next in line. But if you think this is the way to go about it, you've got another thing coming."

"I'm not trying to take your job, Bryant. That's the last thing I want to do."

"Then what? What the hell makes you think that if there was a connection to be made in those cases I wouldn't have already made it?"

"Because there's new information," Shane replied. "Tabitha Barnes came to ACL and told them about a coin."

Bryant scoffed. "Oh, that's right. A coin. Sure." He held Shane's gaze. "You know, the guys around here, they know what you're up to."

"What do you mean?"

A half-cocked smile played on Bryant's lips. "Baylor and you cooking up something about some Fed. Word gets around, my eager friend."

Shane dropped his head. "I get it now." He raised his eyes to meet Bryant's. "You think I'm out to snag one of our own as well? I'm sorry to say that you've been misinformed, my friend. Detective Baylor and I are only tying off loose ends from a months-long investigation. It has nothing to do with this department."

"Sure. You keep to that story." Bryant leaned in. "All's I'm saying is that you need to let me do my job and stop putting your nose where it don't belong. I like you, Sully. You're a good detective. Hell, I wouldn't even be opposed to seeing your pretty boy face up here with the big fellas. But on this count, you're dead wrong."

Shane held up his hands in surrender. "Then I apologize. I thought I was helping out, but I can see I wasn't."

Bryant's eyes softened. "I told those ladies I'd check out their supposed lead with some damn coin. And I will. But I sure as shit don't need your help in doing that. So I'd appreciate you backing the hell off."

"Consider it done." Shane stood. "Anything else?"

"Nope."

"Then you have a good day, Detective." Shane walked out.

Bryant waited for him to leave before turning back to his computer and pulling up the details on the other investigations. He had been alerted to them, but there was little in the way of indicating any connection at all. Of the three, two were girls and one was a boy. All three were aged almost 3 to 4 years older than Hayden Barnes had been. And there was no hint of a suggestion the disappearances involved anything relating to a coin. However, on that last item, nothing relating to a coin had even been mentioned. Maybe it was time for Bryant to take another look at those cases and see for himself.

The first investigation involved a young girl of nearly nine. She'd been abducted from a park near her home while playing there after school. Bryant pulled up her file and studied the girl's school picture. Similarities to the Barnes boy were minimal. Different hair color, eyes. Similar build, though. "Fluffy around the edges," or so his grandmother used to say of slightly plump children. He had been one himself.

The rest of the files populated the screen and Bryant opened the photos of the park. He was going to have to go through each of these cases again and find the proverbial "needle in a haystack," or in this instance, "coin in a parking lot."

Shane peered up at the television mounted above the bar while he sipped on a pint of beer on tap. The message on his phone appeared and as he read it, he glanced over his shoulder. "Hey, man. Good to see you. Take a load off." He raised his fingers in a V to the bartender. "Two more beers." He finished off the last of his pint glass and looked at Baylor. "Is that okay with you?"

"When is it not?" Detective Anton Baylor sat down on the stool next to him. "I thought we weren't supposed to meet up until later this week. What's going on?" Baylor worked in Major Crimes in the general vicinity of Detective Bryant and had been the one to try to put Allison's previous client back behind bars. However, when that investigation took a turn for the more sinister, Baylor came around and now he and Shane were trying to right a wrong committed by a bad federal agent.

"I wanted to get your take on something." Shane nodded when the bartender placed the beers in front of them. "I had words with Detective Bryant, or I should say, he had words with me."

"I know him. He's all right. You catch him on a bad day?" Baylor tossed back a swig of his beer.

"I don't think so. The first thing he says to me is, 'I know what you're doing. You and Baylor.'"

Baylor returned a deadpan stare. "What the hell is that supposed to mean?"

"Exactly. It was like he knew, man. He knew what we were doing."

"No way. Not a chance in hell. Besides the fact that none of what we're working on involves our department or the Tampa police at all. Dave Reddick is FBI."

"I know that, so I have no idea who he's been talking to or what rumors might be flying around. I just want to tell you that we should be careful what we say and who we say it to. We've been at this for months and we're getting closer."

Baylor scoffed. "I am careful. I've been working in Major Crimes long enough to keep shit to myself. It ain't me."

"Well, Bryant's getting information from someone. Is he tight with the Feds?" Shane asked.

"Hell, I don't know. I don't keep tabs on who he shoots the shit with." Baylor appeared to reconsider the notion. "Maybe. He worked on a case a while back. Kidnapping, but it went to the Feds because it crossed state lines or some shit. Nothing I think would tie him to Narcotics."

Shane nodded. "Okay. I guess I'll just have to keep my eyes open."

"We're getting closer. It's called biding your time. Look it up, yeah?" He threw back the last of his beer. "Listen, I can't stay. We'll meet up normal time." He pulled out his wallet.

Shane waved his hand. "I got it. Thanks for coming down, man. See you later." He glanced up at the TV screen again. "Oh, now, come on! That was a foul."

———

IN SOCKED FEET, ALLISON SHUFFLED INTO HER KITCHEN AND rinsed off her empty dinner plate. On tonight's menu—leftover grilled chicken, microwaved long-grain rice, and a warmed-up can of carrots thrown in for good measure. She didn't like cooking and with Nolan out of the house for the time being, there wasn't much point in it anyway.

She turned at the sound of the doorbell and knew who awaited on the other side. Upon opening the front door, she smiled. "Hey, Leo. Come on in." After closing the door behind him, she started back into the kitchen. "Can I get you something to drink?"

"I'll never turn down a beer. Thanks." Leo followed her and dropped onto a stool at the kitchen island.

BETWEEN DARK AND LIGHT

Allison handed him a bottle. "I appreciate you dropping off Nolan's things. Saves me a trip."

"No problem. I'm glad he'll get a chance to come home for a couple of days. The team has a break in their schedule, so it's good timing. And he'll need the extra clothes he's kept at my place anyway. He says he doesn't get a chance to do laundry that often and keeps running out of socks and underwear."

"I'm sure he'll bring everything home for me to wash," she replied. "He's doing so well. It's hard to believe this could be his life, you know?"

"It's a little surreal. All the practices when he was a kid. Little League. Varsity baseball in high school. It's all led up to this."

"You were a big influence on him," she added.

"Maybe, but he has more talent than I ever did." He threw back a swig of beer. "How's work going? Last we talked you had a pharmacy that had hired you to look into an employee?"

"That's over now. We got what we needed. So, onto the next one."

"You have a next one?" Leo peered at her with raised brows. The wrinkles on his high forehead deepened and his round face was made fuller by a broad grin.

"We do. It's complicated." Allison leaned over the counter with her elbows resting on it. "It's a year-old investigation and the mother—she's pretty desperate for answers."

The smile on Leo's face faltered. "What happened?"

"Her son went missing. It's just awful. The detective in charge of the case isn't exactly happy about her hiring us. We're doing the best we can but if we don't get something viable in the next couple of days, we're going to call it. I can't continue to take this woman's money if I know we've reached the end."

"I can't imagine what she must be going through," Leo said.

"Neither can I. She and her husband, who's also the father—

they're in the middle of a divorce. I guess it proved more than they could handle. This one just hits too close to home for me. For Charlie too. Lucy, of course, understands, but she doesn't have kids."

"No. It sounds like this is taking a toll on you. I'm sorry about that."

"I appreciate it, Leo, but we'll get through it. Maybe with answers. I hope with answers." She hesitated for a moment. "Hey, um, when Nolan gets home, we should all grab dinner. I wonder if I can convince Micah to drive home while he's here?"

"That would be nice. We haven't all gotten together since the holidays. I'd like that." He stood up. "Well, thanks for the beer. I should head home now."

Allison led him back to the small foyer to show him out. "Thanks again for bringing his stuff by."

"Any time." He wrapped his arms around her and kissed her cheek.

Allison held onto him for longer than usual. This case had hit home and the thought that this could've happened to one of her own children, well, it just felt right to hang onto Leo a little tighter. When she finally pulled back, she smiled. "No matter what has happened between us, you've always been an amazing father to our kids."

He held her gaze and tucked her hair behind her ear. "You've been an even better mom. Allison, you have a big heart. Just try to remember to protect it against things like this."

"I'll work on it. Goodnight, Leo."

6

Andrew Chumbley worked nights at the grocery store stocking shelves. The 25-year-old dropped out of community college after a year when he realized he had no desire for higher education. His father wasn't happy about it, but he had a job and paid rent. That had changed his father's tune a little.

His shift started at 10 pm and as he looked at his phone, it was 9:45. Andrew stepped out of his old Nissan Pathfinder with faded red paint and brushed away his thick wavy hair that he wore to his shoulders.

Ambition wasn't Andrew's strong point and so he had been meandering through life with no real goals. His lackluster ways had intensified after his mother died five years ago. He'd been devoted to her and watching her suffer from cancer changed him. Nothing really mattered to him that much after that. Life, death—it was meaningless in his eyes.

In the darkness of the parking lot, he walked to the rear

entrance and once inside, made his way to the time clock. With his card in his hand, he punched in. "Hey, man." He nodded to a co-worker.

"Drew, what's up, my man?"

"Earning money," Andrew replied before walking to the employee locker room. Tonight, he was scheduled to restock the meat counter and that required an apron. He pulled it from his locker and tied it around his waist. Before closing the door again, he reached into the back pocket of his jeans. He'd made the trip to the cabin, not realizing his dad's friend, Gary Lucado, was there. Luckily, Gary didn't seem to care so he went inside and retrieved the boots he'd left there the previous weekend. But there was something else he'd discovered and had just pulled them from his back pocket. A handful of change he'd left on the corner of the kitchen counter. "Can't forget these." Andrew placed them on the shelf inside and closed the locker door.

———

THE CLOCK ON THE WALL OF THE MAJOR CRIMES UNIT showed 9:45 pm. Detective Bryant remained at his desk scouring the case files of the three similar abductions that had occurred around the time five-year-old Hayden Barnes went missing. The connection was flimsy at best. He wanted to curse Sully for even suggesting there was a connection at all. Apart from the fact that the abductees were children, Bryant found zero evidence to suggest there was a correlation.

After hours of studying the crime scene photos, not one revealed anything relating to a coin Tabitha Barnes had in her head. A coin or a supposed bald man. "Damn it." Bryant rubbed his bearded chin. No markers matched. He'd wanted to give the partners at ACL a chance. He really did, but this had to be called off. There was nothing new in here that was going to help him find Tabitha Barnes' son.

The thing was, despite what he thought about Allison Hart taking on this case, he believed her intentions were good. She didn't seem like the type to take advantage of someone. And he'd heard about the cases she'd worked in the department, alongside Detective Baylor and the case involving the city's mayor. She was a do-gooder. Something Bryant had been once a long time ago but with age and time in the department, that part of him diminished.

Bryant collected his things and shut down his laptop. In the morning, he would stop in to see the team at ACL and give them the news. They were going to have to shut this down because he couldn't make something out of nothing.

With his carrier bag hoisted over his shoulder, Bryant switched off the lamp on his desk and headed downstairs. As he gazed below, noting the comings and goings of officers, lawyers, and criminals, he spotted Sully. As he reached the first floor, Bryant headed to Sully's desk. "Hey."

Shane peered up from his computer. "Hey. You're here late."

"So are you." Bryant set down his bag in Sully's guest chair and remained standing. "I thought I'd let you know that you opened a can of worms for your friends at ACL and it didn't amount to shit."

Shane creased his brow. "The other missing children cases?"

"Yeah. That's right. I just spent the last six hours reviewing those files. I got nada. Zip. It was a waste of my damn time and now I gotta tell those ladies they don't have squat to go on. And neither do I, for that matter."

Shane appeared taken aback. "I'm sorry. I thought they were similar enough that you might find a link." He knitted his brow. "Are you sure about this?"

Bryant's expression hardened. "I'm sure. This isn't my first rodeo, Sully, in case you forgot. Besides them being all kids, there was nothing to suggest they were related in any way." He pulled his bag over his shoulder again. "I thought you might like to know. Have a good night." He started away.

"Wait." Shane jogged to catch up with him. "Look, I don't mean to offend here, but I only took a 30,000-foot view of those cases and I thought, given the manner in which they disappeared, that might be a solid connection."

"You mean how they were taken from public locations?" Bryant asked. "Let me tell you something, Sully. More than 75 percent of abducted kids are taken by a family member or family friend, usually from a place they're familiar with. The other twenty-five percent are taken from public locations. By your logic, that 25 percent would all be connected. Most abductors don't crawl through a kid's bedroom window and whisk them away. They don't hang around outside the school waiting to snatch them up. They wait until a kid gets lost or is on his own in a park or something. Or even offer them something to lure..." Bryant turned deadpan.

"What is it?"

Bryant hurried back to Shane's desk. "I need you to pull up something for me."

Shane jumped to attention. "Okay. Sure." As he reached his desk, he dropped into his chair. "What do you want to look at?"

Bryant unzipped his bag and pulled out a sticky note. "Pull up the NCMEC database. The file is in there." The National Center for Missing and Exploited Children (NCMEC) acted as a clearinghouse for law enforcement. Each police department had the capability of uploading the files in hopes a match to another investigation somewhere else might offer new leads.

"Here it is." Shane rolled back from his desk to show Bryant. "What do you want to look at?"

Bryant moved in and began typing on Shane's keyboard. "I remember reading a witness statement." He eyed Shane. "You mind?"

"Huh? Oh, no. Go ahead." Shane stood up and allowed Bryant to have a better look. "You remember the witness's name?"

"It was one of only three men. The rest were female witnesses. Hang on." Bryant continued to search for the statement. "Shit, here it is." He zoomed in on the pdf file and scanned over it. "There was something on here. It was...I see it." Bryant smiled knowingly. "Son of a bitch."

"What is it?"

Bryant pulled back. "Take a look for yourself." He pointed to the screen. "Read that paragraph right there."

Shane leaned in and squinted. "Says here this guy, Alan Chumbley, is it? He said he didn't recall seeing the victim at the school fairgrounds, but that he had been in the vicinity when he heard the parents call out for him."

"Right. Right. Go on. There's more," Bryant added. "Go to the next page. I think that was where I saw it."

He clicked the mouse to move to the next page of the statement and continued reading to himself. "Okay, blah, blah, blah. What am I..." Shane stopped and leaned closer, continuing to read. "The guy's a coin collector?" He shot up.

"Son of a bitch is a coin collector." Bryant folded his arms and grinned in triumph. "No one thought anything of it. There's no mention of this man in the other two cases, but that doesn't mean anything."

"The coin Tabitha Barnes mentioned. But how the hell would she have known about it?" Shane asked.

"You got me. Maybe her vision was no bullshit. Hell, I don't know. Point is, Alan Chumbley is worth a second look."

———

ALLISON PULLED INTO THE PARKING LOT OF ACL'S OFFICE building. She spotted Detective Bryant leaning against his newer model charcoal grey Chrysler 300 with a tray of coffees in his hand. "Good morning, Detective." She approached him. "You're a little early. Looks like I'm the first one in this morning."

He held up the tray. "Brought some coffee."

"Thank you." Allison started toward the building and pressed the elevator button.

"Have you talked to your friend, Sully?" Bryant asked, his voice sounding a little hoarse.

"No. I saw your text this morning, but I didn't get a call from him. Why?"

"We'll talk in your office."

They arrived at the door of ACL and Allison inserted her key in the lock. Upon opening it, she flipped the light switch. "Welcome to our little office. You can set those down on the credenza at the back."

She continued to her desk. "My partners should be here any minute."

"Okay. I'll wait until everyone's here." He grabbed one of the paper cups and sipped on the brew. "Damn. I should've brought donuts." Bryant assessed the office. "Not bad. Not a bad little place at all. How long did you say you and your team have been in here?"

"About, oh, 3 months, I guess," Allison replied.

"And before that, you worked for the state in Worker's Comp fraud?"

"I did."

"Reasonable transition. Sort of doing the same type of work." He took another sip.

"How long have you been with Tampa Police?" She asked as she opened her laptop.

"Longer than I can remember. It's been going on for a decade now. Before that, I worked in Boise."

"Boise, huh? How does it compare to here?" Allison added.

"Folks are a lot tanner here."

The door opened and Charlie walked inside. "Morning." She closed the door behind her. "I got Alli's message this morning that you were coming in, Detective."

"Brought some coffee if you want a cup." Bryant thumbed toward the credenza. "It's not too bad."

"Thanks." Charlie set down her bag and eyed Allison. "I thought Lucy would've been here by now." She grabbed a cup. "Did you text her this morning too, Alli?"

"I did. She'll be here soon, I'm sure." At that moment, the door opened, and Allison grinned. "Speak of the devil."

"Good morning." Lucy walked inside.

Bryant walked toward the center of the office. "Well, now that we're all here, I have some news for you three that I think you'll all be interested in."

Allison took in a deep breath. This was what she had been waiting for. She'd spent the entire ten minutes that they'd been alone trying to read him. Was this going to be good news or was he about to slam the book closed on this one, leaving her to break the news to Tabitha? "Please, we're anxious to hear what you discovered."

"I had a chance to review the cases your friend, Sully, mentioned." Bryant opened his laptop and turned it on."

That was the second time he'd said, "Your friend, Sully," as though he was not Bryant's friend. Allison began to lean toward the suggestion that this was not going to go in their favor. "And what did you think?" She asked him.

"At first, I'll be honest, not much. I studied those case files for hours and couldn't find anything that would lead us closer to solving Hayden Barnes' disappearance. In fact, I was ready to call it quits when I stopped by to see your friend, Sully."

There it was again.

"I asked him what made him believe there was a connection, then something clicked." Bryant pulled the laptop near the edge of the table. "Why don't you three come take a look at this?" He had opened the witness statement from Alan Chumbley and highlighted the part about his hobby.

Allison was the first to read the statement. "Wait, is this for real?"

"Yes, ma'am," he replied.

"Charlie, look at this." Allison stepped back and allowed Charlie and Lucy to read the statement.

"Holy crap," Charlie shot back. "And no one thought to look into this guy further?"

"I don't know the investigating officer here, but I'll guarantee you, no one would've had a damn clue or gave two shits that this guy was a coin collector. Hell, it took me a hot minute to realize there could be something here." Bryant turned to Allison. "If it hadn't been for this vision or dream, or whatever the hell Mrs. Barnes saw, I wouldn't be standing here right now."

"Who is this man? Do you have a picture of him?" Lucy asked. "If he's bald too..."

"I contacted the detective first thing this morning. I'm still waiting on a call back, but you better believe I'll be asking to see this man's picture."

"So, what do we do about this?" Allison asked with renewed purpose. "It's the closest thing to a clue we've come across."

"That it is. Of course, this is all acting under the assumption Tabitha Barnes' vision meant something and wasn't some electrical misfire in her brain while she was under sedation." He peered at their eager faces and held up his hands. "Look, first of all, let's keep this in perspective. It's a connection, albeit, tenuous as hell."

"But you aren't going to dismiss it?" Lucy asked.

"Not on your life." He paused for a moment and studied each of them. "I'll be the first to apologize for my behavior. I was more than a little pissed off about Tabitha Barnes bringing you all on. Truth be told, a small part of me hoped I wouldn't find something just to prove my point. But as I stand here, seeing how energized this has made you all, and me, well, I can see you were trying to help her find her son. I can't fault you for that. From this point forward, I'd like us to work together and see if this might take us somewhere."

"Thank you, Detective." Allison looked at her partners. "You don't know how happy that makes us."

"Then first things first. I'm going to touch base with the investigators on all three cases and let them know that we might be opening up old wounds, but that we don't want to step on any toes. I'll take their temperature and see how they want to handle this. Honestly, it wouldn't surprise me if they asked us to get something more solid and then come back to them. Once I let everyone in on the deal, I'll ask you all to do what you do best and take a look for anything where this Alan Chumbley might be connected."

"What should I tell Tabitha?" Allison asked. "I'm sure we don't want to get her overly excited about this. Not yet, anyway."

"You're right about that. Let's hold off until we can rule out— or not—a connection amongst these three investigations, four if you include Hayden."

"Okay. We'll await your go-ahead," she replied. "Is there anything else we can do in the meantime?"

"I don't expect it will take me long to get the complete files for all these, so just sit tight. I don't have anything else for you until then." Bryant closed his laptop and returned it to his bag. "There's one more thing. If this starts to open up for us, I'll do my best to keep you involved, but it's still a police matter and we'll just have to see how this all plays out."

"Of course. We're only here to help Tabitha, not hinder the police in their efforts to find her son." Allison turned to her partners. "Anyone have a problem with that?"

"Nope," Charlie said.

"Not me," Lucy said.

Allison turned back to Bryant. "There you go."

———

Detective Bryant returned to the station and hustled up the stairs to his office when Shane caught up to him.

"Hey, Bryant. You're back," Shane said.

"Good eye, Sully." He stopped and peered at Shane. "Appreciate you letting me handle this deal with ACL. I know you're tight with them and, frankly, I assumed you'd spill the beans on the possible lead."

"It's not my news to tell. I'm glad you're starting to see that they can add value to your investigation. It's been a little bit of a struggle for them to get on the right side of this department."

"It takes time to build relationships," Bryant said. "But from what I've seen so far, Allison Hart and her people seem to have their clients' best interests in mind. I don't know where this will go, but hell, I have to admit, even I'm a little giddy at the news. Listen, if there's nothing else, I have a pile of shit on my list."

"Yeah, of course. Sorry. If there's anything you need, just let me know," Shane replied.

"Will do, Sully." Bryant walked to his office and noticed a

sticky note on his desk. He peeled it up and after reading it, Bryant walked to his lieutenant's office. "Morning, Lieutenant. Got your note. What's going on?"

"Bryant, come in and have a seat."

He dropped onto a chair. "What's this about? I just got in."

Lieutenant Bruce Duran was nearing retirement, though he remained as dedicated and hard-working as he had when he was assigned to Major Crimes in the mid-90s. With eyes peering through thick-rimmed glasses, he began. "I know you've received some new information on the Hayden Barnes investigation."

"I have, in fact, I was just getting ready to return some calls on a few possible connected cases," Bryant replied. "How did you know?"

"I got a call from the captain of the Kissimmee police department. They were notified you'd pulled information on one of their cases, an ongoing investigation of a young boy abducted about three months ago."

"Right. That's the guy I need to see," Bryant replied.

"The captain said the detective in charge passed away about a month ago and gave me the name of the newly assigned detective on the case."

"I see. I'm really sorry to hear that. Was he on the job when it happened?" Bryant asked.

"No, it was a car accident. The captain didn't elaborate but said that the new guy hasn't gotten fully up to speed on the investigation you're inquiring about and that it could take some time."

"L.T., I don't have time to wait. Look, we stand a real good chance that this could lead somewhere. I've been working this case for almost a year and it's been one dead end after another. What can I do? I'm happy to make the drive and see what they have on file if that's okay. I don't want this to die on the vine, too."

Lieutenant Duran appeared to consider the idea before he nodded. "Yeah. That's probably best. But look, Bryant, don't ruffle feathers, you hear me? Just play nice."

Bryant stood and offered a mischievous grin. "I always play nice."

7

Working the night shift at a grocery store wasn't the career path Andrew Chumbley intended on traveling. In addition to college, he'd also tried his hand at selling cars, which had been equally as disastrous. But he had to earn a living. He was an adult still living with his father. It was no wonder he didn't have a girlfriend.

Inside the bar, he hunched over his empty shot glass, staring at it as though it had contained the answer to his general malaise.

The bartender drew near. "What can I do for you, buddy?"

"Another shot," he replied.

The bartender eyed him. "Hey, you know what, man, you should try to slow down a little, yeah?"

Andrew's eyes narrowed. "It's like not even dark yet. What the hell are you talking about?"

"I'm talking about the fact that you've had four since you got here an hour ago. You need to slow down, man. How about a soda for now? Don't make me cut you off."

"The hell?" Andrew shook his head. "I get one night off a week and I can't come in here and have a few drinks?"

"Look, man, it's my license if you get in your car and take off. If you insist on being belligerent, I'm going to need your keys. I suggest you call a friend for a lift."

"I'm not giving you my damn car keys. Seriously?"

"I'm serious." The bartender peered at him. "Either take a soda and chill out or you might want to think about getting someone here, so I don't have to let my boys know you aren't fit to drive."

Andrew rolled his eyes in disgust and reached for his phone. "Fine. I'll get a ride home." He dialed the number. "Dude, I hate to bother you, but I got some do-gooder bartender up my ass telling me I need to leave. Can you come get me? He won't let me drive." He nodded. "At the Gaslight. Yeah, man. Hey, thanks. I owe you." He ended the call and peered at the bartender. "There. You happy now?"

Several minutes passed and Andrew watched the TV above the bar. College basketball. He wasn't much of a sports fan, but it managed to kill some time until a tap on his shoulder grabbed his attention. "Gary. Dude, thanks for coming down. I'm sorry to bother you."

"It's no bother, Andrew. I'd rather you call me than your dad. He wouldn't be as understanding. Come on. Let's get you out of here."

Andrew pushed off the stool, swaying as he did, and peered at the bartender. "Thanks for nothing, dude." He turned back to Gary. "I owe you, big time."

"Yes, you do." Gary led him outside and into his Ford F-150. "You better not puke, that's all I can say."

Andrew laughed as Gary shut his passenger door.

When he returned to the driver's side, he stepped in and keyed the ignition. "Why the hell are you drunk at 7 o'clock at night, kid?"

"It's my night off. Can't a guy have a drink on his night off?"

Gary pulled out of the parking lot. "You need to be thinking about getting out on your own, kid. You're 25 and living with your dad isn't doing you any favors. Look, don't take this the wrong way, Andrew, but I'm your dad's friend. And you're damn lucky he's not here right now. All's I'm saying is it's time to get your shit together. I know losing your mom was tough, but shit happens to everyone. You aren't special."

Andrew scoffed and looked at the center console. "What this?" He picked up the plastic cup full of coins.

"Just some junk I've been trying to unload. They aren't worth anything."

Andrew grabbed one of them. "Are these from that stash you had before?"

"Yeah. That's all I got left. I used a lot of them when we played poker a while back with your dad."

"I remember. I cleaned you out."

Gary chuckled. "Yeah, you did." He glanced at Andrew. "And hey listen, I know what I said before about the cabin, but I'd appreciate a heads up before you go there on your own, okay?"

"You think I'm going to steal shit?" Andrew asked, still slurring his words.

"No, man. It's just that the place is my responsibility and I need to know who's there and when."

Andrew gave him a sideways glance. "Fine. It won't happen again."

———

THE POLICE STATION IN KISSIMMEE WAS A FAR CRY FROM THE downtown Tampa station where Detective Bryant worked. After speaking to the new man in charge of the case, Detective Caleb Santora, he wondered if they had the resources to tackle such a complex case. Never one to burn bridges, Bryant stroked his beard and nodded. "I really appreciate you jumping in on this one, Detective Santora. I know it's a long shot, but after I take a look at your files, we'll have a better understanding of Alan Chumbley and his connection, if any, to the disappearance of your Ian Nygard and our Hayden Barnes."

"Yes, sir. Look, if there's anything else you need, please don't hesitate to give me a call. And, of course, if anything comes of this lead of yours, we'll be ready to move in right behind you. The parents around here are still reeling over this thing."

Bryant stood. "Thank you again."

The detective offered his hand. "You'll probably still hit some traffic, so be sure and get yourself back to Tampa safely."

Bryant nodded and left the station with files in his carrier bag. He stepped into his Chrysler and set down the bag on the passenger seat. After turning the ignition, he glanced at the bag again. "Where the hell was that fairground?" Bryant opened the file to take another look at the location. "Not far." As daylight faded, he considered making a stop at the crime scene where the 7-year-old Ian Nygard was last seen.

Bryant pulled out of the lot and headed south. The skies had dimmed, and streetlights turned on. The fairground was ahead, and he pulled into the parking lot. The grounds were a couple of acres, at best.

The fair had been set up by one of the elementary schools as they had done every year to raise funds. It had been three months since the Nygard boy disappeared from this location, so Bryant didn't hold out much hope he was going to come across something

Detective Santora missed, but it might help to understand if there were any other similarities to his investigation of Hayden Barnes.

Bryant had to see it for himself. That was who he was, and at his age, he wasn't likely to change. Perhaps making a pass here would spur something. It was better than going home with little more than he had when he arrived. No photos had been taken of Alan Chumbley and certainly no fingerprints. He had no idea if the man was bald or not. All he knew about Alan Chumbley was that he collected coins and was in his early 50s. No priors. Not even a traffic ticket. That didn't seem like a man who was a kidnapper. In fact, the more he considered it, the less relevant Bryant thought Chumbley might be. But he owed it to Tabitha and her husband. And it seemed he owed it to Allison and her partners, too.

Bryant moved through the now-empty grounds. Signs of spring popped up in the form of green sprigs of grass and a few clumps of yellow daffodils. The weather was warm, and he removed his lightweight jacket.

One thing Bryant knew for sure was that the grounds had remained empty since the abduction. That hadn't been intentional, it just didn't get much use. Scraps of red paper tickets scattered the area. The kind that had been used for admittance onto an attraction. A few plastic cups and candy wrappers lay about. The occasional cigarette butt, maybe. Nothing that would point to the terrible crime that had been committed in a place where probably 100 adults had been gathered to watch over at least 200 kids. But he knew how things could be. Kids run off wanting to ride on something or eat or join their friends. Bryant didn't have any kids. He was divorced, but he could understand these things. People thought they were safe. That their kids were safe. He knew differently.

Bryant had made it to the rear of the lot where the food vendors and other sellers had been lined up. Even after three months, evidence of their presence remained. Deep impressions where posts had been secured into the ground dotted the area. Tracks from small tires, likely from carts, were still visible. Bryant walked along the back line hoping to find something. It was hope that drove him now, nothing concrete. He aimed the flashlight feature on his phone at the ground. Bryant spotted a penny. Just an old, dirty penny, but he picked it up anyway. And then he picked up the next coin and the next. When he reached the opposite end, something of a miracle occurred before his eyes and a smile danced on his lips. "No way. No friggin' way." Bryant looked around as if he might have been on a hidden camera somewhere or he was being punked like they used to do on MTV. What lay before him was nothing other than a buffalo nickel. A rarity in this day and now he'd seen more of them in the past week than he had in the past ten years. "Well, I'll be damned."

———

AN EMPTY PIZZA BOX LAY OPEN ON THE FOLDING TABLE AT the front of the office. Three empty soda cans lay on top of an already full garbage can. And three women remained seated at their desks, working diligently on the search for Alan Chumbley.

"Hey, Allison, Charlie, I think I might've found something here." Lucy peered at them. "This could be him."

The two walked to Lucy's desk and peered over her shoulder when Charlie began, "Show us what you got."

"This is a Facebook group for coin collectors. I found about half a million of them on here."

"Half a million?" Allison raised her brows.

"Not literally, but a bunch on here." Lucy glanced at her notebook. "This one is number 20. I've been keeping track to avoid duplicates. Anyway, the groups are all private and you have to request to join. Fortunately, whoever the administrator was on each of these, granted my requests pretty quickly. From there, I did a search."

"And the previous 19 turned up nothing?" Charlie asked.

"That's right, but not this time." Lucy pointed to the screen. "Alan Chumbley, Florida." She looked over her shoulder at Allison. "What are the odds there's another Alan Chumbley in Florida who is also a coin collector?"

"I'd like to think pretty slim, but you never know." She slipped on her reading glasses and leaned over. "He's not bald." Allison pulled upright wearing defeat. "He's not bald."

"That doesn't mean anything right now, Alli. I think it's still worth checking this guy out," Charlie said.

"But Tabitha said a bald man with a coin," Allison replied.

"I understand that, but we can't ignore the fact that what she saw could've been a memory coming back to her about that day. Someone she recalled or something her son had mentioned before he was taken. So Alan Chumbley isn't bald. He's still a coin collector and for me, that's meaningful enough that we should press on."

"You're saying Tabitha was half right?" Lucy asked.

"I'm saying her subconscious showed her something meaningful, even if in a different form than what she actually experienced. What else can you see about him?" Charlie asked.

Lucy clicked on his profile picture. "His account is set to private. I would have to be friends with him to see anything."

"We aren't writing off this guy just yet." Charlie returned to her desk and began typing on her computer. "I'm going to friend him."

"What? No. Charlie, you can't do that," Allison said. "What if he is the one responsible? There's no way I'd let you expose yourself to him."

"I'm not going to send him a pic of my privates if that's what you think."

Allison peered at her with some derision. "You know what I mean. There has to be another way. How else can you friend someone without them seeing who you are?"

Lucy winced. "You can't. It's not possible."

"It is if you're not yourself." Charlie raised her hands in surrender. "Don't judge, but I may have created a fake Facebook account once after my divorce so I could see what my ex was posting."

Allison eyed her. "And is that account still open?"

"No. Facebook cracks down on that kind of stuff and I might have been a little too obvious when leaving remarks on certain sites."

Allison shook her head. "Charlie."

"Hey, it was a long time ago. I said don't judge. Besides, I've matured since then. Mostly. Anyway, we're getting off track. My point is, it can be done. I'll just have to make sure I don't end up in Facebook jail." Charlie typed the commands. "I'm doing it. I'm going to join this weird coin-collecting group and then I'm going to friend him. You might be the licensed P.I. around here, but I have ways of getting around the rules to get what I want."

———

TAMPA HEIGHTS WAS NORTH OF DOWNTOWN AND THAT WAS where Shane called home. A one-bedroom apartment on the third floor that overlooked the pool. He lived on a cop's salary and wasn't on the take, so this was about the best he could do.

He keyed the lock and opened the door to a pitch-black room.

A short hall that led from the entryway into the living space had a recessed light above and Shane flipped the switch. He wasn't known for his home decorating skills but managed to throw together some Ikea furniture that gave off a modern vibe.

Upon closing the door, Shane tossed his keys into a bowl on a narrow foyer table steps in front of him. He walked inside and turned on the living room lights. Vertical blinds were pulled closed across the sliding glass door that led to a small balcony. He strolled into the living room and pulled them open to reveal a hint of the downtown skyline in the distance. Below, the pool was lit up and other landscape lighting illuminated the area.

Shane grabbed a beer from the fridge before dropping to his small cream-colored modern sofa and switched on the 65" flat screen mounted above a sleek brown credenza. His thoughts swirled around the newly uncovered detail he and Detective Anton Baylor discussed earlier, outside of the stationhouse. Now that he knew Detective Bryant had heard rumors, it was decided that they would only discuss the issue away from prying eyes and bent ears.

The matter concerned the origin of the wire receipt with the word "Dave" written on it. The two had worked for months trying to track down "Dave's" identity. Turned out, evidence suggesting it was Dave Reddick mounted. Today was particularly concerning in light of the files Baylor received from the Albuquerque narcotics division where Reddick was suspected to have worked with the now-deceased criminal informant Martin Hernandez, a liaison between the Southside Runners and the Columbian cartel.

Now, as Shane stared at the news broadcast, tossing back his beer, he considered where this could all lead. What they needed now was an ally inside the FBI. Someone who would take the evidence, as they gathered it, and present it to their higher-ups to make Reddick pay for his crime. He was a bad agent and had killed a former informant in cold blood to keep him from talking.

He'd thought about what Allison had said on the matter. That it was too much for her to pursue. And she was right. Hell, Shane had begun to think it was too much for him. After all, he was just a bottom-rung detective and here he was trying to bring down a federal agent.

He picked up his phone and considered calling her. Shane had gotten in the habit of talking to her almost daily. It was something to which he looked forward, especially after a day like today. He wanted to hear her voice, to know what she was working on. Shane couldn't recall feeling this way before. Allison was reluctant to give in to what he was sure she also felt. For now, he was in the friend zone and it remained unclear if he could claw his way out.

Shane's attention was drawn from his thoughts when he heard something at his front door. With furrowed brows, he pushed off the sofa and walked down the short corridor. On the floor, shoved under the door, an envelope appeared. "What the hell?" He picked it up and on the front was his name.

Shane pulled open the door and peered down the hall to his left, then to his right. No one was there. He closed it again, securing the deadbolt, and returned to the sofa. The plain white envelope with the name "Sully" written on it, meant whoever it came from knew exactly who he was.

The lump in his throat hardened as he slipped his index finger beneath the lip and tore it open. He unfolded the letter and two words appeared. *"Isabella Gonzales."*

"Who the hell is Isabella Gonzales?"

8

Just as the day began to rear its fervent head into Charlie's bedroom, her phone buzzed on her nightstand. She pulled off the velvety mask that shielded her eyes and checked the time. A guttural moan surfaced at the realization it was 5am. On a workday, Charlie refused to get up before 6 o'clock. Her teenage boys were in high school and old enough to set off on their own. She'd waited years for that time to come and relished in her long-awaited extended sleep. But apparently, not today.

She swiped the phone from the nightstand. The buzz came from a Facebook notification and Charlie suddenly perked up. She rubbed her eyes clear of sleep and opened the app. A smile formed on her lips as she spotted the notification. *"You and Alan Chumbley are now friends."*

It worked. Charlie insisted that Allison and Lucy add her as a friend so that her account appeared legitimate. Lucy was smart enough to realize that would backfire and instead, added bots for friends. Charlie filled out the rest of her profile on her own. Liking pages, particularly ones relating to coin collecting, commenting on posts, all the things needed to make it look as though "Charlie Sweeten" was a real coin enthusiast. And Chumbley took the bait.

Charlie was never one to move with great speed unless her life was in danger, or there was a bee in the vicinity. Neither was the case right now, nonetheless, she hustled out of bed and into the shower. Relaying this new development about a man who could be a suspect in the abduction of Tabitha Barnes' son couldn't wait. And depending on what Detective Bryant had to say, Chumbley could also be connected to the abduction of the child in Kissimmee.

With her keys in hand, Charlie called out to her sons. "Austin? Kendall?" The boys were 14 and 16 respectively and neither had answered. That meant they had already left for school. Charlie was out the door and slipped into her Chevy SUV, headed straight for the office.

On arrival, the clock showed 7:30am. It was a record time for Charlie and on opening the door to the office, she'd beaten Lucy too. Although, neither of her partners would be far behind. She had half an hour, tops, to lay out a plan to present to the rest of the team.

After putting on a pot of coffee, Charlie returned to her desk and opened up her bogus Facebook account. The question as to how she would initiate this friendship with Alan Chumbley lay in the details. If she was too assertive with him, Chumbley could block her. However, too slow an approach would delay the answers they needed in this investigation.

Chumbley lived in Kissimmee. That much they knew. While it wasn't far away from Tampa, it was still a fair distance that sprung to mind how or why this man ended up at the mall in Tampa that day last year. If it was for business, where was that business conducted?

That was where Charlie would start. She needed to search for a reason why Chumbley would have been at the mall that day.

The door opened and caught Charlie's attention. She checked the time and noticed it was already 8 o'clock. Lucy had just walked in. "Good morning."

"Hey, Charlie. You're here early," Lucy replied.

"I wanted to get a jump on a few things." Hardly able to contain herself, Charlie continued, "Alan Chumbley accepted my friend request early this morning."

Lucy set down her things at her desk. "He did? That's great. That's going to open us up to figuring out where he goes and why. If I were you, I'd take a look at his timeline to see if he checked into places that might be of interest to us."

"Checked in?" Charlie asked.

"Yeah. You know, like places he went. That'll tell us a little about his habits." She returned to her desk.

"You're right."

"If we can see where he's been over the past several months to a year, that'll tell us a lot about him," Lucy added.

"You know, you're pretty smart about this stuff." Charlie smiled. "Guess we needed a Millennial on board."

"Honestly, Facebook is out of fashion with us Millennials. But Dad showed me a thing or two about tracking down people. He said people gave away the farm, so to speak, when it came to social media."

"I'm glad you paid attention." Charlie cast her gaze to the door when it opened again, and Allison appeared. "You know, this one over here," she thumbed to Lucy. "She knows what she's doing."

"You think?" Allison smiled. "Good morning." She closed the door and walked to her desk. "By the looks on your faces, you both seem happy about something."

"Chumbley friended me," Charlie said. "I was just talking with Lucy on how we take advantage of this."

"That's good. I wasn't sure this was the right way to go, but now that we're here, let's find out if he should be on the list of suspects. I was hoping to hear from Bryant, but I haven't yet."

"Then it's time to get him up to speed," Charlie began. "Alli, I'm not sure how seriously he's taking all this, and we need to be proactive. If Chumbley is a solid lead, we can't hold off until Bryant says jump. We need to jump now."

"I agree. I'll call him now and get an update." Her phone buzzed on her desk and on glancing at it, she continued. "His ears must've been burning." She swiped to answer the call. "Detective Bryant. I was wondering when we might hear from you."

"Are you in your office this morning?" he asked.

"We're all here."

"Great. I'll be there in ten minutes."

Allison pulled away the phone as he abruptly ended the call. "Well, that was weird. He said he'd be here in ten minutes, then hung up."

"He knows something," Charlie said.

"While we're waiting, show me what you have on Alan Chumbley." Allison walked to Charlie's desk. "Now that he's friended you, what do we do?"

"That's where Lucy had some input," Charlie said. "She said I should check his timeline to see where he's been over the past several months. The places he's visited."

Lucy joined them. "Dad told me that people give away their location on Facebook and other sites and that it made his job a lot easier. I think we should see where Chumbley spends his time."

Charlie logged into the account and clicked on Alan Chumbley's timeline. "I'm particularly interested in what might've brought him to Tampa, if in fact, he came here at all, in the last year. And the mall. If we think he could be a suspect, what brought him to the mall at the same time Tabitha was there with her son?" She scrolled down several months' worth of posts.

"If he was planning on abducting a child, would he have announced on Facebook where he was going to be when he did it?" Allison asked.

"I don't want to convict him before we know anything about him, but you could be right," Lucy said. "Unless it wasn't planned. It was an unexpected opportunity."

Charlie continued to view the screen. "I assume Bryant is bringing in the file he got from the Kissimmee police?"

"I hope so," Allison replied. "It will include Chumbley's witness statement."

"I don't get why no one's taken a serious look at him before now? Are we pulling this out of left-field or is there something legitimate here?" Charlie added.

"We won't know the answer to that until we dig deeper into his background." Allison's attention diverted to the door. "Detective, thanks for coming over." She approached him and offered her hand. "Can I get you a coffee?"

Bryant returned her greeting. "Yes, ma'am. I could use a shot of caffeine." He turned to the others. "Morning, ladies."

"You hustled over here mighty quick," Charlie began. "Does that mean you have good news for us?"

Bryant continued inside and pulled off his suit coat and hung it over one of the guest chairs. "Good news? I don't know about that. News? Yes. I have some news." He reached for the mug as Allison held it out for him. "Thank you, Allison."

She returned to her seat. "What did you find out about Alan Chumbley?"

He sipped on the coffee before answering. "Well, you already know he doesn't match the description Tabitha Barnes offered from her—dream."

"No," Allison replied. "But his occupation seems to fall in line with what she said."

"Yes, it does, which is what brings me here this morning," he replied.

Lucy walked to Allison's desk. "What did you find out?"

Bryant reached into his coat pocket on the back of the chair and retrieved a small evidence bag. He set it on Allison's desk. "Guess what I found at the fairgrounds where Chumbley had a kiosk set up?"

Allison pulled the bag closer to her. "Oh my God." She shot a look to the detective. "Are you kidding me? A buffalo nickel?"

"Yes, ma'am. Seems they're popping up all over the place. Not at all dissimilar to the one you and Charlie found in the parking lot of the mall. I'd call it a coincidence, but I wouldn't want to insult you."

Allison looked at Charlie and nodded. "Tell him about the whole Facebook thing."

Bryant peered over his shoulder at her. "What Facebook thing?"

"I friended Alan Chumbley. We thought it was a good idea to see who he talks to, places he goes, things like that."

"Please tell me you didn't use your real name," he said.

"I didn't." Charlie swatted away the notion. "What am I, some newb?"

Lucy glanced at her with a wide grin.

Bryant nodded. "Well, I'm glad you all didn't waste any time."

Kissimmee, Florida was a small town in comparison to Tampa. The roughly 60,000 residents lent to the small-town feel. Even their downtown business area didn't have any high-rise buildings. Being only minutes from Orlando and the parks there, many people commuted to the touristy area for work. But not Alan Chumley.

He was a slight man whose khaki pants sagged on his backside. On a good day, he reached 5 feet 9 inches and had a head full of dark blonde hair. His square wire-rimmed glasses were for use when he worked on his computer, which he did often. After all, Alan had an online business selling collectible coins and he did well for himself.

He had a dedicated home office near the front of the house. It was a converted formal living room space that had rarely been used as such and when his business went online, he converted the area. Alan was a widower whose wife passed away some five years earlier from leukemia. They shared two children. A son, Andrew, who was now in his mid-twenties, and a daughter, Alana, who was eighteen and had just started college.

Alan's love of coins turned into a career after his wife passed away. Prior to that, he'd worked as a clerk for the city. Now he spent most of his time buying and selling, sometimes trading coins on eBay, and his own website, ChumbleyCoins.com.

He peered at his phone as it rang on his desk. "Hello?"

"Is this Alan Chumbley?"

"Yes, it is."

"Mr. Chumbley, this is Detective Caleb Santora with the Kissimmee police department."

"Oh, hello. What can I do for you, Detective?"

"I was hoping you might come down to the station. There've been a few developments regarding the disappearance of the boy, Ian Nygard, from the fairgrounds a few months ago."

"Oh, I see. Of course. Anything I can do to help with your investigation," Alan replied.

"That's good to hear. If you have time today, I'd certainly appreciate that."

"Today?" He glanced at the time. "Well, I suppose I could do that. I can come down now if that's convenient enough for you."

"That would be fantastic, Mr. Chumbley. Thank you so much and I'll see you soon."

"Okay. Thank you, Detective." Alan ended the call. He clicked on his eBay account to check his sales for the day. He pursed his lips in slight disappointment and powered down his laptop.

"Hey, Dad." Andrew popped his head into his father's office. "Did you say something?" To see the two of them near each other, it was obvious Andrew had taken after his father in terms of his face and hair, though the younger man sported an athletic build.

"I was just talking to myself. I have to run down to the police station. I guess they need to ask me a couple more questions regarding that boy who disappeared from the fairgrounds back in January. I shouldn't be long."

"Oh, okay. I'm pulling a double shift, so I won't be home until late. Unless you want me to come with you? I could call in sick."

Alan pushed in his desk chair. "Oh no. That's not necessary. It's just standard operating procedure. Go to work. I might be up when you get home, or I might not." He wore a crooked smile that bared crowded teeth.

"Okay. If you're sure." Andrew, whose smile was nearly perfect thanks to the thousands his parents spent in orthodontia, nodded in return and headed to his room.

Alan reached for his car keys and walked into the garage to his car. He backed out of the driveway in his white Ford Fusion and headed straight for the police station. During the course of this investigation, he'd only been called in once to offer a statement. Though he understood that the original detective had passed from a tragic accident. This detective, he had never met.

On his arrival, he approached the front desk. "Good afternoon. I'm here to see Detective Santora. I'm Alan Chumbley."

The officer peered at Santora as he neared. "There's someone here to see you, Detective."

"Alan Chumbley? I'm Detective Santora. I appreciate you clearing your schedule for me this afternoon. Please, follow me and we'll talk in my office." Santora, who was pushing 60 and full-waisted with a bald spot on the top of his head, started back into the halls of the stationhouse. "Boy, I sure do appreciate you coming back down here, Mr. Chumbley. You'll forgive me but I'm working real hard to get up to speed on this case since the original detective passed away."

"I heard. That's terrible. And like I said, anything I can do to help," he replied.

"Right through here." Santora held open his office door and closed it behind him before walking to his desk. "I wanted to clarify a couple of points with you regarding your previous statement."

Alan sat down. "Well, I'm not sure I can recall exactly what I said. It was a couple of months ago."

"I am aware of that and I have your sworn statement right here." He pushed the paper toward him. "That said, I'd like to know if you visited Tampa at any time last year."

"Tampa? Last year?" Alan asked.

"That's right. Specifically, around early March. Take your time. Think about it a minute."

Alan creased his brow and gnawed on his bottom lip. "Well, let me see. I do tend to go there when I'm looking to buy a collection or attend a conference."

"You think you might've done that during the timeframe in question?"

Alan shrugged. "It's possible, though I can't seem to recall just at the moment." He peered at the detective. "I'd probably have to take a look at my calendar and get back with you."

"Fair enough. Let's say you did make a trip. Where would you normally go to do your buying?"

"Oh, well, lots of places. Uh, let's see, there's a collector down on the south side of town. Another one near the Bay."

"Any near the old mall that shut down, East Citrus Park?"

"A mall? I don't think so. I can't think of any reason why I'd be going to a mall for anything."

The detective nodded. "Okay. Well, I'll tell you what, why don't you consult your calendar and you let me know if you were in Tampa back in early March. Can you do that for me, Mr. Chumbley?"

"I certainly can, Detective. Although, I'm not sure what that has to do with the incident at the fairgrounds."

"Just looking to rule out something. It's all very routine, I assure you."

"Of course. Is that all you wanted from me today?" Chumbley asked.

"It seems so." He stood up. "But I sure would like a follow up just as soon as possible if that's good with you."

"Just as soon as I get back home, I'll have a look and get back to you." He got to his feet and appeared to hesitate for a moment. "I suppose I'll be talking with you later today, Detective. You have a pleasant afternoon." Chumbley turned into the corridor with a deadpan stare.

9

Allison stood on the front porch of Tabitha Barnes' home. It was approaching midday and an update for her client on what she and her team had been working on was needed. She knocked on the door and a moment later, Tabitha appeared on the other side. "Hi, Tabitha. How are you?"

"Doing okay, Allison. Come in." Tabitha stepped aside. "You'll have to forgive the mess. I'm still not quite 100 percent and the doctor told me I couldn't do any heavy lifting." She chuckled. "I think I'm really just using that as an excuse not to do housework."

"I understand completely," Allison replied. "I'm not much for keeping a tidy house myself."

"Please, have a seat." Tabitha gestured to the living room sofa. "Can I get you anything to drink?"

Allison sat down. "Oh, no thanks." She waited for Tabitha to take a seat. "I wanted to give you an update on what we've been working on."

"Okay." She appeared hesitant, as if expecting bad news.

"I realize this past year has been hell for you and your

husband. And while I don't have definitive updates for you, I wanted you to know that Detective Bryant is fully on board and has actually been a great help in running down new leads based on what you told us on our first meeting."

"So, I wasn't crazy? The things I saw actually meant something?" Tabitha asked.

"It certainly seems that way, but we're being cautious not to jump the gun without getting a clearer picture first. Another similar investigation is ongoing in Kissimmee. A young boy disappeared from an elementary school fair that had taken place a few months ago." She paused for a moment. "You remember the buffalo nickel we found in the mall parking lot?"

"Of course I do," Tabitha replied.

"Well, Detective Bryant found another one at this fairground. I realize it's an ambiguous connection as I'm sure there are thousands of these coins floating around. But the fact of the matter is that two of them were discovered at locations where children went missing. This is not something to be dismissed and deserves our full attention."

"What do you plan on doing then?" Tabitha asked.

"The other investigation has a lead on a suspect and we're coordinating with them. Detective Bryant made the trip to see the other detective yesterday. I wanted to come here to tell you this because I think what you saw in your dream, in that state of unconsciousness, might have been something you had seen in real life. Coins, an unknown man who happened to be bald. I was hoping you might think about retracing your steps from that day to see if you can recall anything else," Allison said. "I do believe there could be more hidden away in your head that, if given the chance, might reemerge now that the worst of the shock and pain have subsided."

"How would that be possible? The mall is closed," Tabitha said.

"Detective Bryant is looking to get the owner of the property to let us revisit." Allison paused again. "I'm asking if you'd be willing to relive the events of that day in an effort to recall more relevant details."

Tabitha appeared to consider the request. "I'm not sure I can do that, Allison."

"I don't pretend to know what you went through and I understand if you don't want to do this..."

"But if you think it could help, I have to try, don't I?"

Allison smiled warmly. "I'll tell you what, think about it. Detective Bryant would still need to get permission from the mall owner. Give it a day. If you agree, we'll move forward and get it out of the way as quickly and painlessly as possible."

———

SHANE WASHED DOWN HIS BURGER WITH A GUZZLE OF SODA before he continued, "You're sure you want to put her through that again?"

Allison peered through the window of the restaurant that overlooked the downtown skyline. "What we have right now is promising, but we really need more. This man, Chumbley, he was just a witness for the Kissimmee investigation you matched to ours. Even Bryant believes there could be something to it but believing and knowing are two very different things. I guess we're hoping there's another element to this that she might remember if put back in the situation."

"And Bryant agrees?" Shane pressed on.

"It was his idea. He wants us to run on that with Tabitha while he works with Detective Santora in Kissimmee on background details for Alan Chumbley."

"I can see you already believe he's a suspect." Shane took another bite. "You gotta be careful about that stuff. You don't have a shred of evidence."

"I understand that, Shane. What will turn a corner for us is if we discover Chumbley was in Tampa and at the mall when Tabitha's boy went missing. For me, that'll seal the deal. Case closed."

"I wouldn't count on it being that easy, Allison. Look, I'm glad you've been able to open up a possible lead, but you guys have a long way to go on this. With Bryant backing you, you stand a good shot, but don't count your chickens, you know?"

"I get it." Allison tucked a French fry into her mouth. "So what about you, huh? What's been going on? Are you working on any new cases?"

"Someone shoved an envelope under my apartment door last night." He slurped on his soda.

"About Reddick?" Allison lowered her tone to a whisper.

"Oh yeah, definitely. It was a name and I'm working on it."

"But you're not in any danger, right? Whoever gave this to you, is it a friend or foe?"

"Ah, now, that's the real question. If it was a foe, I doubt I'd be sitting here with you right now. I'll be fine."

"And you're sure you want to keep at it?" She asked. "Even if it could jeopardize your future and Baylor's?"

"If we don't, then who will?" Shane wiped his mouth with a napkin. "If you guys need anything, you know I'm here for you, right?"

"We know, and it's appreciated."

"What are you going to do after this?" he asked.

"I'll head back to the office and update the girls on what I discussed with Tabitha. Charlie's been working her own angle on Alan Chumbley."

"Oh, she has?"

"Yeah." Allison smiled. "She can be quite creative given the opportunity and, in this case, I'm completely on board. We'll see if anything comes of it." She eyed the time and pulled out her wallet. "Listen, I need to head back."

"I asked you to lunch. Put away your wallet," Shane insisted.

"You don't have to do that but thank you."

He reached for her hand that rested on the table. "I'm proud of what you've built, Allison. In a short amount of time, you've managed to keep yourself and your staff above water. That's tough for any business to do. The reason people come to you is your compassion for their plight. That was why Tabitha Barnes knocked on your door. The old couple who owned the pharmacy, too. Don't ever lose that. This type of work can leave you feeling jaded. I'm sure Tommy Boyce said that to you as well. Just remember the good you're doing for these people who've come to you for whatever reason."

Allison let her fingers slip away from his. "Have you lost that compassion?"

"Not yet. Then again, I don't see a lot of good people in what I do. But I know I'm helping. That's all I have."

Allison grabbed her purse and started to rise. "You should come over for dinner again sometime. I wouldn't mind the company. I'll see you later."

Shane smiled. "Yeah. Sure. See ya."

———

CHARLIE GRABBED HER PEN AND JOTTED DOWN THE

locations where Alan Chumbley had checked in on Facebook. "I don't think this guy gets out much."

Lucy glanced at her from her desk. "You haven't sent him any messages or anything, right?"

"No. I've liked a couple of his posts, but I learn from my mistakes. I don't intend on getting blocked. So far, from what I've seen, he's attended a few conferences in his industry. One in New Orleans, another in Boston."

Allison opened the door and walked in. "I'm back."

"How'd it go?" Lucy asked.

"With Tabitha? She's considering the request." Allison walked to her desk.

"And with Sully?" Charlie asked with a raise of her brow.

"Fine. We had a nice lunch."

"I'll bet you did," she snickered.

"The joke's getting old, Charlie." Allison dropped to her chair. "I'm waiting to get word back from Bryant on whether Alan Chumbley relayed his schedule to the Kissimmee detective. He was supposed to get back to him about whether he'd been in Tampa last March. I assume you haven't had any luck figuring it out?"

"Nothing yet, but I'm still working on it," Charlie replied. "You know, Alli, it might be a good idea for me to try to get a little closer to him."

"That's the exact opposite of a good idea, actually," she replied. "If this man did what we think he might've done, there's no chance I'd let you get anywhere near him."

Charlie stood up and paced the office. "I'm starting to rethink that assumption. I mean, look at this guy. He's an average guy. Kind of geeky, but otherwise, he seems pretty normal. Maybe we're looking in the wrong direction."

"Normal looking people are the ones to be concerned with, in my opinion," Allison replied. "I'm not ruling him out until we know for sure he wasn't in Tampa when Hayden Barnes went missing. Until then, Charlie, I just don't think it's a good idea for you to do anything more than what you're doing. Don't engage him. Please."

Charlie raised her hands. "Fine. I won't."

"I can see the look in your eyes. I know what you're like. Promise me," Allison insisted.

"I promise, okay? Is that good enough for you? I won't engage Alan Chumbley." Charlie walked back to her desk but not before winking to Lucy.

"I saw that," Allison said. "You're not the only mom in this room. I have eyes in the back of my head, same as you."

"What?" Charlie laughed. "Fine. I hear you. I hear you."

Allison's phone rang. "That's our man now." Picking up the call, she began, "Detective Bryant. Good to hear from you."

"I have some good news and some not so good news," he replied.

"I have the rest of the team here so I'm going to put you on speaker and let's start with the good news." She set down her phone and pressed the speaker button before waving over Lucy and Charlie. "Okay. You're on."

"Good afternoon, everyone," Bryant began.

"Afternoon, Detective," Charlie replied.

"It's Lucy. Hi there, Detective."

"Now that the pleasantries are over, let's hear what you have," Allison said.

"The good news is that Alan Chumbley got back with our detective in Kissimmee. Turns out, he was in Tampa in March of last year. When the detective pressed him on an exact date, he couldn't come up with one but made mention he could go back and check his bank for details on purchases. Apparently, he made a sizeable purchase."

"That sounds good for us, pending an exact date. What's the bad news?" Allison asked.

"The bad news is that he says he was never at the East Citrus Park mall at any time during his visit."

Charlie's shoulders dropped. "He's sure about that? Because he doesn't even seem sure of when he was in Tampa."

"Well, you're right, but he insists he would've had no business being at the mall. So, I'm not sure how much farther we can go on this particular lead," Bryant said.

Allison looked to her team. "Any ideas?"

"Detective Bryant, it's Charlie here. What is the detective in Kissimmee saying? He's got a similar investigation. Does he even remotely consider Chumbley a suspect based on what you found at the fairgrounds?"

"He already knew Chumbley was there, which was why he was interviewed in the first place. Several people were interviewed when it happened. So, finding a coin doesn't seem that big of a deal to him yet. We're going to need more if we want to push this. My main concern is about our case here."

"Let me ask you this, Detective. It's Allison again. "You seemed to think along the same lines as we did. That it was pretty tough to ignore the fact that we made those coin discoveries at two sites where children went missing. What are your thoughts now?"

"I can't argue the odd connection, but if Chumbley wasn't in the right place at that right time, what can I do about that? Look, I think the best thing to do now is to let Mrs. Barnes know what's going on. Let her know that we might be back at Square One. Now, I can give her a call, if you'd like..."

"No," Allison began. "Let me do it. She came to us and I told her I'd keep her in the loop on everything. What about the visit to the shuttered mall? Have you gotten permission?"

"Again, Allison, I'm not sure it's worth it if what she saw before turns out to have meant nothing."

Allison appeared to disagree but didn't say as much aloud. "Let me get with the team here and see what our next steps are. Thank you for doing what you could do, Detective."

"I'll keep following up with Kissimmee. Who knows? Something else might pop up. I'll speak with you ladies soon. Goodbye."

Allison ended the call. "Well, now what? The guy says he wasn't at the mall."

Charlie marched back to her desk. "I don't accept that. Come on, Alli. We have some compelling evidence here. I understand where Bryant is coming from. He's under certain constraints. We aren't. We can do certain things he can't."

"Such as?" Lucy asked.

"Such as me making contact with Chumbley. It has to be done. I need to know who he is. The more we know about him, the more conclusive we can be as to whether he can be ruled out. Does anyone believe he could be lying about his whereabouts? What if he lied about not being at the mall? I don't accept Bryant's notion to pull the plug on the only real lead we have on this case."

Allison turned to Lucy. "What do you think?"

Lucy shrugged. "First of all, it sure would've been nice if that damn mall was still open. But since it's not, I think Charlie could be right. A guilty man would lie regarding his whereabouts."

"An innocent man would tell the truth," Allison added. "You've put him in the 'guilty' category already?"

"I don't know. I guess not." Lucy looked at Charlie. "But if she can just get a little closer to him and try to learn what kind of man he is, we'll be better off than we are now."

Allison nodded. "Tell me how you want to approach this."

Charlie appeared re-energized by the idea. "Here's what I was thinking. The man's single. We know that. He's older. What, like in his fifties?"

"That's what the file said, yes," Allison replied.

"Okay, and not exactly a chick magnet, you know? He's just an average, maybe a little on the small side, kind of man. I'm an average, maybe on the small side, kind of woman. A little older, not quite 50—yet. Maybe he needs to find out a little bit more about Charlie Sweeten."

"Who's that?" Allison asked.

Charlie furrowed her brow. "Me. It's me. That's the name I chose to set up the account."

"Oh. Okay, I'll go along with this on the condition that you don't meet with him personally. No face-to-face, you got it?"

"Sure." Charlie swatted her hand. "I got this."

10

The porch light burned white as Allison waited for Charlie to answer her door. She heard the deadbolt unlatch and the handle turn and instinctively stepped back a few inches until she saw Charlie on the other side. "Hi."

"Alli, come in." Charlie stepped aside and shut the door behind her. "Thanks for coming over. I didn't interrupt your evening, did I?"

"No, of course not," Allison replied.

"The boys are with their dad. I thought it'd be better if you came over so I could show you what's been happening." Charlie walked toward the kitchen, which was on the small side, but decorated in white and light blue and had a sort of coastal charm. She didn't get much in the divorce, but she got the house.

Charlie opened the fridge. "You want a beer or a glass of wine?" She peered inside. "Looks like I have a chardonnay."

"That'll do. Thanks." Allison pulled out a chair at the kitchen table where Charlie's laptop lay open. "I guess we're in this now, huh?" She sat down.

Charlie returned with two wine glasses and set one down in front of Allison. "Oh, we're in this now. I honestly didn't think I'd get such a quick response."

"Well, we shouldn't keep the man waiting." Allison moved next to her. "Show me the conversation."

Charlie logged into the fake account and opened the messages box. "Right here. Like we talked about, I sent him a message. Nothing too personal or that might make me seem crazy, which, by the way, was a tough task." She smiled. "I asked him how long he'd been a collector." She pulled up the dialog box. "Here's his response."

"Mainly since my wife passed away a few years ago. It keeps me busy, earns me a bit of money, and makes me feel like I have something to look forward to every day."

Allison pulled back. "Oh, man. He's a widower."

"I know." Charlie took a drink of her wine. "I kind of feel bad for doing this."

"You won't if we find out he's our guy," Allison replied.

"What do you think I should say in response? I was thinking I could lighten the conversation with my usual on-point wit."

"You could do that, or you could use his vulnerability against him. And yes, I know how that sounds." Allison peered at her. "If he took Hayden Barnes and the other kid, then it will have been worth it, right?"

Charlie nodded. "Yes." She inhaled a breath. "Okay, so what do I say?" She placed her hands on the keys. "What about something like 'I'm sure your wife would want you to be happy and fulfilled,' or maybe something like…"

"What about asking if he has kids?" Allison asked. "The whole purpose of this is to find out who he is."

Charlie nodded. "Okay, I think I got it." She began typing. "What do you think of this."

Allison looked at the screen and smiled. "Perfect."

"You're sure?" Charlie's index finger hovered over the "enter" key. "I'm only going to get one shot at this. If he thinks he's being played, we lose."

"No, this is good. This is great, actually." Allison looked at her again. "Do it. Press the button."

"Okay. Here goes nothing." With a cringe, Charlie pressed "send." "That's it. We'll see if he bites."

"Then we wait." Allison sipped on her wine. "I'm still expecting Tabitha's answer regarding another visit to the mall. I know Bryant didn't want to follow through with it, but I'm going to need him to back us up on this one. It's our last shot, Charlie."

"Bryant has been working on this investigation for almost a year. He doesn't have anything to lose by going through with it."

"What are the odds she'll recall something worth looking at?" Allison asked.

"You want the truth? About as good as me finding a date."

Allison tossed back her head in laughter. "Please. You don't even try, so how can you complain about not having any dates?"

Charlie buffed her fingernails on her shoulder and peered at them. "I shouldn't have to try. They should be lining up at my door." She laughed in return. "You know, like they do for you."

"What? Right. Yeah, I got a line of men just waiting for their chance."

"You have at least one that I know of," Charlie replied.

"Stop already." Allison's cheeks flushed a pale pink.

"Oh, hang on. What's this? Are you blushing? Oh, that's new. I hit a nerve there, didn't I? Do I sense there's something you're not telling me?"

"We were supposed to have dinner at my house tonight, but just as friends," Allison replied.

"Wait. Shane was going to your house and you canceled on

him to come here? If I'd known that, I could've handled this myself, Alli. I just thought you'd want to see what kind of response we got from Chumbley. I'm sorry."

"Don't be. It's no big deal. This is far more important. Besides, I'm still leery of that whole situation. I'm not sure I'm ready..."

Charlie pulled to attention as the notification sounded on her laptop. "Hold on to your britches. Looks like we got ourselves a reply here."

"What did he say?" Allison pulled closer with renewed interest.

Charlie turned the screen so they could both read Chumbley's response.

"You seem very kind. I'm glad you reached out to me, Charlie. It's nice to talk to someone with compassion. Most people don't see me. I'm invisible to them. But I'm still a person."

Charlie appeared stunned. "Okay, how big of a piece of crap do I feel like right now?"

"He seems sincere," Allison replied.

"Cripes." Charlie shook her head. "This guy's a killer? Really?" She pointed to the remainder of the message. "He says he's got two kids."

"Yeah, both adults. One who still lives at home." Allison studied the screen again. "He could be playing on your sympathy, Charlie. Maybe that's how he gets the kids' attention. He makes them feel sorry for him. Just like we do now."

Charlie pulled off her dark-rimmed glasses and rubbed her full cheeks. "I don't know."

Allison perked up with an idea. "I got it. What if we tell him you live here in Tampa and ask if he ever has reason to come here and if he plans on doing so in the near future."

"I'd basically be asking to meet him," Charlie said. "I thought you didn't want to go that route."

"I don't. What I want to know is if he comes to Tampa on a regular basis and why. We need to know what he was doing here last March. We need to stay focused on our goal."

"Yeah, okay. I got it." Charlie typed again. "I'll ask him now and make it sound like the next time he's here, we should meet up."

Allison nodded. "Okay. We'll see what he says to that."

Charlie pressed send and waited. "I feel like I can't breathe."

Allison placed her hand on Charlie's thigh. "You can. We haven't done anything wrong. If we don't get to the bottom of Chumbley's intentions..."

"I understand but I'm starting to hope that we're wrong about this."

"Maybe we are. Time will tell." Allison tossed back the last of her wine. "I could use another. You want a top up?" She grabbed both glasses and walked back to the fridge and poured out the rest of the bottle.

"Alli, come quick. He already responded," Charlie said.

Allison marched back to the table. "Well? Did he bite?" She dropped into the chair next to Charlie.

"I'd say so. Take a look."

"I do travel to Tampa on occasion. Usually if there's an event or a conference. There's an exhibit again later this month. If so, it sure would be nice to have someone to go with."

"Holy crap." Charlie shot a look to Allison. "He wants to meet up."

"Let's find out what this exhibit is and when. We might've just discovered if he had an alibi when Tabitha's son went missing."

ALAN CLOSED HIS LAPTOP AND SMILED. HE COULDN'T believe his luck, friending a woman who also happened to be into coin collecting. As he pushed off his sofa, he headed toward his bedroom to change for bed.

Along the way, he noticed Andrew's door was ajar and a light was on inside. "Son, how many times have I told you to turn off the lights when you leave a room?" He would've thought his 25-year-old son wouldn't still need to be told these things, and he walked inside to turn it off.

Andrew was at work and Alan had wanted to share the news of the woman but didn't feel quite comfortable yet. After all, she hadn't even agreed to a date yet.

"Maybe picking up your dirty laundry would be useful, too." Alan scoffed as he stepped over numerous pairs of socks and some t-shirts balled up on the ground. He made his way to the nightstand where the lamp burned.

The drawer beneath was closed but something was caught in it. Alan pulled open the drawer and noticed it was a ticket. "What in the world?" He unfolded the yellow copy of what appeared to be a parking violation. "Oh, come on, son. How old is this? I'll bet you haven't paid this either." Alan shook his head before turning off the light. "I'm sure I'll have to do it for you."

He walked to his bedroom and pulled on a t-shirt. Charlie had already made his heart soar, but he couldn't shake the ordeal with the police detective. He'd given him vague details that would certainly be scrutinized. This new detective wasn't going to just let Alan fade into the background. However, coming clean about where he was and what he was doing in March of last year would implicate someone besides himself.

———

WHEN ALLISON ARRIVED AT THE OFFICE, BOTH SHE AND Charlie realized they had uncovered significant details about their supposed suspect. But before they ran to Detective Freddy Bryant with the news, they needed to be certain it held value for him. Their credibility was at stake and they had no room for error. The relationships they built now would help them on future cases, but if they made Bryant jump through hoops for nothing, that bridge would be burned.

"Any luck on the name of this expo or conference Chumbley was talking about?" Allison asked as she peered at Charlie from her desk. "I haven't found anything yet."

"I've been searching his Facebook, but I don't see any reference to it," Charlie began. "So, I'm going through the coin collecting group to see if anyone posted about it from last year."

"What about asking him the name of it?" Lucy said as she poured a cup of coffee. "He seemed pretty willing to open up to you last night. You didn't follow up with that?"

"Alli and I thought it was best not to seem too urgent about it. That somehow it might make me look too desperate."

"I guess so, but you said yourself he was kind of a loner. Maybe he's the desperate one?" Lucy added.

"You might be right, Lucy," Allison continued. "But I think I'd rather us find out when this conference took place to see if it put Chumbley here at the right time. If not, then there's no point in having Charlie lead him on."

Lucy returned to her desk. "I get it. What can I do in the meantime to help out?"

"It's probably a long shot, but everything about this case has been. What if those coins found at the crime scenes hold some value, or better yet, were associated with an owner? I'm certainly no expert, but I'm wondering, could there be a paper trail of ownership?" Allison asked.

"I'm sure I could find out," Lucy replied.

"There's a collector's shop on Wilmhurst Drive," Allison said.

Lucy grabbed her bag. "I'm on my way."

———

LUCY ARRIVED AT THE NEAREST COIN SHOP THAT WAS ALSO A collectibles store for other items such as baseball cards and sports memorabilia. She pulled to a stop and parked her car, or rather, her dad's car, which was an old black Monte Carlo SS. The time showed 9am and the store had just opened. She flipped back her dark hair before stepping out with a carrier bag slung over her shoulder. Inside that bag were the coins.

Lucy pushed open the bar on the glass door and a bell rang above her head. The store had no customers. Inside were items encased in glass, rows of shelves with assorted memorabilia and in the far corner, behind the cashier desk, was a display of coins. Lucy was completely unfamiliar with regard to coin values and now she was going to have to play to the notion that she actually knew something about these buffalo nickels.

"Good morning, miss. How can I help you?" A man who appeared to be in his late forties stood behind the counter wearing a pleasant smile. His plump belly touched the glass case in front of the register.

"Hi there." She approached. "I had some questions about buffalo nickels." Lucy reached into her bag and pulled out the two that were in separate Ziplock baggies. "I have an uncle who gave these to me a long time ago, actually, and I just came across them again when I moved. They look to be in not so great a shape, but could you tell me if they might be valuable in some way?"

"Are you looking to part with them?" he asked.

"No, I don't think so. They have sentimental value. I was just wondering, for insurance purposes, if I should maybe keep them in a safe or something."

"Well, let's see what you have."

Lucy placed the baggies on the glass counter and unzipped them. "This one, I think is older, but I'm just not really sure." She pulled the first one out of the bag. It had been the one Allison and Charlie discovered at the mall. The second was in slightly better condition and she set it beside the other.

The man picked up the one from the mall and examined it. His eyes narrowed as his index finger and thumb twirled the coin. "There's no date on this one." He looked at Lucy. "I'm afraid that means you'd be lucky to get ten cents for it." He set it back down and picked up the coin Detective Bryant found at the fairgrounds. His eyes narrowed into mere slits as he pulled the coin toward his face. "Now this one..." he continued to study it. "This one might just have a date. It's almost gone but I think I see some indication here." He pointed to it. "You see that?"

Lucy nodded.

"That little bit of raised feature suggests the date is probably still legible if I were to clean it with a solution."

"And could you do that?" She asked.

"Well, I could, but I'll tell you, that would negate any value at all. You see, the solution tends to damage the coin in the process of revealing a date. So, it's a bit of a Catch-22."

"I see." Lucy appeared defeated. "And if either of these coins had a date, would they be, oh, I don't know, registered or something?"

He pursed his lips before continuing. "Well, no. That's not really how these things work. You'd register a coin collection for sure. They're valuable and you'd want it to be covered under insurance. Think of something like getting a piece of jewelry appraised. That would be kind of the same thing."

"And if a collection was registered, where would that information be kept?" Lucy pressed on.

"Do you have a collection, miss? I'd love to see it. I could offer you a valuation."

"I don't. But since I found these, well, I guess I think it's kinda cool, you know?"

"Oh, I know how that goes. Believe me. I fell in love with coins many years ago. In fact, I have a few collections, myself." He turned and pointed to a shelf behind him. "You see that one there? That is worth almost $2000. I put it in a safe every night, just in case."

"Wow. That's awesome." This was about as far as she was going to get with this guy and she still hadn't had much in the way of answers. "So, this registration process. Is there like a database or something where people could see other coins other collectors might have?"

"Well, I'll tell you what, there is an association of coin collectors. I'd check there if I were you. They'll give you the lowdown if you're really interested in becoming a collector."

11

L inking Alan Chumbley to either of the coins found at the crime scenes was a hundred-to-one shot and hadn't panned out. Another blind alley on route to more dead ends.

Disheartened, Lucy returned to the office and presented the information. "What I did find out was that there is a registry for coin collectors. Two main ones, actually. One is called the PCGS, the Professional Coin Grading Service, and the other is called the NGC, the Numismatic Guaranty Corporation. If a collector wants to register his collection, it would have to be certified by one of these two groups."

"And the collections are traceable to an owner?" Charlie asked.

"They are. We could join online and search collections to confirm whether Chumbley is a member," Lucy replied.

"That doesn't help us with the coins we have," Allison pressed on.

"They aren't worth more than a dime and they wouldn't be

included in anyone's collection." Lucy sighed. "It wasn't the answer we needed."

"No way to tie either of them directly to Chumbley. It was a longshot to think we could find an owner, but we can check out the rest of it. It was still good work, Lucy," Allison replied. "Not all is lost. Charlie, tell her what we found on the exhibition."

"Tampa hosts an exhibition every March called the Tampa Coin Expo. Turned out, it wasn't that hard to find details on it. Now I can go back to Chumbley and speak with some intelligence on the matter. After all, I'm supposed to be a coin enthusiast," Charlie said. "Here's the kicker. This event was held during the same week last year that Hayden went missing."

Lucy appeared to have renewed hope. "He was here when it happened."

"Which means he's lying to Detective Santora in Kissimmee," Allison added. "So now comes the hard part. Now it's on us to prove Chumbley was at the mall the day it happened and not at the expo."

"How are we going to do that?" Lucy asked.

Allison took in a deep breath. "I'm open to suggestion."

———

GARY LUCADO SIPPED ON A CUP OF COFFEE WHILE HE WAITED for Alan Chumbley. His friend had requested the impromptu meeting but failed to offer a reason for it. There wasn't much time before he needed to return to work, having made up an excuse to leave in the first place. He took another drink when Chumbley arrived. "You're late."

"Sorry. I got here as quickly as I could." Alan sat down.

"What's this about, buddy? Why the urgency?" Gary asked.

"I'm treading in deep water with the police right now."

"What?" Gary set down his mug and revealed concern.

"You remember when that little boy was abducted from the school fair back in January?" Alan asked.

"Yeah, I remember. Everyone remembers."

"You know the police talked to me once already because I had the cart set up there that day."

"Sure, I remember that too." Gary held his gaze. "What's that got to do with anything?"

"The detective, he knows I was in Tampa last March. I don't know why he asked me about it, and I tried to avoid an answer, but he persisted. I ended up telling him roughly when I was there but not an exact date."

Gary pulled up at attention. "Wait. The cops are asking you about Tampa last year?"

"Yeah. That's what I said. Look, Gary, I don't want to drag you into any of this..."

"How did you leave things with this detective?"

"I told him I'd have to look around for documentation of when exactly I was there. I told him I couldn't recall."

"So you lied?" Gary shook his head. "Not the smartest thing you've ever done, my friend."

"What else could I do? I needed time to come up with something, but I think that has run out now too. He's not going to let this go."

"What the hell does that have to do with the kid from the school fair?" Gary persisted.

"You got me, but someone knows something, or it would never have come up. What am I going to do?"

"What about Andrew?" Gary asked. "Does he know?"

Alan shook his head. "Not yet. I don't want to tell him until I know how to handle it. Please don't say anything to him. I know you two are close."

"I won't say anything. You have my word."

Alan stood up to leave. "Thank you."

"Hey man," Gary began. "Don't let that detective get into your head. Don't let him rope you into saying something you'll regret."

"I regret all of it anyway." Alan turned and walked away.

Gary picked up his phone and typed a text message. *"We need to talk."*

———

ALLISON DROVE BACK TO THE SHUTTERED MALL WITH Tabitha in the passenger seat. The silence between them nearly broke her heart. She couldn't imagine what Tabitha had suffered and hated keeping details from her. There was just no proof yet that Alan Chumbley committed this awful crime, so there was no point in mentioning they were looking into him. He wasn't even a suspect in the kidnapping of the boy from the fairgrounds three months ago. It was a drastic measure to pursue this lead, Allison knew that, but she had nothing else. Tracing ownership of the coins had been a bust. Detective Bryant had convinced Santora to question Alan Chumbley but the results of that were still up in the air. Bryant had also warned Allison again about giving Tabitha false hope. If there was one thing she hadn't yet learned about this job, it was this; don't promise results that might be impossible to deliver.

"This is it." Allison pulled to a stop near the mall entrance. "Are you still doing okay?"

"I am. I'll be fine. It's not like I haven't been here since that day. Believe me, I spent the first few months sitting in this parking lot, staring at that building, and wondering how I could've let someone take my child." Tabitha opened her car door and stepped out into the temperate air. She peered with squinted eyes at the sun before turning to Allison. "The steel shutters are new. I won't be able to see inside."

"A representative of the property owner is meeting us in a moment. There's an employee entrance around back. He'll let us in and give you time to do whatever you can do. Then we'll just have to take it as it comes. If you can manage to glimpse in between the darkness of your grief and the light of your memory, you might remember something." Allison reached for her arm and led her to the front of the store.

Tabitha gazed at the storefront. The sign had been removed, leaving behind only shadows of the lettering. Signs were posted stating the property was private and no one was allowed inside.

Allison peered at her. "Take your time. We're in no rush at all."

———

CHARLIE WALKED INTO THE DOWNTOWN TAMPA POLICE station on the hunt for Shane Sullivan. She wore a dogged expression and approached the front desk. "Hey, Felix. I'm here to see Sully."

"Charlie, it's nice to see you." Felix smiled. "You're looking lovely today."

Flattering remarks weren't bestowed upon Charlie often and she'd come to accept that. So it was nice when a friendly cop threw her a bone, but acknowledging such compliments wasn't easy for her and she used humor to deflect them. "Then it seems my master plan is working, which is to woo you with my keen sense of style." She grinned. "You mind if I head back?"

Felix chuckled. "Go on. He's at his desk." As she continued through the bullpen, he added, "Consider me wooed."

Shane spotted her arrival. "What was that about? You and Felix have a little thing going I don't know about?"

"We're just messing around. Hey, thanks for making time for me, Sully. Allison's busy with the client and I wanted to follow up on a few things and as it turns out, I need your help."

"I'm not sure you've ever said that to me before. I feel honored," he replied.

"Don't let it go to your head." She reached into her bag. "I was wondering what you could find for us on this guy here."

Shane reached for the file Charlie placed on his desk and pulled it closer. "What am I looking at?"

"That's Alan Chumbley and he's our only lead right now. Detective Bryant has been cooperative and we're grateful for that, but we're losing the battle on this lead and his support for it."

"That could be for a good reason. I assume you don't have anything solid," Shane replied.

"Not yet. That's why I'm here. We want to arm ourselves with as much evidence as we can muster and take it to Bryant to convince him to move forward."

"What kind of evidence do you have?" he asked.

"We know Alan Chumbley was in Tampa around the same time as our client's son went missing. However, he's already told the detective in Kissimmee he wasn't at the mall that day."

"And you're convinced he was?" Shane asked.

"I don't want to take what he says at face value. Call me a cynic."

"You, Charlie Wells, a cynic?" He smiled wryly.

"Normally, I'd be prepared with a quick retort but I'm fresh out today. Sully, we can't place him at the crime scene, and we need your help."

He studied her. "What can I do then?"

"Can you get security footage from a coin expo held in Tampa last year?"

"I gotta be honest, first of all, the odds that footage would still exist after a year are slim," he began. "Secondly, I'm not sure how willing the venue owner would be to offer it up without a warrant, should it still exist. Why do you want it?"

"It's the only way we can prove if this man was at the expo. And if he was, we need to find out if he was there the entire time."

Shane examined the photo again. "Say the video was in some archive somewhere. Great. I could maybe get my hands on it somehow. We could even go so far as reviewing it to see if this man was there, but how easy would it have been for him to slip out of view and insist he was in a place that wasn't captured on the video? My guess is that cameras would be in the open area of the expo hall where all the exhibitors were located. But what about the bathrooms? The lobby? The parking lot? He could say he went outside to eat lunch in his car, or whatever." Shane eyed her. "What I'm getting at is that if we saw him on the video, it would prove he was there. But what it wouldn't prove was if he left for a certain amount of time, say the time it would take for him to drive to the East Citrus Park mall and abduct a kid and then return to the expo. It's unlikely, but the possibility still exists and I'm sure a jury would see it that way too."

In one fell swoop, Shane stuck a pin in her idea, deflating it altogether. "Well, thanks for shooting me down."

"I'm just trying to be honest with you," Shane began. "The only thing that would truly help is if you could get security footage from the mall."

"Bryant already did that when he started his investigation. Apparently, the mall had security footage but not the store itself and there was nothing in the parking lot either. So, I guess that's it for that brilliant concept."

"Not so fast. There could be another way."

Charlie leaned in and placed her hand under her chin. "Tell me more."

———

THE HEAT OF THE DAY REACHED ITS PINNACLE WHILE Allison waited for Tabitha to call on her memory. It appeared to have turned into nothing more than an act of desperation that had forced Tabitha to relive the single worst day of her life.

"It's okay. You gave it your best. It's all anyone could ask for." Allison stepped toward her. "We can leave now."

"No, I don't want to leave. I can keep trying," Tabitha replied.

Allison backed off. "Maybe just a few more minutes if you think it will help." She'd begun to feel increasingly guilty for putting Tabitha through this. Bryant was right. It was a mistake and she should have listened to the detective who'd been through cases like this more than once. There were times when Allison believed she knew what was best. This wasn't one of those times.

Tabitha finally dropped her head into her hands. "I'm sorry. I just can't remember anything else. It all happened so fast. The panic set in. All I could feel was fear. Even under the anesthesia, when Hayden showed me the coin, and talked about the bald man, I honestly don't remember seeing any of that at the time."

"It was obviously deeply rooted in your memory. It's what the mind does, right? Helps us to forget," Allison replied.

"What if it didn't mean anything? Just like Erik believes. That it was all just part of the process of being under anesthesia. It meant nothing."

"That's not true."

"How do you know, Allison? So you found a buffalo nickel. Big deal. They're everywhere."

"It is a big deal. You remembered something about it. That matters to me."

"How are you so sure of it? Do you know more than you're letting on?"

Allison sighed. "You remember me telling you about Bryant going to see a detective in Kissimmee, right?"

Tabitha nodded. "Yes."

"Well, afterward, he drove to that crime scene that happened months ago. Tabitha, he found another buffalo nickel."

"And you're only now mentioning it?"

Allison's face masked in regret. "Because I needed to learn more. It could have been a coincidence."

"You don't think that's the case, do you?" Tabitha pressed on.

"I'm not sure what I think right now. I wanted you to recall something that could put it together for me. I was hoping for a miracle."

Tabitha folded her arms. "What now? Are you going to give up?"

"No, I won't give up on you. I just need time," she replied. "At the very least, I need to rule out that these coins are relevant."

Tabitha turned squarely to Allison. Her eyes reddened and welled with tears. "I know you'll find something. I came to you for help because I had heard what you did for that young man. I saw the news stories. I read what he said about you and ACL. He said you and your team always believed in him. Never once did you falter. That's why I'm here with you."

"Come on, we should go back now." Allison pushed through the exit and started toward the car while Tabitha followed.

Allison started the engine. "Do you want me to stop and we can grab a quick bite to eat? You must be hungry."

"No, thank you. I'm fine." Tabitha gazed through the window.

Allison headed toward the loop road of the mall. She didn't

know what words she could offer and figured there weren't any. The team would just have to continue plodding through the unsubstantiated lead until it was exhausted. After that, who knew what would happen?

"Wait!" Tabitha gripped the arm rest of the door. "Stop the car!"

Allison slammed on the brakes. "What is it?"

"Go back. Go back to the store entrance. I remember something." She shot around. "Allison, hurry!"

She turned the steering wheel hard to the right and headed back to where they'd just left. "Tabitha, what is it? What do you remember?"

"Just go. I'll show you. Hurry, please!"

Allison pressed down on the gas pedal and sped back to the entrance before slamming the gearshift into park. "Okay. What..." But before she could say another word, Tabitha was out the door and was running back toward the entrance of the store.

Allison jumped out of the car, running to catch up to her. She hurried until coming to an abrupt halt where Tabitha stood. "What do you..."

"Shhh. Give me a minute. I need to think." Tabitha searched high and low, examining everything around the entrance. "I remember the cops standing around here. People huddled in small groups in the parking lot. The police tried to keep them away." She walked to the doors. "I was standing here with Detective Bryant, answering his questions. I don't remember the questions, but I know I stood right here. I know that because I looked over there." She pointed to a large planter that no longer had a plant inside. "There was a man."

"A bald man?" Allison asked.

"I don't... no, I don't think so. He was a small man. Mousy, you know? The only reason I remembered him was because of the look on his face. He was almost in tears. I thought that he must've been a father and he could feel the pain I was in." Tabitha paused for a moment, then placed her hand over her mouth, letting out a small gasp. "Oh, God. He held this frame. I thought it was strange that it wasn't in a store bag or anything. It was just out there." Her eyes widened and she turned to Allison. "It was a frame with coins in it."

"Like the kind a collector might have?" Allison's tone was laced with anticipation.

"Maybe, yeah."

"Do you think, if you were shown a picture, you'd be able to say, 'yeah, that's the guy'?"

"I think I could. Maybe," Tabitha said. "You think it might be the guy you've been looking into?"

Allison nodded. "If it is, then you just ruled him out."

12

As far as Allison and her team were concerned, all signs had pointed to Alan Chumbley, the coin collector, as the most logical suspect in the abduction of Hayden Barnes. Not anymore. Tabitha's revelation had forced a course-correction. One in which Allison hadn't wanted to let Detective Bryant in on just yet. There was still more to learn.

Getting to the heart of why Chumbley was at the mall that day was pertinent now more than ever. When Allison returned to the office, she pulled the team together to come to some understanding as to why he would lie about it.

"You're sure you want to pursue this, Alli?" Charlie asked. "Tabitha essentially proved Alan Chumbley's innocence."

"She proved he was there and lied about it, Charlie. There is something else at play and it's up to us to learn what that is."

"I think I'm going to have to agree with Allison on this one," Lucy said. "We know the Kissimmee detective straight up asked him about being at the mall and he denied it. You can't tell me it was that he forgot. Who forgets about being on the scene of an abduction? No one."

"I say we find out why he was there," Allison continued. "Tabitha said he had a shadow box or something like that in his hand. There must've been a coin collector store at the mall, and he made a purchase."

The mall is closed now," Charlie replied.

"We can find out what it was called and who owned it." Lucy hurried to her desk. "I'll call the property owner now and find out."

Charlie pulled Allison aside. "How's Tabitha doing? Is she all right?"

"I think so. It's hard to know for sure," Allison replied. "Charlie, I'm right about this. I can feel it."

"Feel what exactly?"

"I think Chumbley lied because he was protecting someone," Allison said.

Lucy returned with a sticky note in her hand. "Collector's Paradise. Owner's name was Ed Reilly. And guess what? He has a new location."

"I'm going there now." Allison grabbed her keys.

"Not alone, you're not." Charlie swiped her bag from her desk. "Thanks, Lucy. You mind holding down the fort?"

"I guess not."

"Actually, I hate to disappoint you both, but I'm going to have to handle this on my own."

"No way," Charlie replied.

"First of all, if this man is still in contact with Alan Chumbley, the odds are good that our visit will get back to him. Charlie, if the owner describes you, it won't be hard for Chumbley to add it up. And Lucy, I need to approach this solo because if he feels in any way that we're after him, I don't know what might happen. I know nothing about him." She fumbled with her keys and started toward the door. "Sorry guys. This time, it's gotta be me."

Charlie pursed her lips and turned to Lucy. "I hate it when she's right."

————

ALLISON DROVE FOR SEVERAL MINUTES BEFORE COMING UPON a newly built retail center anchored by a Target store. This was Ed Reilly's new location.

Allison pushed the door and walked in. "Hello."

"Hi, there. What can I do for you today?" A man who was roughly 6 feet 2 inches tall stood behind the counter. His medium build appeared concealed behind an oversized Hawaiian shirt.

Allison pulled off her sunglasses and peered at him. "Is your name Ed Reilly?"

"Yes. Do we know each other?" His heavy brow knitted.

"Did you used to own a place like this inside the East Citrus Park mall before it closed down?" she asked.

"I did. I'm sorry, what is your name?"

Allison approached the counter. "Sorry about that. I'm Allison Hart. My husband is an avid coin collector and mentioned your store a while ago. Well, wouldn't you know, it's his birthday and I went to check out your place to get something for him only to discover it's closed. Luckily, I tracked you down."

Reilly still appeared mildly cautious. "Well, what is it that you're looking for then?"

"Coins, of course."

He nodded slowly and kept his eyes on her. "I see. Are you a collector?"

"Me? No. Again, this would be something for my husband. I'd been keeping an eye out online for a deal, but I just don't trust buying online, you know? Certifications can be faked. I guess what I'm saying is that I don't want to be taken advantage of."

"Of course not. I can assure you everything I sell in this store is certified and has been evaluated for authenticity," Reilly added.

"That is good to hear," she replied.

"So, what is it you're looking for, Mrs. Hart?"

"What do you have?" She smiled flirtatiously at him. "I'm interested in something nice. Something of value that he can hold onto and see a decent return on someday."

"Sounds like you know what you want," Reilly answered. "I think I might have something along those lines in the back. Let me take a look."

"Thank you." Allison felt confident a place like this wouldn't keep anything too valuable in plain sight. Too much exposure. This was the opportunity she needed to check out the operation. She meandered around the area in search of cameras. She picked up on three right away. In fact, they looked to have been placed as a deterrent. Considering there were also racks of comic books, it was probably intended to remind kids they were being watched.

What Allison was more interested in, however, was the collection of coins just right of the register, mounted on the wall inside shadow boxes. Her attention was captured when Reilly reappeared.

"Let me show you what I have, Mrs. Hart." He returned to the counter and laid out the binder.

Allison walked back to him. "The collections in the cases up there, are they valuable?"

"Somewhat, yes. Why? Do they interest you?"

"I was just curious. You know, I hear people do a lot of trading online too. Do you ever do that?"

"Sometimes, sure," he replied. "Let me show what I have here."

"Do you ever go to the coin expos? I'll bet you know a lot of people in the industry. I've only done some research, but it seems like kind of a big deal around here."

"Not particularly." He held her gaze. "Mrs. Hart, are you really interested in making a purchase?"

She inhaled a breath. "You know, the more I think about it, the more I think maybe I should keep looking. I came across a website of a coin collector. Oh, I can't recall it offhand, but it seemed to have some pretty good deals, just based on some of the research I've done."

"Well, I can match my competitors, assuming we're talking like quality and value," he replied. "You don't remember the website name?"

Allison cast her eyes toward the ceiling. "Let me think." She snapped her fingers. "Oh, that's right. I remember now because it was such an unusual name. Chumbley coins dot com. That's what it was."

Reilly smiled and peered down for a moment. "I know who you're talking about. Let me tell you, I'd think twice about making an online purchase from that site."

"Why is that? Please, enlighten me because I'm absolutely terrified of making a mistake and my husband would never forgive me if I paid more for something than it was worth."

"Let's just say the guy who runs that site, in my opinion, should be in jail."

"Oh. I see. Well, thanks for the warning. I had no idea. You must know him personally?"

He only shrugged. "You know what, take your time. Look around. If you're still in the market, I'm open six days a week. I'd love to work with you."

He'd just shut her down. No way was he going to say anything more, which was suspicious enough. "Thank you again, Mr. Reilly.

I appreciate your straightforwardness. I'm sure we'll be doing business soon." Allison pushed the bar on the door and walked outside. As she made her way to her car, she picked up the phone. "Charlie, it's me. There is definitely something up with Alan Chumbley. It's getting late. Why don't you guys meet me at Bayside in half an hour? I'll fill you in."

———

AS EVENING SET IN, ALLISON AND HER PARTNERS SAT INSIDE the Bayside Restaurant located in the north of the city near Tampa Heights. Shane walked in and found them sitting in the booth. Allison peered up at him. "Hi. Thanks for joining us. I thought you should be here too." She scooted over to make room for him.

"Your message sounded important."

"Alli thinks Chumbley is some kind of crook," Charlie said.

"What?" He peered at Allison. "What did you find out?"

Allison relayed the details from her encounter with Ed Reilly as well as what Tabitha remembered from her visit to the mall. "I told the girls that we should reconsider our position on Chumbley. He doesn't seem as innocent as we thought."

Charlie sipped on her gin and tonic. "Based on what our client recalled, he's at least innocent of taking Hayden Barnes. There's no way he could've taken that boy and been only feet from Tabitha as she talked to Detective Bryant."

"Maybe not but it sure makes it more likely he was protecting someone when he lied to Detective Santora about being in Tampa."

"I get what you're saying, Allison," Shane began. "But Charlie's right. You're looking for an abductor. It doesn't sound like Chumbley's it."

"Are you folks ready to order?" A young waitress approached with a wide smile.

"Could we get just a few minutes?" Allison asked.

"Of course."

"Hang on," Shane began. "I wouldn't mind a beer. Landshark." When the waitress disappeared, he continued. "We can't forget either that Chumbley was never a suspect in Santora's investigation in Kissimmee. He was only questioned as a favor to Bryant. I'm sorry, Allison, but even if he's a shady coin dealer, or whatever you want to call it, we're looking for a kidnapper."

"It's connected," Allison said. "One way or another, there's a connection we're not seeing right now."

"What about the expo in a few days?" Charlie began. "We know he's going to be there."

"How do you know that?" Shane asked.

"I sort of made contact with Chumbley." Charlie held up her hands. "In my defense, it was Alli's idea." She shot her a glance and revealed a grin. "No. It was my idea. I made up a Facebook account. Anyway, I managed to friend him, and he said he was going to this coin expo in a few days. He asked me to go with him."

"It's in a few days, huh?" Shane nodded.

"I told her I didn't want her to meet him face-to-face," Allison said. "I don't think it's safe and I'm even more convinced of that now."

"We already know he didn't take Hayden Barnes, Alli. What am I really risking here? I think it's important to know why he lied. Maybe he was covering for someone. A friend or something. I don't know why, but I agree with you that he lied for a reason. I think I should try to learn what that reason was," Charlie replied.

"Allison, you believe that Alan Chumbley visited Ed Reilly's coin store at the mall the day of Hayden's disappearance," Lucy began.

"That's right. I couldn't confirm it with Reilly, but Tabitha spotted what appeared to have been a purchase of coins. Where else would he have gotten them if not that store? And we already know what Reilly thinks of Chumbley."

"I think Charlie should go to that expo with him," Lucy added. "And I think Allison and I should look into why Ed Reilly says Alan Chumbley is a crook. Allison could be right. My gut is telling me there's a connection there and we just need to find it."

"You're Tommy Boyce's daughter. Far be it from me to question your hunches. That said, if you guys want to go down this road, you have to bring Bryant into the loop," Shane added. "You're wading in some murky waters right now."

"Agreed," Allison said. "We have to bring him up to speed now. I don't see any other way."

Shane nodded. "As far as meeting with Chumbley? I'm not sure it's worth the risk. If he discovered you lied about who you were, that would be a problem. We don't know anything about this guy, even less than we thought from what Allison's said."

"Oh, come on," Charlie began. "He collects coins for Pete's sake."

Shane held her gaze. "He lied, Charlie. That's a problem. And right now, we have no idea why."

———

HE WANTED TO HAVE THE ANSWERS FOR THEM, BUT THEY already knew exactly what they wanted to do. They didn't need his help. Shane might've been there as a sounding board, but it was clear, this was their investigation. But that didn't mean there wasn't something he could still do for them. For her, if he was honest.

Shane returned to the station to garner whatever evidence he could to support the ACL team in their pursuit of the Chumbley lead.

He logged into the Sex Offender Registry. If Chumbley was an offender, that would be red flag number one. Shane entered the name and waited for the system to run it. He peered at a colleague who walked by. "Hey."

"You're here late," the officer replied.

"Paperwork. What can you do?" Shane added.

The officer smiled and continued on. Meanwhile, he returned his attention to the screen and the answer appeared. "Nothing. Not on the registry." He felt relieved but it almost would've been easier if Chumbley had been on there, just to have proof that Charlie needed to steer clear.

His next move was to do a background check. Criminal, civil, any and all things related to Alan Chumbley. "Son of a bitch. He's squeaky clean." Shane rubbed his smooth chin and peered at the screen. "Why did you lie concerning your whereabouts?" he whispered.

There had to be something on this guy. Not even a traffic ticket. Shane typed again on his laptop. "What about financial problems, huh?" He pulled up any records on foreclosures or bankruptcies. "Nothing. Shit."

"Hey, Sully. What the hell are you doing here?" Lieutenant Bruce Duran approached him. "It's late and you looked pissed. You working a case or something?" Duran was the lieutenant in charge of Major Crimes and would be Shane's boss sometime in the near future.

"Lieutenant." He closed his laptop. "Just filling out reports. I had forgotten to file one of them and I was just having some trouble with the system." Shane put on a smile. "What are you doing here so late?"

"Bullshit paperwork. It doesn't change just because you wear the bars." He sat down at Shane's desk. "Since you're here, I should tell you that Haskins just told me he's planning to retire in a few months."

Shane sat at attention. "Oh, wow. That's great, for him, I mean."

Duran smiled. "Uh-huh. I think it could be great for you, my man. This is your shot to move upstairs. That's what you've wanted, right?"

"Yes, sir. Very much so," Shane replied.

"Then maybe we should get things moving in that direction. But you know, there is one thing."

"What's that, Lieutenant?" Shane asked.

"I'm gonna need your full attention when you work for me."

"Of course. I wouldn't have it any other way."

"Well, I am glad to hear that, Sully. So, I guess you won't need to be spending as much time with Baylor as you have been. In fact, I'll be reminding him of his priorities as well." Duran wrapped his knuckles on Shane's desk. "You should go home and get some sleep, Sully. You've looked better."

Shane watched as Duran walked away, dumbstruck. He knew. Somehow, Duran knew what he and Baylor had been doing, or at least, he knew something was up. But how? Bryant had known as well. Why the hell would either of them give two shits about what some bad FBI agent was doing? And now it sounded as though if he kept at it, all hopes of him moving to Major Crimes would turn to dust. He'd been one of the good guys. An honest cop, like most of them, and now he was being punished for something that didn't affect anyone in his department. "Unless it does."

He packed up his laptop and files and headed out to his car. It was getting late, almost 11 o'clock, but he had to see her. He needed to tell Allison what had happened and thought maybe she could offer sage advice. Or maybe he just wanted to be with her right now. If he was being honest, he felt intimidated. Maybe Agent Dave Reddick had more friends than he knew about. Baylor needed to know too, but right now, Shane wanted a friend he could vent to. There was more to it than that. Shane "Sully" Sullivan, who could get just about any woman, wanted Allison Hart. Maybe the time had come to tell her.

———

ALLISON HAD ALREADY CHANGED INTO A T-SHIRT AND SHORTS when she got the text from Shane. He was coming over and would be there soon with news. What this news was remained a mystery. She was glad to be seeing him anyway, even if it had only been a few hours since they last met.

So far, Allison had spent the evening preparing for Nolan's return tomorrow night. She'd cleaned his bathroom and put fresh sheets on his bed. That was what moms did. They went the extra mile to make things just right for their kids. And the extra mile didn't bother them one bit. It was how Allison's own mom had been, except when she was drinking. Allison never liked to think about those days. Only Leo knew what her mother had been like when she was a child. Her children didn't know. Besides that, Allison preferred to stay focused on the good times and not the bad, since her mother was no longer here. She passed away before Micah was born. Her kids never knew their grandmother. Sometimes that bothered her. Sometimes she considered it a blessing.

The doorbell rang and Allison hopped off the sofa and padded to the front door. "Hi."

Shane walked in. "Hi. Thanks for letting me drop by. I hope it's not too late." He shoved his hands in the pockets of his jeans. "Hey, um, you got any beer?"

"Is that a question that needed to be asked?" She laughed. "Come on. I'll get you one." She walked into the kitchen, her blonde locks flowing down her back. "You said you had some good news. After our dinner earlier, I wouldn't mind some good news." She popped open two bottles of beer. "Here you go."

"Thanks."

Allison furrowed her brow. "You okay? What's going on?" She leaned against the center island and folded her arms.

"First things first." Shane pulled out a stool to sit down. "I went back to the station and decided to look a little deeper into Alan Chumbley because I know Charlie. She's going to meet with him at this expo, isn't she?"

Allison appeared guilty. "Um, yeah. Look, Shane, it's just..."

"No. It's okay." He held up his hands. "I figured that would happen. And based on what I found, it's probably harmless anyway."

"Why? What did you find?" she asked.

"The guy is clean as a damn whistle. I found Jack Squat. I did a criminal background, civil, hell, I even checked the Sex Offender Registry. Nothing." He took a long gulp of beer, nearly finishing half the bottle.

"That seems to fall in line with what we know of Chumbley so far. Although, Lucy and I have to get to the bottom of whatever happened between Reilly and him."

"That's true. That could be serious, Allison. Do you really think it's worth Charlie going to see this guy? I'm starting to wonder what the point of it is," Shane pressed on.

"It all goes back to the tiny white lie, doesn't it? Maybe it wasn't so tiny or white. All I can say is that we're grasping at straws because we have nothing else. And I did put in a call to Detective Bryant and told him what Tabitha recalled."

"What did he say about that?"

"He was disappointed. I think he wanted a valid lead as much as we did. I also mentioned we could use some of his contacts to take a look at Chumbley's business dealings. He isn't as confident it will net us the results we need, but he said it's worth a shot."

"One thing that's been bothering me," Shane began. "Do we know if Santora mentioned the mall abduction to Chumbley?"

"I don't know if he said anything about that at all, actually, but I'll ask Bryant. I think if he had, and Chumbley was protecting himself or someone else, we'd see some movement from him, and we haven't so far." She held his gaze. "Why did you want to come over? You look like you have something else on your mind."

Shane lowered his gaze for a moment. "There is some other news."

"Oh?" Her elbows rested on the kitchen island and she leaned closer. "Spill it, Sully."

He smiled. "You never call me that."

Allison shrugged. "What can I say? It's growing on me."

Shane nodded. "Lieutenant Duran, you know, the man who would be my boss when I move up to Major Crimes?"

"Uh-huh. What about him?"

"He said there's a spot opening up in a few months. Another detective is retiring."

"Oh my God. That's great, Shane. That's what you've been waiting for." She studied him closer. "Why aren't you happy about this?"

He pressed his lips together until they turned white. "He said if I wanted to make the move that I should stop hanging around Baylor so much and focus my efforts."

"Wait. What?" She pulled back. "What's that supposed to mean?"

"It means he knows what Baylor and I are doing. That's what

it means. It was a threat, Allison. If I don't stop looking into Agent Reddick, I can kiss my transfer goodbye."

"I don't understand. How would he know?" She touched his shoulder. "Shane, I'm so sorry. I just can't..."

"Neither can I." He placed his hand over hers. "I just wanted to come here and tell you. I guess I figured you'd get it, you know?"

"Of course, I do. We're friends, Shane. You can talk to me anytime about anything. And especially this. I was the one who dragged you into that investigation."

"You didn't make me pursue it. In fact, I'm pretty sure you cautioned against it." He peered at her. "Allison, I'm glad you consider me a friend. I consider you one, too. But, do you think, maybe somewhere down the road, we could be more?"

13

Allison should have handled it better. The middle of an investigation was hardly the time for a budding romance but what Shane was going through compelled him to act on his emotions, leaving her caught light a deer in headlights.

Now, in the light of a new day, Allison was full of regret. Shane had been vulnerable, concerned his entire career was about to go up in flames for reasons he couldn't understand. People much higher on the food chain had come down on him in ways he couldn't have predicted. So when he expressed wanting to become more than friends, Allison did the only thing she could do—kick the can down the road. What remained was unspoken hurt feelings that were shoved under the rug and would undoubtedly be exposed later. But later was better as far as Allison was concerned. She'd insisted there would be time to discuss such things but that now was not that time. Her logic was sound, and he agreed, though it was clear his heart had come to no such arrangement.

As she drove to work, Allison tried to put her focus back on the investigation. A meeting had been scheduled with Detective Bryant and as Allison arrived at the office, he was already there. "Good morning. I hope you haven't been waiting long." Allison walked to her desk and set down her things.

"Not at all. In fact, I was just enjoying a nice breakfast." He held a bagel in one hand and a coffee in the other.

"Lucy's good at keeping us all fed around here. So, to what do we owe the pleasure of your company today, Detective?"

"I happen to have some interesting information on Lucy's hunch about the relationship between Alan Chumbley and Ed Reilly."

Allison nodded. "Is that so? We would love to hear what you found out."

Bryant sat on the corner of Allison's desk while Lucy and Charlie huddled around him. "I went in early today to get a jump on it and then I had a chance to make some calls. Turns out, Ed Reilly has had a few businesses over the past several years. A couple of stores that lasted maybe a year or more before something mysterious happened."

"Like what?" Lucy asked.

"Insurance claims, robberies, that sort of thing," Bryant replied. "At least, that was what Reilly claimed happened. Police never could find any real evidence of robberies."

"What does that have to do with Alan Chumbley?"

"I'm glad you asked, Charlie. Our Mr. Chumbley was partnered with Reilly on two of those stores. One, right after his wife died. Lasted a couple years. The second was the mall location."

"You mean it didn't shut down because the mall closed?" Allison asked.

"No, ma'am. It went belly up around the time of the closure, but not because of the closure. Reilly filed for bankruptcy."

Charlie folded her arms. "Did Chumbley file as well?"

"He did not. Reilly bought him out for a rather large sum of money only months before he filed, at least, according to his former accountant, to whom I also spoke."

"That is interesting," Allison said. "Why was he there that day, though? What brought him to the mall? He had a small collection in his hands at the time Tabitha recalled seeing him."

"I wish I knew. That remains outside purview at the moment."

"Sounds like they're both crooks then. Not that it helps Tabitha," Allison said.

Bryant nodded. "No, it doesn't. However, it sheds new light on who Alan Chumbley truly is. Makes me think he isn't the man he portrays himself to be."

Charlie paced the room. "What about going back to the company that owns the mall now and see what additional footage they might provide?"

"There simply isn't any more video that will show us anything from the mall. Believe me, I went to every store that was still open and asked them. Just in hopes that one of them might have spotted the abductor pulling Hayden Barnes away. But this mall, it was shutting down. The retailers were going broke and couldn't pay for the security anymore. It was the perfect situation for a person to take advantage of," Bryant replied.

"There was one other thing we haven't mentioned to you yet, Detective." Charlie glanced to Allison and Lucy. "I have an opportunity to attend this year's coin expo in a few days with Alan Chumbley."

"I'm sorry, what? You've been in contact with him directly?

Look, I was okay with you faking the Facebook connection, but this?" Bryant said.

"We needed to learn more about him, Detective," Allison began. "Charlie searched his Facebook to find details but there was just nothing there. We had no choice but to take that next step."

Bryant rubbed his eyes. "No. Tell me you didn't. Why? Why would you do that, Charlie? And now you want to meet him in person?"

"It's a public place. Charlie has no intention of putting herself in a dangerous situation alone with him. It's simply an opportunity for her to understand more about him," Allison added.

"With what I just learned, I am going to strongly disagree." He turned to Charlie. "I get that your heart is in the right place, but it's too risky and it would accomplish what exactly?" Bryant turned back to Allison. "Before you go rogue on me, here, Allison, let me get with Santora. There's still the situation of his open investigation. Let me talk to him and see if it's worth bringing Chumbley in again to question him a second time, especially with what we know now. You better believe I'll be looking more closely at his business dealings. I appreciate that you want to get answers, but I think I can do that in a more productive, and safer way. Will you give me that?"

Allison glanced at her team. "Can it happen in the next 48 hours?"

"I assume you're asking because this expo starts after that?" Bryant asked.

"It does."

"Fine. I'll get answers inside of 48 hours." He stood. "Thanks for the bagel and coffee. I'll be in touch." Bryant walked out the door.

Charlie waited for him to leave. "Are we really just going to sit here for two days and wait for Bryant to spoon-feed us information? That's not us doing the job our client hired us to do."

"I understand that. But there's something else we haven't thought about yet," Allison said.

"What's that?" Lucy asked.

"Charlie, can you look at Chumbley's Facebook account and check out who his friends are?" Allison asked.

"Yeah, sure."

"If details of that day are returning to Tabitha, then I have to assume that somewhere during that time, she came across a bald man. Maybe she spotted him in passing or even standing near her son. We've pushed aside that idea and put our focus solely on Alan Chumbley because of the coins. But there could be more to this and now is the time to pursue it before Charlie meets him in person."

Charlie pulled up the account and searched Chumbley's friend list. "This won't take long. He doesn't seem to have many friends." She scanned through the list and clicked on the names of the men. Within moments, she had a hit. "Uh, hey guys, I know there are a lot of bald men out there, but Alan Chumbley happens to be friends with at least three. You want to check this out?" She picked up her laptop and carried it to Allison's desk. "Lucy, come take a look." She set it down on the desk and turned the monitor. "This man here lives in St. Petersburg."

Allison peered at the image. "He's a possibility. Anyone closer to Kissimmee?"

Charlie moved on. "This one here. He looks promising. Okay, so yes, he's bald, but more importantly, take a look at the posts he's interacted with Chumbley on."

Allison put on her reading glasses. "He's about the same age as Chumbley."

"Looks like they share the same interest in coins," Lucy said. "That's important."

"Yes, it is, but then take a look here." Charlie pulled up the posts. "He doesn't mention the Tampa expo, but it looks like they both went to an expo earlier in the year in Boston."

"Boston," Allison said. "Didn't he say something to you in a message about going to Boston?"

"He did. Could it be this friend went with him to Tampa too?" Charlie added. "Why is there no mention of the Tampa expo anywhere?"

"Charlie, can you search this man's posts to see if he checked into the Tampa expo?" Allison asked.

"I'm not friends with him. I don't know if his account is private. Let me see." Charlie clicked on his wall. "It's private, Alli. I can't see any of his posts except for the comments he's made on Chumbley's."

"Okay. Okay, let me think here for a minute. So the bald guy went to Boston with Chumbley. When was that?"

Charlie peered at the post. "It was about eight months ago."

Allison nodded. "Can we see where he lives?"

Charlie shook her head. "No. Again, I don't have access to anything on his wall except for the profile picture and he conveniently left out a city. Just says Florida." She paused for a moment. "We have resources, Alli. We could find out more about this man. Where he lives, where he works. We need to learn who he is."

14

Alan Chumbley worked in his home office and checked his eBay sales. The day was going well so far, and he hoped to keep the momentum. However, his thoughts drifted to the detective who kept hounding him about the dates that he'd been in Tampa last year. How long could he put off Santora before it raised a red flag?

"Hey, Dad. You working?" Andrew stopped in front of his office. "I was just going to head out to hang with a friend."

"You're not on the schedule today?" Chumbley asked.

"Nope. Got the night off, so I'm going to grab a bite with Denny."

"Okay. I'll see you later. Drive safe." Chumbley returned to his monitor and pressed the refresh button. "One more sale." It was almost time to make some new buys. That was the main reason he attended the coin expos. It was where he bought his inventory. He looked forward to the expo but even more so now with the prospect of seeing the lovely Charlie Sweeten. He smiled at the thought of her. She had been so friendly and funny and all the things he liked in a woman. It had been a long time since he felt this way. His heart fluttered and his cheeks flushed. He liked this woman and he hoped she would consider meeting him there.

———

THE LONE PALM BAR THAT ANCHORED A RUNDOWN STRIP mall was where Andrew Chumbley turned up a short while ago. Under the pale green glow of the pool table light, he leaned down to take his shot. His hair fell in his face and he shook it away, aiming his cue near the white ball. "Right corner pocket." Andrew pulled back the cue between his thumb and forefinger and closed one eye. With a quickfire thrust, the white ball sailed across the table, nicking the outside edge of the striped ball he aimed for. "Damn it." A swing and a miss.

"Nice try, man," Denny replied.

"I need another beer. You want one?" Without waiting for an answer, Andrew headed toward the bar. What he hadn't expected was to see Gary Lucado bellied up to it. "What the hell are you doing here?"

Gary turned to him. "You've been avoiding me. I told you we needed to talk."

"How did you know where I was?" Andrew asked.

"There are only 3 bars around here. Process of elimination. Your dad said you were out tonight, so I took my chances." Gary peered over his shoulder at the pool table where Denny waited. "Finish up whatever you're doing. I'm not leaving until I have my say."

"Fine. One more game."

"I don't think you're understanding me, kid." Gary looked at the bartender who had arrived to take Andrew's order. He waved him off.

Andrew held his gaze, but quickly backed down. "Okay. I'll tell my friend to leave." He started back to the table. "Denny, I got some business to take care of. I'll catch up with you later?"

"Are you sure, man? Is everything okay?" Denny asked.

"Fine. I have to do this. Sorry." Andrew returned to the bar. "He's leaving."

Gary peered back at the young friend and waited for him to leave. "Good." He returned his eyes to Andrew. "Your dad's stepping into something that's going to shine a spotlight on things."

"What kind of things?" Andrew asked.

"The kind you wouldn't want the cops to get wind of." Gary tossed back his beer.

"Cops? Wait, I don't understand. What are you talking about?"

"I'm talking about Tampa last year, for starters. Look, son, I've been considering ways of protecting our interests and while I was contemplating our options at my cabin, a funny thing happened. Not so much funny as troubling."

Andrew cast down his gaze for a moment.

"You got something you want to tell me, son?" Gary began. "Why don't you start by telling me what the hell you did at my cabin?"

———

ALLISON PULLED OFF HER GLASSES. "GARY LUCADO. 53, LIVES in Kissimmee." She peered at Charlie. "They live near each other."

"That makes things easy for us. What else you got?" Charlie strolled to Allison's desk. "Please tell me he's got a shady past and we can easily pin this all on him."

"Oh, you thought this was going to be easy, did you?" Allison replied. "Hey Lucy, tell Charlie over here how easy these cases come together. You know, because I'm sure your dad said it was all just a piece of cake."

Lucy smiled. "Well..."

"Yeah, yeah. I get it. It's not going to be easy," Charlie replied. "I've tasted my own medicine. Let's move on." She elbowed Allison. "Anything else that tickles the hairs in your nose?"

"I'm running a DMV search now. When I get that, I'll have an address and a car registration."

"Should we tail him?" Charlie asked.

"Not unless we have a reason to. Being bald isn't a good enough reason, either," Allison replied. "I'm about to run a criminal background now. Who knows? He might be in on whatever it is Chumbley and Reilly had going. I'm starting to think Chumbley could be guilty by association. Could be used as leverage if he does know what happened to Hayden Barnes."

"Let's not jump the gun yet. We're a long way from shady business dealings to kidnapping and murder," Charlie replied.

Allison keyed in the information and waited for the data to be returned. As the screen populated, she pulled on her reading glasses again and leaned in. "Looks like back in 2010, a bench warrant was issued."

"Really?" Charlie studied the screen. "Oh. It's for missing a traffic court date. Hardly makes one a kidnapper."

"I'm still looking. Hold onto your pants." Allison scrolled through the information. "Oh, here we go. A misdemeanor charge for drunk and disorderly. That was in 2012." She looked at Charlie. "Maybe he's a drunk?"

"Maybe. Although that would only make him less capable of kidnapping if he was drunk. Keep looking."

"Fine." Allison continued to peer at the screen. "2017. He was arrested for domestic battery."

"That's not good," Charlie said. "That's not good at all."

"No." Allison typed again. "Let me look up records on a marriage certificate and any divorce filings."

Charlie walked to the credenza and poured a cup of coffee, sticking it in the microwave to warm it up. "Someone with a history of violence raises the hair on the back of my neck."

Lucy nodded. "Dad dealt with a lot of cases like that. When he was a cop, I mean."

"Yeah, well, I've had my share of dealing with that crap and I wouldn't do it again, that's for damn sure," Charlie replied.

Lucy peered at her with concern but didn't pursue the meaning of her cryptic statement.

"According to the Clerk's office, Gary Lucado was married in 2000 and divorced in 2017," Allison said.

"Must've been after the arrest," Charlie replied.

"Probably. I don't see any other criminal records here, but I'm definitely interested at looking into this man a little more. He's a supposed friend of Alan Chumbley and he's bald. That doesn't make him a child abductor, but it puts him on my list of shady friends of Alan Chumbley."

"Shady friends always bring trouble," Charlie said. "Just look at what you've done to my reputation?"

Allison scoffed. "Sure. It was me who ruined your reputation."

"Okay, so what are we going to do here?" Charlie asked. "We promised Bryant we'd give him time to come up with a more suitable suspect than Chumbley. If not Ed Reilly, then I think he'd be pretty interested in Gary Lucado."

———

ALLISON ARRIVED AT THE STATION AND STOPPED BY TO SEE Shane on her way to meet with Detective Bryant. "Hi, there."

"Hey, Allison." Shane peered up at her. "What are you doing here?"

She pulled out the chair and sat down. "I wanted to go over some things with Detective Bryant, but I thought I'd stop by to see you first."

Shane peered at her. "You wanted to check on me to see if I was doing okay after your brutal rejection?"

"Brutal?" Guilt quickly masked her face.

"I'm kidding. No, it's fine. We're all good. Just busy today."

"Oh, I'm sorry. I didn't mean to interrupt you," Allison replied.

Shane appeared stoic. "You didn't. I'm just. It doesn't matter. You're dealing with this case."

"No, tell me. What is it?" She pressed on.

"Nothing, really. I'm just still trying to figure out who left that envelope for me. I've been working on the name, but nothing's come up so far. Baylor and I are meeting tonight, and I'll see what he can do with it." Shane cast his sights around the bullpen. "Point is, I have no idea who gave it to me and that makes me a little nervous. Especially with what Lieutenant Duran said and even what Bryant mentioned. People who shouldn't know, know."

"I'm sorry, Shane. Here I was thinking this was about me. Sounds pretty selfish if I do say so myself."

"It's got nothing to do with that. Well, it might have a little to do with that." A grin appeared but quickly faded. "So, tell me, why are you here to see Bryant?"

"The girls and I are working on tracking down more leads. We found what appears to be a friend of Chumbley's. He matches Tabitha's description and he's definitely a shady character."

Shane nodded. "Sounds like Alan Chumbley hangs out with the wrong people."

"It certainly looks that way."

He peered at the time. "You should go meet with Bryant. Let

me know if there's anything I can do. And about last night, pretend I never said anything, okay?"

Allison held his gaze. "How about we just put a pin in it—for now."

He smiled half-heartedly. "Sure. Go on. We'll talk later."

She headed toward the staircase, making a final turn back to smile at Shane. It was clear to her now that she had hurt him last night. It was probably made worse by the fact that she glossed over it afterward, moving right on to the case and not acknowledging it further. Allison approached Detective Bryant's office.

"Allison. Come in." Bryant pulled up in his chair. "Thanks for coming down. We could've discussed this over the phone if it would've been easier for you."

She walked into his office and sat down. "No, I think it's best if we look at this together and you can decide if it's worth our time. I think it is."

He peered at her with interest. "Show me what you have."

Allison opened a manila folder and laid out the contents, including a picture of Gary Lucado and his criminal record. "I'll state the obvious first. We found our bald guy."

Bryant dragged the file toward him and picked it up. "Who is he?"

"He's a friend of Alan Chumbley and appears to be a fellow coin collector, 53, and lives in Kissimmee. The two have attended coin expos together in the past." Allison explained how she came across Gary's details through Charlie's Facebook account. "I did say that Charlie was resourceful. Here's the criminal record I ran earlier today."

Bryant studied it. "Domestic battery charge. That's noteworthy."

"A little bit," she added. "It doesn't mean he's a suspect, but at this point, anyone associated with Alan Chumbley, in my opinion, is worth a deeper dive. We found our bald guy. We found our coin collector. I'm sure now more than ever that Tabitha Barnes, what she saw in her dream, was just little reminders of what lay in her subconscious."

"You know she believes her son is still alive and that he showed her the coin and talked about the bald man," Bryant said.

"I'm not so sure about that, but I think we both realize that it's unlikely Hayden Barnes is still alive. I don't mean to sound pessimistic..."

"You sound realistic to me. And as much as I hate to think it too, I know what the odds are that after this long we'll find that little boy." He nodded. "But this? I'll give you this one. We should take a peek." He set down the file. "You know, Allison, I don't think I've given you and your partners enough credit. Your methods are unconventional, but I can't dispute the results."

"Where do we go from here, Detective?"

"Well," Bryant leaned back and laced his fingers over his stomach. "It looks like we have a couple of directions to take this."

"How do you mean?"

"I mean, you've got Chumbley and now you've got his friend, Lucado. You've also got some business dealings that don't appear quite above board."

"I agree. What about the other detective? Santora, was it? You wanted some time to get finer details on his open investigation?"

"I'm working on that, but I have a feeling, given this new information, you and your partners are going to run with the idea of having Charlie meet up with Chumbley on Friday. That said, we need to come up with a plan to keep her safe and determine what she'll need to get from him to move forward. Can we do that?"

"Yes, sir. We absolutely can."

———

THURSDAY NIGHT HAD ARRIVED, AND WORD HAD BEEN SENT that Charlie Sweeten, aka Charlie Wells, was going to meet Alan Chumbley at the Tampa Expo on Friday at 11am. Now, the team huddled in Allison's kitchen to review the plan.

"Detective Bryant is on his way back after meeting with Santora about Gary Lucado. He should be here soon to give us an update." Allison looked at Charlie. "Are you still feeling confident about this?"

"I'm going to a coin collector show with a bunch of coin collectors. I think I'll be fine. There's no need for Shane to be there."

"Yes, there is," he replied. "I'm not letting you go in there alone. I'll only be there as a backup and to keep an eye on you."

"It's for your safety, Charlie," Lucy began. "I don't know what I'd do if something happened to you."

Charlie placed her hand on Lucy's back. "Nothing's going to happen to me. I promise you. I might die of boredom, but apart from that, I'll be fine."

A knock sounded on the door and drew their attention.

"I'll bet that's Bryant," Shane said. "I'll get it." He walked into the foyer and opened the door. "Just the man we've been waiting for. Come in."

"Do you always answer the door at someone else's house?" Bryant stepped inside.

"Sometimes. Everyone's in the kitchen and there's pizza too." Shane led the way. "Looks like we're ready to get the ball rolling."

"Detective Bryant, thanks for coming over. You want something to eat?" Allison grabbed a paper plate. "There's plenty of pizza."

"I wouldn't mind a couple slices of pie. Thank you. A beer too, if you have one."

She opened the fridge. "There's always beer in this fridge. I keep it stocked for Shane." When Allison closed the door, she turned and spotted Nolan standing in the foyer. "Oh my God. Nolan. You're home!" She rushed to him and pulled him into a long embrace. "Are you eating? You look thin."

"I'm eating, Mom. They're just pushing me hard. Working out all day long. What's going on in here?"

"Oh, well, you know, we've been working on a case and we're just hashing out a few things over pizza. Why don't you go and get settled in and I'll bring you some food? You want a Coke too?"

"That'd be great. Am I going to get a chance to talk to you tonight?" Nolan asked.

"Oh, we won't be long. An hour, tops." She turned to the others. "Right?"

"Sure thing. How you doing, kiddo?" Charlie asked.

"Doing good, Charlie." He peered at Lucy. "Hey, Lucy. It's nice to see you."

Her cheeks flushed. "You too, Nolan. I forgot your mom said you were coming home for the weekend."

"Yeah." He nodded at her awkwardly. "We should catch up later, huh?"

"Sounds good."

He turned back to Allison. "I'll go off to my room now like a child." He grinned. "I know, I know. It's part of your job. That's fine. I need to shower anyway. I haven't taken a real shower in a month."

"Okay, sweetheart. We'll talk after this is finished." Allison returned to the kitchen. "Okay, so where were we?"

Charlie kept her eyes glued to Lucy. "Hey, Lucy, you with us?"

"Huh? Yeah. Sorry."

Charlie unveiled a crooked smile. "Good." She turned back to Allison. "So anyway. Now that Detective Bryant is here, we should talk about Gary Lucado."

"Right." Bryant wiped the pizza sauce from his mouth. "Santora is interested in following up with him. He's working on finding a way to bring him in for questioning while Chumbley's here in Tampa. Less likely for the two to converse on the matter."

"On what grounds? He wasn't with Chumbley at the fair, was he?" Allison asked.

"I don't know. I think he's going to ask him about it, among other things. Let's turn our focus on how we approach tomorrow morning. Charlie, you're still good with going through on this?"

"I am. I want to do this."

"Okay then, here's the deal…"

15

For most of Charlie Wells' working life, she had found herself behind a desk performing mundane tasks that left her feeling uninspired and insignificant. Since her divorce, the pressure was high as bills mounted and her teen boys grew. Sure, her ex-husband kept the kids every other weekend, and did pay some child support, but she quickly learned to rely on herself.

When a shift in the direction of the Tabitha Barnes investigation arose and it became clear that Alan Chumbley had an as of yet uncertain connection, Charlie relied on her own intuition. Meeting with the seemingly mild-mannered coin collector had been Charlie's idea. Now that idea was about to be put into action.

It almost felt like a date. Meeting Chumbley, a man who Charlie had only communicated to through Facebook, brought back memories of the last time she went out with a man. Yikes. That was almost two years ago, and it hadn't gone well at all.

In the back of her mind, Charlie believed Alan had nothing to do with the abduction. He was just an average man, a widower. How could he have taken a child, let alone two? Then again, she never was a good judge of character when it came to men.

Charlie stood in her master bathroom and pumped the hairspray on her hair. Each spikey section froze in place, the bangs perfectly angled on her forehead. She spritzed on a mild floral perfume and walked into the kitchen to grab her things. She was set to arrive at the office first to meet with Shane, then drive to the Tampa Convention Center downtown. The plan was to meet Chumbley at the Riverwalk entrance number three on the bayside of the building.

On her arrival at the office, her partners waited. "What are you two doing here so early?" Charlie began. "Did we have a meeting I didn't know about?"

Allison bore a worried expression. "We're getting our ducks in a row, as they say. Did you sleep?"

Charlie grinned in an attempt to ease her friend's concern. "Yes, just like I do every night. I'm fine, Alli. I'm not worried about strolling around the convention center with a coin collector. You shouldn't be either."

"I know you're right. Shane will be there keeping an eye too, so there's nothing to worry about."

"And that's what you need to remind yourself. I'll get the answers we're looking for, Alli. Have a little faith." Charlie's attention turned to the door as it opened.

"Morning. Wow, Charlie, look at you. You have a date or something?" Shane stepped inside.

"Funny. You're a funny guy, Sully," she replied.

"I think you look great, Charlie," Lucy added.

"See? Lucy gets it. I don't need to be there until 11, so should we go over the plan again?"

"I'd actually like to come up with an escape plan," Allison

said. "Not to be an alarmist, but if you need to high-tail it out of there, we should know how to make that happen."

"Why would I need to leave?" Charlie asked.

"I'm going to side with Allison on this one," Shane began. "If Chumbley starts to get suspicious of your questions, he might get spooked. And because we don't know who he is, or how he'll react, I'm not prepared to take any chances."

———

IN THE SMALL, KEY WEST STYLE BUNGALOW WHERE ALAN Chumbley called home, he smoothed the collar of his blue polo shirt and rubbed his freshly shaved cheeks, slapping a dash of aftershave on them. He was excited to meet Charlie in the flesh. The rush of butterflies in his stomach was something he hadn't felt in more than twenty years. It was like he was a teenager again. Since his wife died, he hadn't been out on a single date. Now that a woman had shown interest in him, he felt exhilarated. He even managed to cast aside his growing fears of what the police might uncover about what had happened in Tampa last year—for the time being.

Chumbley returned to his kitchen and turned off the coffee maker. The time was almost 9:30 and while they weren't scheduled to meet until 11 o'clock, he wanted to arrive early and get ahead of any possible traffic delays. The drive to Tampa was only thirty to forty minutes, but Chumbley was nothing if not prompt, and especially where an attractive woman was concerned.

He walked down the hall to his son's bedroom and gently opened the door. Andrew was still asleep. The kid worked mostly nights and so Chumbley didn't bother waking him to tell him of his plans. Although he wouldn't return until late tonight if he pulled it off. The idea was to convince Charlie to have dinner with him after the convention. He still planned on attending Saturday but didn't think any woman in her right mind would want to go to a coin collector's event twice in a row. Chumbley loved it, but he was realistic. Most people didn't understand or share his enthusiasm.

He closed the door again and gathered the tickets and his binder which documented his collection and certifications. Trades were often made at these events and he needed to be prepared. On his way out the door, the cloud beneath his feet carried him to his car and he drove away.

———

CHARLIE PULLED INTO THE PARKING GARAGE AT THE convention center and parked on the third floor. Shane was behind her and found a spot a few yards away. He stepped out and met her at her car.

"You'll need to stay ahead of me," he began. "And don't worry, I won't let you out of my sight."

"I'm not worried," Charlie replied.

Shane gently reached for her arm. "I know you like to play the tough guy. Don't get me wrong, you are tough, but it's okay to be a little nervous about this. You don't need to put on a hard front with me."

"I appreciate that, Shane, I really do. But I'll tell you, after what Alli and I have been through over the past six months, this really feels like a cake walk. I don't have to worry about drug gangs or crooked politicians or dead FBI agents. I'm okay. I really am. Come on. We should go." She started ahead.

Shane waited for her to get thirty or so feet in front of him before he followed.

Charlie inhaled a breath and while she'd just assured Shane of her confidence, it was a little bit of an act. Nerves were on end and although it wasn't that warm, she felt trickles of sweat run down the back of her neck. But she had to remember that she wasn't alone. Shane was looking out for her and if there was anything that she'd learned about him so far, it was that he'd do everything in his power to keep her safe. He would do that for all of them. That put her mind at ease as she made her way to the Riverwalk.

With the muggy air coming off the bay, Charlie had begun to regret her choice of attire. Her thick thighs rubbed together beneath the long skirt. "Wear a dress. Look like a girl for once in your life. Sure. Good call, Charlie," she said to herself.

The sign for Entrance 3 came into view. She was almost there, and her heart beat just a little faster. A quick turn of her head and she spotted Shane well behind her. He'd already warned her not to keep checking around for him because it would appear suspicious, but just this once.

In the distance, sitting on a concrete bench in front of the entrance, was a man with thick dark blonde hair, a thin build, and wearing a blue polo shirt. Charlie swallowed down the lump in her throat and pressed on, knowing it was him. As she neared, he stood and smiled.

Charlie forced a smile in return as she approached him. In a tender voice she hadn't used in many years, she peered at him with caution. "Alan?"

"Charlie." He stepped toward her with an outstretched hand. "It's so nice to finally meet you. Wow. Your profile picture doesn't do you justice."

"Thank you. It's nice to meet you too, finally." She accepted his hand. "Well, here we are."

"Here we are." Chumbley appeared nervous. "Oh, here's your ticket." He pulled it from his pants pocket.

"How much do I owe you for that?" Charlie reached for her wallet.

"Oh, nothing. Honestly, they weren't that expensive, and I get a discount since I'm a member." He pulled open the door. "Shall we?"

"Absolutely."

———

GARY LUCADO WALKED INTO THE KISSIMMEE POLICE station. His slumped shoulders and plump midsection barely visible beneath a Tommy Bahama button down and baggy cargo khaki pants. He approached the front desk. "Good morning, or is it afternoon already? I'm here to see Detective Santora."

"And you are?" The officer asked.

"Gary Lucado. He asked me to come in."

"I'll call him up now. You can take a seat if you'd like, right over there."

Gary turned to see the wall of chairs where only one other person sat. He meandered toward them and took a seat on the chair at the end.

After several minutes, the detective appeared. "Mr. Lucado?"

Gary looked up. "That's me."

"I'm Detective Santora. Come on back." He peered over his shoulder to see that Gary had trailed him. "I appreciate you coming in this afternoon."

"Sure thing, but I'm not sure what help I can be." Gary shuffled along in his white Reeboks.

"This is all just routine questioning. Nothing to be concerned about." The detective opened a door. "Right through here."

Gary appeared hesitant as he realized the room looked a lot like an interview room.

"Is everything okay, Mr. Lucado?" Santora asked.

"I somehow feel like I need a lawyer or something."

"Why?" He glanced inside. "Oh, this room? Sorry about that. It can be intimidating. It's just that my office is in a noisy part of the station and I thought it best to have someplace quiet where we could talk. I assure you, you're not in any trouble, Mr. Lucado."

Gary hesitated a moment longer and finally stepped into the room.

"Great. Go ahead and have a seat." Santora closed the door and sat across from Lucado. "Like I mentioned on the phone, this is just routine questioning I'm doing regarding the missing boy from the school fairgrounds back in January. Your friend, Alan Chumbley, was there that night."

"Okay. What's it got to do with me then? Shouldn't you be talking to Alan? And, I'm sorry, but how do you know that he's a friend of mine?"

"He mentioned it the last time he was in here. Said you were with him at the fair that night. Is that not true?" Santora asked.

Gary appeared as though this was news to him. "I was there. He had a little stand set up. I offered to give him a hand since I had nothing better to do. Alan likes to help out the community when he can and decided whatever sales he made, he'd donate a portion to the school that hosted the fair."

"Sounds like an upstanding citizen," the detective replied.

"He's a good man," Gary added. "You say you've talked to Alan already?"

"That I did. So that night at the fairgrounds, did you stay with Mr. Chumbley the whole time or did you go off and have some fun on the rides and such?"

"The rides were made mostly for the kids and last I checked, I'm a little long in the tooth for that type of thing. That said, I did a little walking around. Checked out the other vendors, grabbed some food. Things you'd do at an event like that."

"Sure, sure. So you couldn't account for Mr. Chumbley's whereabouts the entire time you were there?"

"No. Like I said, I wasn't with him the whole time." Lucado folded his arms. "Is Alan some kind of suspect or something?"

"Not at all. I asked you here to help me piece together a timeline of events leading up to when the boy was taken. Do you recall seeing anything out of the ordinary that night?"

"Out of the ordinary? Well, no. Kids running around, dropping food and screaming and shouting as kids do. I wouldn't say that was out of the ordinary, Detective."

"Do you have kids, Mr. Lucado?" He flipped a page on his notepad.

"No, I don't. Just a nephew."

"So you and your wife, excuse me, ex-wife, no kids there, huh?"

Gary's face turned deadpan. "No, sir."

"Huh. Probably just as well. Sounds like you two didn't part on friendly terms. Let's get back to Mr. Chumbley. He's a coin collector if I recall. More than just a hobbyist, I gather."

Gary appeared to hesitate, but finally continued, "Yes, sir. He makes a fairly decent living out of trading coins."

"How long have you two been friends?"

Lucado cast his gaze to the ceiling. "Oh, I'd say since he started collecting on a more professional basis, shortly after his wife died."

The detective nodded. "And are you a collector too? Is that how you two met?"

"I used to be, but I made some unwise purchases. Got fleeced and learned my lesson. So, no, I don't collect anymore, not even as a hobby. And yes, that was how we met. A mutual friend has a collectibles store in town, and we happened to be in there together once. Been friends ever since." Lucado appeared to grow frustrated. "You'll have to pardon me, Detective, but can you just ask me what it is you want to ask me? I feel like you're doing your best to beat around the bush and I'm sure there are better things we can both be doing with our time."

Santora nodded. "You know, Mr. Lucado, you're right. My goal is to find out who took that little boy three months ago. Time is no longer on my side or the victim's. So the best I can hope for now is to narrow down who might've seen the man or woman who took him. That's what I'm trying to get at now."

"Then that means you do think Alan took him?"

"It doesn't mean that at all. It means I need to rule everyone out that I can and see who's left standing. That's why you're here. I'll ask you just one more question, Mr. Lucado." The detective inhaled a deep breath. "You a fan of the buffalo nickel?"

He smiled. "I'm sorry, what?"

"The buffalo nickel. They sure are interesting. In fact, I had a look at Mr. Chumbley's collection he has registered online through one of the official certification companies. Turns out, he has some that are quite valuable. Though I hear most aren't worth more than face value. But what an interesting thing to show off, am I right?"

"Show off?" Lucado shrugged. "I guess so."

"Do you have any in your possession?"

Lucado turned down his lips and shook his head. "Nope. Like I said, I don't collect anymore."

"Anymore. Can I ask what you did with the collection you had? Sell it?" Santora asked.

"Some of it. Alan bought a few things from me. The rest I gave away."

"Okay then." Santora stood up. "Well, I sure thank you for your time. Oh, there was one other thing. You ever spend any time in Tampa with your friend, Alan?"

Gary held his gaze and was quiet for a moment. "No. Not that I can recall anyway. Why do you ask?"

"Again, just looking to gain an understanding of Mr. Chumbley. I figured, since he said he was there back, oh, I think he said back last March, I thought maybe you made the trip with him."

"Last March, you say?" Lucado rubbed his chin. "Doesn't ring a bell."

"Well, Mr. Lucado, your cooperation is very much appreciated."

"I can leave?"

"Yes, sir. You are free to go." The detective opened the door. "Have a good rest of your afternoon."

Gary walked through the station and exited through the front doors. He returned to his car and stepped inside, reaching for his cell phone. With his phone to his ear, he made the call. It went straight to voicemail.

"Alan, it's Gary. We need to hash this out. I know you're at the expo, but you need to call me. Shit's going off the rails, man."

———

INSIDE THE CONVENTION CENTER WERE ROWS OF EXHIBITORS. Charlie had no idea the coin collecting industry was so big. She'd never seen so much metal in all her life hanging in frames and shadow boxes. Some inside binders, each with their own little pockets. "This really is something."

Chumbley turned to her. "It is. I feel like a kid in a candy store when I come to these things."

"How many are there in a year?" Charlie asked, trying her best to feign interest. She needed to make him feel comfortable around her so she could ask the important questions. The ones that would tell her who this man really was.

"Oh, I'd say at least three or four. Mind you, I don't go to all of them. Some are on the other side of the country and I'll be honest with you, I don't make the kind of money from it that affords me the luxury of frequent travel."

Charlie laughed in her most non-offensive manner. She was usually a full-on belly laugher, but she couldn't embarrass either of them with her true personality. "Do you usually bring girls with you?"

"Despite what you might think, I'm not much of a, what do they call it? A lady's man." He chuckled. "No, I'll come with a friend of mine on occasion. In fact, he was here with me last year. Sometimes my boy comes along too. He's not much for this sort of thing though. He says he does it ironically." Chumbley used air quotes on that last word. "Whatever that means."

"I have a couple of teenage boys. I've heard that word more often than you might think."

Alan smiled at her. "Then we have that in common too."

Charlie walked beside him and spotted Shane in the distance heading their way. Her brow furrowed just for a moment, but she continued on as if he was only a stranger. As they neared each other, Charlie was careful not to let her eyes meet his.

After he passed them, she exhaled. It seemed a risky thing to do, but maybe it was his way of trying to tell her something. Maybe she needed to make a call to him. She turned to Chumbley. "You know what, I see a restroom just ahead. I think I'll make a quick pit stop."

"Sure, of course. I'll meet you back here." As Charlie walked away, he peered at his phone and noted the voicemail message.

Within a few minutes, Charlie returned, and the look on Alan's face concerned her. "Is everything okay?"

"I need to step away for a moment. I have a call to return."

"Okay. I guess it's my turn to wait." Charlie smiled, but once Chumbley disappeared, her smile faded, and Shane approached her. "I replied to your text. What's going on?"

"Listen, the detective in Kissimmee called Bryant. Bryant reached out to me a few minutes ago. Chumbley's friend, Gary Lucado, he's connected to this after all."

"What about Alan?" Charlie asked. "I need more time with him. He's just starting to open up to me."

Shane appeared to consider this. "Fine. Let's give it another hour and then try to get out of here. Start by finding out how close he is to Lucado. We need to ascertain the nature of their relationship."

16

Standing on the outside and peering in was never a position in which Allison felt comfortable. She and Lucy waited in the office while Charlie took the lead on gathering intel on Alan Chumbley. When 6 o'clock was about to roll around and both were at their wit's end, Allison's phone rang. She was quick to answer. "Shane, tell me you guys are leaving now."

"I agreed to give Charlie another hour to get more information and that hour is just about up. I just wanted to check in on you two."

Allison placed the call on speaker. "Lucy and I are sitting here biting our nails waiting on you two to come back."

"So you haven't talked to Detective Bryant?" he asked.

"He dropped by a few hours ago and said he was waiting on a call from Detective Santora. Why? Did he call you?"

"He did. According to Santora, Lucado used to be a coin collector, like Chumbley. Guess what that collection used to include?"

Allison closed her eyes. "Buffalo nickels."

"You got it. But here's the thing," Shane continued. "He gave them away. He told the detective that he sold some of his collection to Chumbley, but the stuff that didn't have any value he said he gave them away. Oh, and what is probably the most important aspect here, Lucado was with Chumbley at the fairgrounds."

"What are you saying? They're working together?" Allison asked.

"That's what we need to prove," Shane replied.

"Shane, this is Lucy. Is Charlie in any danger?"

"No, and certainly not while I'm here with her. Santora couldn't say with any certainty that Lucado and Chumbley were in collusion. It's just one hell of a striking coincidence their stories appear to be intertwined. I told Charlie we'd meet back in the parking garage by 6 o'clock. Fifteen more minutes."

"I'll feel a lot better when she's back," Allison said.

"I won't let anything happen to her," he replied. "We'll see you both soon."

———

As Charlie walked alongside Alan, he had become noticeably quieter. She knew time was running out. The convention would be over for the evening and Shane had given her a deadline. That deadline was about to strike. "I sure did have fun today. More fun than I expected to, in all honesty."

Alan turned to her. "Really? You had a good time?"

"I did. I'm so glad we did this. But you know, it's just about over. We should maybe think about heading toward the exit."

He checked the time. "I hadn't realized it was so late. I guess time really does fly when you're having fun."

Charlie gently reached for his elbow and pulled him to a stop.

"Is everything all right? It seems like that call you made earlier, and I don't mean to pry, but it seems like it was bad news."

He turned down his gaze. "Just a friend of mine. I think he might be getting caught up in something. I'm just a little worried about him, that's all it is." He captured her gaze. "But I have enjoyed today. Very much, in fact."

"Well, this friend, is he in some real trouble or is it just a misunderstanding?"

He looked at her with minor curiosity. "It's nice that you're concerned, but he'll be fine. I'll stop by his house later tonight and have a word with him just to see that he's all right." He inhaled a breath. "Which brings me to another problem. I had intended to ask you to have dinner with me after this, but now..."

Charlie smiled warmly. "It's okay. I understand. I would've loved to have dinner, but I'm sure we can do it another time. Your friend sounds like he could use a shoulder to lean on. Are you two close?"

"Yes. He's the one who came here with me last year. In fact, he used to be a collector himself until he made a couple of bad buys. But we get together at least once a week and play poker at my house. My son joins in sometimes too. I guess I am a little worried about this. Well, anyway, would you consider a rain check? I'll be here tomorrow too, but I wouldn't put you through this again."

"Stop. I told you I had fun, but I do actually have plans for tomorrow. I'll take a raincheck on dinner, though. Definitely."

"Great. I'm glad to hear that, Charlie. How about I walk you to your car?"

———

ALLISON JUMPED TO ATTENTION WHEN CHARLIE RETURNED with Shane. "You're back. Thank God." She watched as Charlie meandered inside and dropped onto her chair. "Well? How did it go? Was it worth the effort?"

Charlie pulled off her low-heeled shoes. "What's worth it for me right now is to take off these damn sandals. I really should've worn tennis shoes with all the walking I did today. And I'm tired of standing. Cripes, it's good to be done with that."

"Charlie, what happened?" Allison walked to the mini fridge and pulled out a bottle of water. "Here."

"Thanks." She was about to put the bottle to her lips but stopped short. "I did have a fantastic lunch. Great food there."

Shane raised the corner of his mouth in a crooked smile. "I think they'd like to know if you found out anything worthwhile today, Charlie."

"I'm getting to it." She took another drink and eyed Allison, who had been standing in front of her with arms crossed. "Okay, okay. I can see you're anxious about this."

"You think?" Allison replied. "Lucy and I have been waiting here all day for this news. So, let's hear it."

Charlie pulled up in her chair. "Well, I don't think Alan Chumbley could hurt a fly let alone kidnap and murder a child."

"But can we pull him out of the equation altogether? And should we now be focusing on Gary Lucado?"

Shane perched on the edge of Charlie's desk. "Bryant and Santora think it's worth looking into him. Charlie, you said Chumbley told you his friend was with him at the expo last year, right?"

"He did, but he didn't give me a name. It was pretty easy to put two and two together, though."

"And yet, according to Santora, Lucado claimed to have never been in Tampa last March," Shane added.

"So he lied," Allison said. "Both of them lied about being in Tampa last March. And we already know that Chumbley has business dealings that might not be completely legitimate. I understand that doesn't make him a kidnapper, but it's starting to feel like he's trying to cover for his friend, Lucado."

Charlie nodded. "The possibility exists that Alan might have been covering up for his friend, yes."

Allison traded glances with Lucy before adding, "You just called him Alan."

"I guess I did. I've just spent the last seven hours with him. I got to know him," Charlie replied. "Alli, look, I was with him all day, and he was the nicest man. If it had been a real date, I'd be planning the next one already."

"But you know you can't do that, right?" Allison said.

"I know where the line is. I'm just saying, he's a good guy. Now, as far as his friend, what I can also tell you is that he said he and Lucado are close. They get together once a week for poker with Alan's son. It all appears very normal."

"He never actually used the name, Gary Lucado?" Allison asked.

"No. Again, it was clear that he was talking about Lucado based on what Shane just said. He had gotten a call from him and Alan was concerned about his quote-unquote, friend, being mixed up in something."

"How did you leave things with Chumbley?" Lucy asked.

"He wants to go out to dinner at some point," Charlie replied.

Allison noticed the look on Charlie's face. There was no doubt she had taken a liking to Alan Chumbley. It was as though she couldn't see that he could still be a threat. Maybe he hadn't done the crime, but the possibility remained he could be helping someone cover it up. "Charlie, there are too many unanswered questions." She looked at Shane. "What do you think?"

"I think you should consider pumping the brakes on Chumbley for a while," he replied.

"Okay, I get that I can't date the guy. Fine. I can also accept there could be another role he played in this. But if I cut him off, and especially since I made it clear I wanted to see him again, don't you think that could raise a red flag with him? Like he might start to think he was being played."

"He doesn't know who you really are, Charlie," Allison continued. "He doesn't know where you live, where you work. That said, I do think it's safe enough for you to continue to message him on Facebook. Details on his friend are what we need now."

"So, I'm supposed to use him?" Charlie nodded. "Okay then. I'll keep in contact with Alan, but I won't meet up with him again. I'll make up whatever excuse I need to make up. Hell, he thinks I'm Charlie Sweeten, so I could disappear off the face of the planet and he'd never know."

"We should start by learning what he and Lucado did here last year during the expo." Lucy turned to Charlie. "Did they stay in a hotel here? Was his friend with him the whole time? And what about the mall footage from last year?"

"Lucy, we've gone down that road already. Bryant confirmed as much," Allison replied.

"True. I know Bryant looked through that already, but he wasn't looking for a bald guy. He was looking for someone who took Hayden and he didn't find that. What if we can spot Gary Lucado in that footage? We know Chumbley was there based on what Tabitha said. If his friend was there too, that looks bad. And let's not forget the fairgrounds."

Shane nodded. "That's a hell of an idea if it still exists. After a year? Not only is the mall closed down, but it's in the hands of new owners. Tracking down that video might be next to impossible, and that's assuming it still exists."

"I'll work on that," Lucy said. "I'll do whatever I can to track it down or get proof it's no longer available. If it does exist, however, I'll find it."

———

As Alan Chumbley turned onto his street, he spotted Gary Lucado's car parked alongside the curb fronting his home. It appeared his friend was anxiously awaiting his return. Upon pulling onto his driveway, he stepped out and met Lucado at the steps of his front door.

"We should go inside and talk," Lucado said.

"I was thinking the same thing." Chumbley unlocked his door and closed it behind them. He turned on the lights in the living room. "If you're hungry, I think I have some leftover pizza in the fridge."

"Food hasn't been on my list of priorities today, Alan, but you know what has? The cops."

Chumbley walked into his kitchen. "How about a beer, then?"

"Yeah, I'll take one of those." He took the bottle from Chumbley and chugged it down. "What was the expo like today?"

"Same as last year. You didn't miss much," Chumbley replied.

"And the lady you met there?"

Chumbley smiled. "She was nice."

"Uh-huh. The look on your face says she was a little bit more than nice. You gonna see her again?" He took another drink.

"I hope so. But that doesn't address our current situation."

"No, it doesn't. That Detective Santora is after you. He pulled me in there asking all sorts of questions about the fairgrounds. Oh and get this, he asked if I was in Tampa last year too. You tell him I was?"

"No, of course not. I said I was there but that I couldn't

remember exactly when. Hang on, he asked you about the fair? I never told him you were with me."

"Then how the hell did he know?"

Alan shook his head. "He waited to talk to you. It was as though he knew I was going to be gone for the day. There's no way he would've known you were with me at the fair."

"Someone's talking to him or he just made it up to see what reaction he'd get from me. Man, this is no joke. What we did...they find out..."

"What I don't understand is how the detective knew we were friends," Chumbley said. "I don't understand why they're so concerned about me being in Tampa either. The dealings we had with Reilly, it's like they know all about it. Reilly gave us his word."

"I think we have bigger fish to fry than worrying about counterfeit certifications. That cop is after you thinking you murdered some kid from the fairgrounds. Screw Reilly. Reilly's a piece of shit who would do anything to save his own ass. You and me? We gotta get our stories straight. What about the kid?"

"Andrew?" Alan asked. "He doesn't know anything, and it needs to stay that way."

17

Spending Saturday afternoon at a McDonald's hadn't been on Lucy's agenda for today. But when Nolan called and asked to meet her, she would've gone anywhere he wanted. Her old black Monte Carlo SS rumbled into the parking lot. Lucy parked her dad's beast of a car and stepped out. She had gotten used to the looks from people when she drove it. He'd loved this car, but it wasn't Lucy's style. Regardless, she hadn't had the means to trade up and the idea of selling something her father loved didn't feel right either.

Lucy walked inside, put in an order, and spotted Nolan right away.

He smiled as she walked nearer. "Hi."

"Hey." Lucy slipped into the booth. "It's nice to see you again."

"You too. Did you order?" Nolan had a Quarter-pounder with cheese and a large fry in front of him. "I can wait..."

"No, it's fine. Mine should be up in a minute. So, how's training going?"

"It's great. I love it. The guys are a lot of fun. The coaches ride us pretty hard, but it's nothing I didn't expect. What about you?"

Lucy smiled. "I'm happy working for your mom. I've learned a lot and I think I contribute a lot too. And I guess I feel like I'm keeping my dad's legacy alive, you know?"

"Sure. Yeah. No, I think it's awesome. You're smart. I know Mom thinks so too."

Lucy heard her number called at the front. "That's me. I'll be right back." She grabbed the tray at the counter. On her return, most of Nolan's food was gone. "Wow. That was fast."

"I was hungry." He slurped on his soda. "You mentioned something about you having to check out a property owner today?"

"Yeah. This case we're working—there's a lot to it. I feel like we're running in a bunch of different directions, but I think that's just the way it goes sometimes."

Nolan studied her and grinned.

"What?" She asked, suddenly feeling self-conscious.

"Nothing. It's just cool. You look happy, Lucy. It's nice to see that."

She wanted to tell him that she'd been seeing Logan Carr off and on. It hadn't become serious, but she liked him a lot. She liked Nolan too, but he was going to be absent until the end of summer when baseball season was over. It wasn't hard to see that Nolan liked her too. She saw it in his eyes now. "I'm starving." Lucy took a bite out of her chicken sandwich and swallowed it down. "You're going back tomorrow evening?"

"Yeah. I have to get back to camp, but I wanted to see you."

"You didn't just come back to see your mom?" Lucy asked with a smile.

"To be honest, she hasn't had much time for me with all this going on. We're supposed to have dinner tonight with my dad, and then I think she wanted to go out to breakfast, just the two of us in the morning before I leave. Lucy..."

"Wait. I have to tell you something. I don't want to keep anything from you, and I know it's not like we're going out or anything, but it's only right that I tell you I've been seeing Logan Carr—sort of."

"Sort of?" He asked.

"We went out a couple of times. He's a good guy. I mean, I know his history doesn't do much for him."

Nolan wore his disappointment like a thorny crown. "Oh. That's awesome."

"It's not what you think," Lucy added.

"Hey, you're right. It's not like we're dating. I mean, we've been texting and stuff, but you should be getting out there, you know? It's not like I'm not super busy right now anyway. I totally get it."

Lucy's heart sank. "Nolan, I like you and I think you like me. I'm telling you this because I'd never want to keep anything from you or lie to you. You have a shot at an amazing career in baseball. I wouldn't want to interfere with that, like at all."

Nolan shrugged. "So, what's this mean? Are we just going to be friends or what?"

She held his gaze. "Is there a way to be anything more?"

The question hung heavy in the air. Neither one seemed to know the answer. And now, Lucy had to leave. "I'm so sorry, but I have to go. I don't want to be late for the meeting."

"Sure. I'll walk you out." Nolan slipped out of the booth and followed her to the door.

As they reached Lucy's car, she opened the driver's side door and turned to him. "It was good to see you. Thanks for making time to hang out."

Nolan moved toward her and rested his hand on the door

frame. "If things were different. If I was here more, would you go out with me? Would you stop seeing Logan?"

Lucy studied him. "Does it matter what I answer? It's not the way it is or is ever going to be."

Nolan placed his hand on her cheek and leaned in, touching her lips gently with his. A moment later, he pulled back. "It matters to me. Lucy, it doesn't have to be so cut and dry. I can do both, see you and still play ball." He turned away briefly. "You know, I don't think I realized just how much I wanted to be a part of your life until just now. Being faced with the alternative puts it in perspective. Tell me you'll think about it?"

Lucy nodded and wore a tender smile. "I'll think about it." She slipped onto the driver's seat and closed the door. As the engine roared to life, Lucy drove away.

On the way to the commercial real estate firm, Lucy replayed the kiss in her mind. It was only a split second and it was done. She hadn't expected it but welcomed it, nonetheless. Her heart soared. The fact remained, however, that Nolan had a job that meant he would travel for a good part of the year. Maybe she was jumping the gun and she should just give it a chance. But then there was Logan.

It was too much to think about now as she prepared to meet with the owners of the mall. She needed that video and there was still the grim possibility it no longer existed. If it had nothing on it the police needed at the time, it could very well have been destroyed.

Lucy pulled into the parking lot of the mid-rise building and stepped out. The afternoon sun warmed her skin and she shed her light sweater, tying it around her slender waist. She continued inside and reached the front desk. "Good afternoon. Lucy Boyce with ACL Investigative Services. I'm here to see Ryan Hawley."

"Of course." The receptionist called back. "It'll be just a moment."

"Thank you." Lucy wandered the lobby, gazing at the artwork, and glancing at the magazines on the table. A woman soon appeared wearing grey dress pants and a soft, pale pink blouse.

"Lucy Boyce?" She offered her hand. "I'm Ryan Hawley. Nice to meet you."

Lucy wasn't expecting this blonde-haired woman with a boyish build who now stood before her. "Ryan. Nice to meet you too."

"I can see you were expecting a man. It's the name. I hope you're not disappointed."

"Not at all," Lucy began. "It's a pleasant surprise. I want to thank you for coming in on a Saturday for me."

"Not a problem. I tend to work Saturdays anyway. Follow me. Would you like a glass of water or a coffee?"

"No, thank you. I'm fine." Lucy trailed her.

Ryan opened her office door. "It's such a shame they still haven't found that poor boy or whoever took him. Please, take a seat."

Lucy sat down in a guest chair. "Yes, it is."

"You say the mother of the victim hired your P.I. firm?" Ryan took her seat. "I assume after this long, she's desperate for answers, as any mother would be. I have a daughter. I just can't imagine..." she trailed off. "But you're here to find answers for her, so how can I help?"

Lucy retrieved the file from her carrier bag and set it on the desk. "My firm has been tracking down leads and after revisiting some previously unclear circumstances with our client, we're pressing forward on a person of interest."

Ryan nodded and crossed her arms. "You seem like a very intelligent and well-spoken young woman. Forgive me, but I wasn't expecting that from someone who looks like she's about twenty or so?"

"I'm twenty, yes. And thank you. My father was a P.I. for many years. Before that, he was a detective. I grew up around this sort of stuff. I learned from him. So, going back to this man here." She pointed to a photo of Gary Lucado. "When the detective running the investigation first met with the previous owners of the mall, before it closed down, he and his team reviewed the video footage and didn't find what they had hoped."

"This man here," Ryan began. "He's now a person of interest?"

"For us, yes. That's why I'm here. I am hoping—praying, actually—that you might still have the security footage from the mall that the previous owners had in their files."

"That was captured almost a year ago?" Ryan inhaled a breath and cast her gaze to the window. "There is actually a slight chance." She turned back to Lucy. "We acquired their cloud servers. I'm not an expert in that sort of thing, but I have people who could take a look and see if what you want is available."

Lucy sighed with relief. "That's great news. How long would it take for you to retrieve the files?"

Ryan pushed up from her desk. "How about we go and ask the person in the know? Come with me."

———

Tabitha Barnes had been at the forefront of Allison's mind since the beginning of this investigation. She related to her in a way she hadn't to her previous, albeit few, clients. They were both mothers and there was a kinship there. So while it was an otherwise beautiful Saturday in the city, Allison had no intention of sidelining the investigation for personal errands or otherwise.

Allison arrived at Charlie's house and knocked on the door. "Are you ready to go?" She asked Charlie.

"I'm ready." Charlie walked outside. "Are you sure this is the right thing to do? There's so much we don't know about Alan Chumbley yet and now we're tailing him?"

They stepped into Allison's car and she started the engine. "How are we going to learn more about him if we don't watch him?" She backed out of the driveway. "He mentioned he was going back to the expo, right?"

"That's what he said yesterday," Charlie replied.

"Perfect. Gives us a chance to take a quick drive." Allison made her way to the highway and traveled to Kissimmee. As they drew near, she turned to Charlie. "Could you check out that address for me again?"

Charlie pulled up the file. "792 Sandpiper Trail. According to Google Maps, it's the second street on your right." She looked at her. "Are we just going to sit in front of his house? He's not there."

"I know. I want to see where he lives. I want to get a sense of *how* he lives."

Charlie peered at her. "This feels a little like we're reaching, Alli. We're going after a man who in all likelihood had nothing to do with our client's case."

"He had something to do with it. We just don't know what that something was. Just humor me, would you, Charlie?" Allison pulled onto the street lined with small, older homes. Mostly bungalows. "792? That's it up there. We'll wait back here and just see what happens."

Charlie unbuckled her seat belt. "Okay. Wake me up when it's over." She leaned against the door and closed her eyes.

AFTER WHAT FELT LIKE HALF A DAY BUT HAD ONLY BEEN about an hour, Allison spotted the garage door opening. "Charlie." She nudged her. "Something's happening."

"What is it?" She pulled upright in the passenger seat.

"That car backing out of the garage. That's not Chumbley's, is it?" Allison looked at the file again. "What's it say he drives?"

"A 2012 Ford Fusion. White." Charlie looked to the home. "That's not his car. I'll bet it's his son's."

"That's right. He has a grown son living with him." Allison zoomed her phone's camera in on the car. "Let's get a shot of those plates."

"Hey, Alli." Charlie peered through the windshield. "There's a truck heading this way."

Allison turned her attention to the truck as it neared. "He's slowing down. Any idea who that is?"

"Not a clue."

The Ford F150 pulled behind the faded red Nissan Pathfinder in Chumbley's driveway and stopped.

"What's he doing?" Allison asked. "He stopped behind the kid."

"I can see that." Charlie looked on with interest. "Who is it?"

They waited for whoever was inside the truck to step out and when he did, they turned to each other.

"That's Gary Lucado." Allison grabbed her phone again and snapped more pictures of the two together. "What do those two need to talk about?"

"You got me. And when Alan's not there. This doesn't look good," Charlie said.

"See? I told you this wouldn't be for nothing."

"You got lucky this time," Charlie grinned. "This could still mean absolutely nothing."

"We'll see," Allison replied. "Oh, looks like Lucado's walking back to his truck."

"The kid doesn't look happy. What the hell is going on between those two?" Charlie asked.

"I don't know, but it's up to us to figure it out."

———

Lucy followed Ryan to the first floor where the company's IT department was located. A large room near the end of the corridor appeared to house several workstations and tall servers.

"This is where we keep our equipment," Ryan began. "Our IT department consists of ten people, most of whom scour the nation in search of properties that have been listed for sale. While we own much of the properties ourselves, including the East Citrus Park mall, we also act as brokers to find properties for clients." She continued through the room. "Back here is the man I want to introduce you to. Sig, this is Lucy Boyce. She's interested in finding out whether we have the East Citrus Park mall's security footage on file."

Sig raised his eyeglasses to the top of his head and used them to push back his shoulder-length black hair. He looked to be around Lucy's age, give or take a few years. "We haven't scrubbed their data yet, so there's a good chance it's still there." He looked at Lucy. "I hope you have a time frame narrowed down or we'll be here for a while."

"I do, actually. March 17th of last year. Maybe the day before and the day after, just to be on the safe side."

Sig nodded and looked at Ryan. "Do I have permission?"

"Absolutely."

"Then let me take a look here now." Sig logged into his computer and entered several commands.

Lucy felt a spark of hope after believing that the odds of them having this had been stacked against her. Her anticipation must've been obvious as Ryan appeared to notice.

"If it's here, we'll get it for you," she said.

"Thank you. You have no idea what it would mean to us."

Sig continued to type in commands. "Okay. I think I found what you're looking for. I assume you want this on a flash drive?"

Lucy shot a hopeful look at Ryan.

"Yes. Please burn a copy for her." Ryan turned back to Lucy. "I hope you find what you're looking for."

18

After Allison dropped off Charlie at home, the deal was they would wait for Lucy to return from her visit to the property owner. They hadn't yet heard back from her on when that might be. So, Allison was going to head back home and then they would meet up at the office later.

Whatever had transpired this morning at the Chumbley home drew new concerns for Charlie. While nothing pointed to wrongdoing, as all the men did was have a face-to-face, it seemed dubious and especially in light of the senior Chumbley's absence.

The directive given to Charlie yesterday was to only communicate with Alan through Facebook and on a limited basis. But how was she supposed to learn more about this incident through messages?

She swiped her car keys from the side table. The boys were at their father's and Charlie was glad she didn't have to explain any of this to them. They knew she worked at the P.I. firm and had grown used to her odd and sometimes long hours, but they never asked much in the way of questions. Not like Nolan did to his mother. It wasn't that her boys didn't care. She believed it was that they hadn't fully understood her job. It was fluid at any given moment. Sometimes she pretended to be someone she wasn't and sometimes she spent hours in a County Clerk's office hunting down documents. It was tough to explain that.

With her keys in hand, Charlie was going to take the initiative. Sure, she might be jumping the gun. After all, they still needed the mall footage from Lucy to establish whether Lucado had been there that day. Nothing else mattered if they couldn't prove he had been at the scene of the crime, as he was when the Nygard boy was taken. But she knew where Alan Chumbley was today, and she had just asked to meet him there for a late lunch.

Charlie stepped into her Chevy crossover and backed out of the driveway before heading into downtown. Admittedly, she wanted to see him again. The idea that she'd fallen for a suspect was troublesome, to say the least. And she couldn't be honest with Alli about it either, though she suspected Alli knew already and had chosen to ignore that small, but potentially destructive reality.

This was the solution—to get the necessary answers and put this to bed once and for all. Either Alan was in on it, or he wasn't. And if he wasn't, well, Charlie would learn whether his friend was. One thing was certain, Alan Chumbley was protecting someone.

She arrived at the convention center and parked in the same garage. It appeared to be a little less busy than yesterday. Maybe a lot of people could only stand one day of looking at coins. She'd be hard pressed to spend another 8 hours here, that was certain.

Her hair was perfect, and her clothes were neatly pressed. She'd opted for capri pants today being Saturday and looking casual would be a reasonable thing to do. Not to mention that her thighs were still chaffed after wearing a dress yesterday. She wore tennis shoes too, foregoing the notion of sandals after several blisters appeared on her feet from all the walking.

The meeting point was the same. Riverwalk entrance number three. The upside was that the food here was surprisingly fantastic, so she was in for a good meal if nothing else. The other risks, she elected not to contemplate.

As she arrived, a smile arose on her lips when Alan stood from the same bench that she'd seen him stand from yesterday. "Hello, there. Long time no see."

"Hi, Charlie." Alan leaned in and kissed her cheek.

She quickly pulled back at the unexpected show of affection. "I'm so glad we could do this."

"Me too. I was glad to hear from you. Should we go in?"

"Yes, please. I'm starving." Charlie walked inside.

They reached the food court and placed an order. Alan led the way to the tables and sat down. "It's a little quieter around here today. It's been kind of nice, actually."

Charlie set down her tray and sat on the bench across from him. "I see that. I guess I thought since it was the weekend, it might be busier than yesterday."

"Well, a lot of the people who come here have stores of their own and are looking to wheel and deal. The first day sees the best bargains. Most of the good stuff is gone after that."

Charlie tucked away at her salad. "Then why did you come back?"

"Oh, I love to window shop. I'm not really in the market this year, but I like to see what's happening with the industry and look for trends."

"You know a lot about this stuff," Charlie said.

"It is my job."

"I suppose it is." She took another bite and prepared to get down to business. There was a limited time to get what she needed, and it was best to just go in for the kill. "You mentioned you were here last year with your friend. Why didn't he come here with you again this year?"

Alan smiled. "Honestly? I thought it might scare you off, having a third wheel." He appeared embarrassed. "I hope that's okay."

"Yeah, of course, but I would've been fine with it. Did you guys stay through the whole weekend last year? Make a boy's trip out of it? Unless your friend isn't single like you and had to get back to the family."

"Oh, no. He's single, too. Divorced, actually. We did make a fun trip out of it. I know the drive isn't far from where we live, but we thought it'd be nice to get a change of scenery. Tampa's such a big city in comparison."

Charlie took another bite and considered the next question. "There are so many great hotels around here. I love staying downtown. I don't get to do it much. What do you think is your favorite hotel here?"

"Uh, let me see. There are some great ones." Alan sipped on his soda. "Well, last year, we stayed at the Hyatt. Now that was fun. It was close to here, too, so it worked out well."

Charlie nodded. "Very nice. I'll bet you two lived it up, huh? Maybe stayed up a little too late. Drank a little too much? I know that's what I would do."

He laughed. "That's not really my scene. Now, Gary, he's the partier. I know I was in bed long before he was on both nights."

Charlie picked up on the name. It was the first time he'd said it. He was definitely warming up to her.

Alan took another bite from his sandwich and washed it down. "You know, here I am talking about myself and I still don't know anything about you."

"Well, you know that I have two sons who are still in high

school. Good kids." She stabbed her fork into a piece of grilled chicken mixed into the salad. "You have a son too, right? I think you mentioned he liked to play poker with you and your friend."

"That's right. My son's a good kid too. His name is Andrew. He's 25 and still lives with me." He held up his hands. "I know how that sounds, but since he lost his mother, well, I haven't had the heart to push him out of the nest. He gave college a try, but it didn't work out for him. Now, my daughter, on the other hand, Alana, she's a very good student. Very independent. She's in her first year at Penn State."

"Wow. That's great," Charlie added. "So, it's mostly just you, and Andrew, and your buddy sometimes, huh?"

"Yep. The three amigos. In fact, I don't know if I mentioned this, but Andrew actually came with us here last year too."

"Really? No, you didn't mention it. That's nice. I'll bet the three of you had a great time."

"We did." Alan's cheeks flushed. "But you know, I think I'm having a better time with you if that doesn't make me sound like an awful person."

Charlie smiled. "Not at all, Alan. It makes you sound like a very kind, fun person. Just the type of man I like."

———

THE SHIP'S NEST RESTAURANT WAS ON THE EDGE OF downtown and was usually packed during the week but on a Saturday, after the lunch crowd, several tables were empty.

Allison hadn't gone home as she promised Charlie. It hadn't been intentional, but an idea struck and if it worked out, she could present it to the team on Lucy's return. She spotted Milo Nash sitting in a booth and started back.

"Well, Miss. Allison." Milo slipped out of the booth wearing a salmon-colored button-down and khaki pants. "How nice it is to see you."

"No suspenders today, Milo? I'm shocked." Allison moved in for an embrace.

"It is a Saturday. I like to keep it casual when possible. Please, sit down. Let's get some drinks ordered, shall we?"

"I'm game," she replied.

"Perfect." Milo waved to the waiter. "Hello, sir. I think the lady and I would like two of your finest IPAs if you'd be so kind."

"Of course. Will you be ordering lunch today?" he asked.

"I would absolutely love a plate of your nachos," Milo replied.

"Just the drink for me, thanks," Allison said.

"Then I'll be right back. Thank you," the waiter replied.

After he walked away, Milo began, "This sounds serious, Allison. No lunch?"

"I am a little preoccupied with this investigation I'm working on," she replied.

"Do tell."

Allison relayed the details they had up to this point including what had happened this morning. "So, here we are. I was hoping you might be able to help us out."

Milo nodded. "I see. What an awful thing, losing your child in such a way. I simply can't imagine what that poor mother has gone through, or father, frankly."

"No, I couldn't either," Allison replied. "What do you think, Milo? Any chance you'd be able to get me Chumbley's financial records? He's involved in some shady dealings with a man by the name of Ed Reilly. What I want is to get hold of that information and use it to get Chumbley to talk. Milo, I'm sure he knows what happened to my client's son. Like I said, I ran a credit check, criminal background. Did all the things I could do and the best I have is that Chumbley incurred some serious debt in those first few months of last year, then all of a sudden, poof! The debt vanished and he was whole again."

Milo reached his hand around the back of his neck and rubbed it as though he suffered from mild stiffness. "I'm afraid that's just not possible, not without jumping through some very narrow hoops. Firstly, a warrant would need to be issued. Secondly, your suspect would then be notified of said warrant well in advance. Now, I assume you don't want the subject of your investigation to know that he's under investigation. At least for the time being."

"I understand the limitations I have," she began. "However, the D.A.'s office has a greater reach. I was hoping there might be a workaround—legally speaking."

Milo scratched at his round belly and cleared his throat. "Well, I'll tell you what, best thing you can do, as I understand it, is to ask Charlie to get the answers you need. Legally, your hands and mine are tied as it relates to the matter of financial records. Unless, of course, you wish to convince your detective to go after a warrant."

Allison's shoulders dropped.

"I'm sorry to disappoint you, Allison, but that's just the cold hard truth of the matter. The good news is you have something to run with. You can point Charlie in the right direction to ask the right questions. You both did good with the information you had to work with. Now that you're armed with that, I suggest you use the relationship she has cultivated with this gentleman and bring this case to closure."

"Look, we understand that Alan Chumbley is a bystander in all this. At least, all facts seem to point to that," Allison said. "The timeline, as recalled by Tabitha Barnes herself, puts Chumbley practically in front of her face only thirty minutes after her son went missing. I have to get Detective Santora to bring Chumbley in for questioning again. He can bring up what we've uncovered about him to date. The dealings with Reilly—all of it.

"But you say that has nothing to do with Santora's ongoing investigation, which is of a similar nature?" Milo asked.

"Nothing I have right now suggests any connection other than the coins. This is where you come in. Outside pressure on Santora to conclude his investigation, which would leave him no other option than to bring in Alan Chumbley. The guy will crack. I know he will under that sort of pressure. He won't want to be blamed for the murder of two children."

"Oh, how I wish I could be of further assistance to you, Allison, I surely do. That being said, should this case evolve, and charges end up on my desk, now we're talking a whole different ballgame. I'd have a lot more leeway in that instance. Until then, I'm afraid I'll have to stay in the dugout until you call me in to pitch the last inning."

———

CHARLIE SET DOWN HER FORK AND PEERED AT ALAN. "THAT salad was absolutely delicious. I'm so glad we could do this today."

"You know what, Charlie, me too." Alan dabbed at the corners of his lips and set down his napkin. "With everything that's been going on, I really needed this."

Charlie had spent the last few minutes thinking of how to ask the real questions and now it seemed he might've just opened the door for her. She inhaled a breath. "Forgive me for being intrusive, but I wanted to ask you about yesterday. Your friend, the one who you had been so concerned about, did all of that turn out okay?"

Alan knitted his brow for a brief moment as if pondering the question. "I'll be honest with you, Charlie, because I feel like I can be, I've had some past business dealings that it seems have recently come into question. My friend, as you probably guessed, Gary, well... You know what, it doesn't matter. Point is, he's fine, but there are some things we have to figure out. Nothing too serious, I promise you. But I appreciate you asking. It's nice to know you were paying attention to me. So many people these days, they only think about themselves."

"I understand." He wasn't going to bite. Not hard enough to reel him in, anyway. Charlie needed something else to coax him.

Alan pushed aside his tray. "We should talk about more pleasant things."

"Well, Alan, I do need to be heading out. I have to run to the mall to get a birthday present for a friend of mine. I'm taking her to brunch tomorrow and of course, I waited until the last minute. I think I'll hit the East Citrus Park mall. I hear they're closing, and I'll bet there are deals to be had."

Alan cocked his head. "I'm pretty sure it's closed down already."

"Really? Oh, that's too bad. You've been there recently?"

"Oh no. I just remember something about it on the news a while back. A year or so, I think," Alan replied.

"Wow. I should try to keep up on what's happening in town, huh? You don't even live here, and you knew it was closed," Charlie nodded. "Oh, well. I'm sure there'll be plenty of sales elsewhere."

Alan stood up. "I'll see you out."

"I'd like that very much. Thank you."

As he started ahead, Charlie's smile faltered.

19

The coordinated effort to gather promising information that could aid in the Barnes investigation had proven both useful and a waste of valuable resources. By late afternoon, the team had reconvened at the offices of ACL. Allison also requested the presence of Detective Bryant who had begun to lose faith that their one and only lead had evaporated. She needed to make him see otherwise.

"First of all, thank you, Detective, for meeting with us this afternoon," Allison began. "The last we spoke, our forward momentum had all but dried up. Today, however, I think we were able to pull together some evidence that could push us over the hump."

"All I can say is that if you managed to do that, maybe you all should be lead detectives," Bryant replied. "Show me what you got."

Lucy stepped forward and held the flash drive between her thumb and forefinger. "I met with the current owners of the East

Citrus Park mall and they were able to find the mall's security footage on their cloud servers."

"Excuse me, Lucy, but I believe I had mentioned all of that had been scoured by me personally," Bryant said.

"Of course, but at the time, you weren't aware of Gary Lucado," Lucy said. "As I was saying, they'd purchased all the servers from the previous owners and hadn't even had the chance to review the material. Good news for us." She opened her laptop and inserted the flash drive. "I asked them to download mall footage for the day prior, the day of, and the day after Hayden Barnes was taken. In the event the abductor scoped out the area in advance of his plan, we might see that here."

"Have you looked at this yet?" Allison asked.

"No. I did mention to the firm's representative that this was in regard to the abduction and she was more than willing to help out." Lucy loaded the files.

"Let's take a look at the day in question." Bryant moved in and studied the monitor. "I reviewed this footage myself for hours and as we all know, the boy wasn't on any of these tapes suggesting he was taken through the store while his mother waited at the checkout counter."

Lucy forwarded the video to 2:47pm on the day Hayden Barnes went missing. The footage covered the main mall areas only and not the individual stores. "This is from inside the main concourse but outside the store where Tabitha was." She zoomed in on the area in front of it. "Time is 2:47pm." She let the video play.

Allison moved in next to Bryant. "I'll bet this looks familiar."

"You have no idea. I started dreaming about this place almost every night." He folded his arms. "I'll tell you though, if I'd seen anything out of the ordinary, regardless of who it was, it would've been flagged. So I'm not sure we'll find our bald man, Lucado, on this video."

"He was with Alan Chumbley at the Tampa Expo last year," Charlie said. "And they stayed at the Hyatt near the convention center."

Bryant shot her a look. "How did you find that out? Santora said Lucado denied being in Tampa at all last March."

"Alan told me."

Bryant peered at her with concern. "You're still in contact with Chumbley?"

Charlie nodded. "I met him for lunch today."

"What?" Allison whipped around. Her eyes said what she didn't want anyone to hear. Not that it should have come as much of a surprise. Charlie was her own person and doing what she thought was right was who she was.

Lucy kept her eyes fixed on the screen and Bryant leaned in. "Hold on." He pointed to the screen. "Stop it here. Let's see who this guy is."

"It's pretty grainy given the distance." Allison leaned in a little closer.

"I don't have a way to clean it up either," Lucy said. "Where's a picture of Gary Lucado?"

Allison walked to her desk and retrieved the file. "Here." She held the picture next to the screen. "What do we think?"

Lucy turned to her. "This man in the video is bald. It's possible that's Lucado."

Bryant nodded. "I can take this to Forensics and get it cleaned up, but it doesn't prove anything. I can't arrest someone because they were at a mall. We need more folks."

Allison peered at the monitor. "Where was Lucado when the incident took place? Can you forward the video to 3:21pm when Tabitha made the 911 call?"

Lucy nodded and scanned the video to the time in question. "This is before Tabitha stood outside and talked to Detective Bryant and noticed Alan Chumbley nearby." Lucy again played the video. They studied the screen and waited for Lucado to appear. Several minutes passed and still nothing. "We're at the time when Tabitha was outside. Lucado is nowhere to be found, or at least, who we think could be Lucado."

"Damn it." Bryant placed his hands on his hips. "I appreciate what you went through to get this, Lucy, but we don't know any more now than before."

"I disagree," Allison said. "If you can use your resources to confirm that the man we saw at the 2:47 timestamp is Gary Lucado, then you have both possible suspects at the location when the child was abducted. And you already know they were both there when the other child was taken three months ago from the fairgrounds in Kissimmee. Detective, that isn't a coincidence."

"She's right," Charlie said. "I realize that all you have is two people at the locations in question and nothing more. But the more we learn about them, the better we'll understand if there's a connection. What Alli and I saw this morning, Gary Lucado and Alan's son, that's germane to all this. Not to mention the shady dealings Lucado and Alan seemed to have with Ed Reilly." She paused for a moment. "Lucado appears to be some sort of ringleader. He's running this show and he has a history of violence. Alan is nervous. He looks like a man whose walls are closing in on him."

"Here's something we haven't thought of," Lucy began. "Let's look at the same footage for Chumbley's son. Do we know what he looks like?"

"I could pick him out of a lineup after seeing him this morning," Charlie said.

"Same here," Allison added.

"Good. Then if we find him here too..." Lucy added.

"Then we have three men and no idea how they connect to the missing children," Bryant said.

"Clear as mud, right?" Allison said.

Lucy scanned through the video again. "I'm going to see if he was around Lucado. Hang on, I have to go back." She reversed the video until Lucado appeared on the screen. "Here it is."

The team watched closely until Allison jumped. "Stop! That's him. That's the son. Lucy, zoom in."

She zoomed in on the frame. "He walked past Gary Lucado but didn't stop to talk to him."

"That's him, Detective." Allison peered at Charlie. "Right?"

"Oh, yeah," she replied.

Bryant inhaled a breath and nodded. "God damn it. Instead of clearing up anything, all we've succeeded in doing is muddying the waters. Now you're talking a third person?"

"We just need a positive ID on Lucado at the mall and the pieces will fall into place," Charlie said.

"We have the license plates on both of their vehicles. We haven't even considered the son in all this until now. Detective Bryant, you have no other lead on Hayden's disappearance. I understand we've been going back and forth with this. But look at the video. Look at the material we've uncovered so far. We've got our bald man and we've got our coin collector."

"Yes, from a woman who recalled seeing one in a dream and then later recalled seeing that person near her when she was speaking to me. That was why she dreamed it."

"There are no coincidences," Allison added.

Bryant nodded. "Fine. What do we know about the son? Hell, we've thrown in everything and now the kitchen sink. What do we have to lose?"

———

Milo Nash was the special assistant attorney for the state's Attorney General's office. He was responsible for prosecuting cases tied to financial crimes such as money laundering, bribery and the like. It made sense that Allison came to him earlier today. Nevertheless, the information she sought was unattainable insomuch as they would need to inform Alan Chumbley of such an intrusion. It was no wonder why she didn't want to go that route. Scaring off your only possible lead meant the case would slip through their fingers. Milo was quite certain that Allison had no intention of letting that happen. He'd been there with her through the investigation that eventually led to the arrest of the city's mayor and had aided her as well during the Logan Carr investigation that brought drug runners and dangerous gangs to her door.

This case, though, Milo knew, had hit close to home for her. After all, she was a mother and what parent could ever conceive of such a thing? So as he returned home, kicked off his shoes, and put his feet up on his hand-carved cherry coffee table, Milo considered if there was another way. Something that he could do to help her and her client.

The confines of the law could feel like a noose around his neck sometimes. As an attorney, he understood those laws were there for a reason and that was to protect American citizens.

He reached for his cell phone and placed the call. When the line answered, he began, "Well, I wasn't sure you'd answer your phone on this lovely day."

"Milo Nash. I always answer my phone for you, weekend be damned. What can I do you for, sir?"

"Chuck, I am in need of your assistance. Said assistance might require walking a thin line."

"Now, Milo, you and I have walked that line many times in the past. So long as we stay on the right side of it, I'll do what I can for you."

"I do appreciate that, Chuck. As you work for the Osceola County prosecutor's office, I was wondering what information you might have regarding a missing person case out of Kissimmee."

"As much as I hate to admit it, Milo, we have many such cases. Can you offer specifics?"

"A boy named Ian Nygard went missing from a school fair about three months ago," Milo replied.

"Ah, yes, I am familiar with that as it struck a chord with a lot of people. It's received a good deal of attention from the press. Why might you be interested?"

"Turns out, we got us a similar case here in Tampa that's about a year old. Went cold from what I gather, and the family went and hired a P.I. firm. I happen to be a good friend of the woman who runs that firm. They believe they might have some new evidence that links those two cases."

"Is that so?"

"Yes, indeed." Milo lowered his feet from the coffee table. "I'll tell you what, how about I send you what I have, and we can converse further on the topic at your earliest convenience."

"Before I agree to that, Milo, let's get down to brass tacks. You said your request teeters on the edge of what I assume are legal complications. How about we get that out of the way first, and I'll tell you whether this is something I'm willing to take on."

Milo nodded. "Fair enough. Here's the deal. We got ourselves a couple of men who happened to be in each of said cities at the times these kids went missing. The P.I. firm is already looking into these men, however, there are things they cannot touch."

"Milo, I appreciate your love of words, but verbosity is not what I need right now."

"I do apologize. What I need is a complete history on one Alan Chumbley. Including, but not limited to, bank records, tax returns, and lastly, insurance policies taken out on his valuables, specifically, his coin collections."

"Criminy sakes, Milo, how the hell do you expect me to get the financial records of this man? Is he currently under investigation in my county?"

"Not officially, although I believe he is a person of interest. However, I'm hoping you might convince the detective in charge that he should be recategorized. That'll open up all sorts of doors for you. You know I can't get that information, not unless or until the case reaches my desk. I need your help here, Chuck."

The sound of a deep sigh bellowed through the phone. "Are your private investigators in touch with this detective?"

"Not directly, but a Tampa police detective here is. However, he's been just a little on the hesitant side to move forward on this individual as they've found no real connection."

"So I'm supposed to convince the detective here that he has a case?" Chuck added. "I'll tell you what, have your man talk to the detective here. Convince him to open an official investigation into this Alan Chumbley. I'll fall in line and back him up. That should give the detective a level of comfort to push forward. I'll get you what you need after that. Agreed?"

"One hundred percent. Yes, sir," Milo replied.

"Good. Can I get back to my golf now?"

"Wouldn't think of delaying you any further, Chuck. Thank you again." Milo ended the call.

———

AFTER REVIEWING THE VIDEO FOOTAGE LUCY OBTAINED, NO other sightings of Gary Lucado were noted. Not before Hayden

Barnes was taken and not after. They had one shot at this. One thin strand to connect these men to the disappearance of the boy. And if they could do that, odds were good a connection could be drawn to the Nygard boy as well. Detective Bryant had agreed they needed details on Alan Chumbley's son to determine if he might have been intertwined in whatever it was his father or his father's friend appeared to be involved in.

Bryant pulled up the records on Andrew Chumbley and the young man had no priors.

"He's as clean as his father," Allison replied.

"None of these people have a record," Bryant continued. "That makes things a lot harder to piece together."

Charlie grabbed a bottled water from the mini fridge and returned to her desk. "I can find out more about his son. They seem very close. Alan takes his son to these coin collector shows. The two live together and from what I've learned, seem to get along very well. I can learn more."

Bryant noticed a call coming in on his cell phone. "Detective Bryant," he answered. "Yeah. Uh-huh." He peered at Allison. "Yes, I am, actually. Okay. Sure thing, Lieutenant. I'll get right on it." He ended the call and looked at Allison. "I can only assume this must've been instigated by you."

"What do you mean?" she replied.

"You met with a friend from the Attorney General's office today," Bryant pressed on.

"That's right," Allison replied.

"Lieutenant Duran says I need to put in a call to Detective Santora and ask him to open an official investigation into Alan Chumbley for the abduction of Ian Nygard."

"The directive came from your boss?" Charlie asked.

"Duran got a call from this prosecutor friend, who in turn, promised that the Osceola County attorney would throw his support behind the investigation. They're leaving it up to me to talk to Santora."

Allison's face masked in relief. "Milo was able to help. I don't know how he convinced the other prosecutor."

"Take this as a win, Alli. Milo came through," Charlie replied. "Then I'm going to need to make myself available to Alan. When he's told he's under investigation for something like this, he's going to need me. I'll be his shoulder. He'll talk."

20

Since Allison started the agency, Leo had backed off on what had been overprotective measures. It was as though he still believed the two were married and it was his duty to protect her. First of all, Allison could protect herself. Secondly, Leo had lost any claim as her protector. Still, it seemed he had come to terms with her new identity—a private investigator and business owner. Hell, if things continued on this path, she might even end up bringing home more money than he did.

Nolan cut the juicy steak into a large piece and shoved it in his mouth. The kid could eat steak like no one's business. So when Leo suggested this little family gathering, he also offered to pay for it, and Nolan's $40 steak dinner. "This is delicious."

Leo sipped on his wine and smiled, deepening the lines on his cheeks and crow's feet at his eyes. He had been almost solely responsible for helping Nolan train and make the Triple A team. His ability to be a great father was never in question. It was his ability to be a great husband that hadn't panned out. "I'm glad you like it. It sure is good to see you, son. I'm glad you could get away for a couple of days. Too bad Micah isn't here."

"Spring break doesn't start for another couple of weeks," Allison replied.

"I'll be starting the season by then and won't be home for a while," Nolan replied, swallowing down his food. "Besides, it's nice to feel like an only child."

"I'm sure it is." Allison drank of her wine. "I'm glad we could all get together. It's been too long."

Leo eyed her. "Nolan says you're working on an investigation right now. Is it the same one you mentioned the other day about the boy?"

"It is, yes. It's been a little crazy lately, but today opened up what could amount to a real break in the case. So, I'm happy about that."

"And how's Charlie doing?" Leo asked.

"Very well. Lucy too."

Nolan shot a look to her but didn't say anything.

"This case you're on," Leo continued. "Is your detective friend helping you?"

Allison detected a hint of jealousy in his tone and felt somehow vindicated. "He helps out when he can. I'm glad to have him in my back pocket."

"Well, it makes me feel a little better knowing you have law enforcement backing you up."

There it was again. She was hard pressed to contain her glee, but it wouldn't be right in front of their son. Not that anything was going on between Shane and her anyway, but there was no point in clarifying the issue.

Leo cleared his throat. "Do they think the boy is still..."

Allison shook her head. "It's not likely."

"It's okay, Mom, you don't have to soften the blow. I

understand what happens when kids go missing sometimes. I'm not a child anymore. I have a job and everything."

"I know you do, honey. I don't mean to treat you like anything but the adult that you are. It's just tough. You'll understand one day when you have kids of your own," she replied.

"Well, on a lighter note, I do actually have some news for you guys," Leo began. "I was hoping to share this with everyone, including Micah, but I'll just have to call her, I suppose."

Allison's phone buzzed with a call. "Oh, I'm so sorry, but can you both excuse me for just a moment?" She stood from her chair. "Hold that thought, Leo." Allison made her way toward the restaurant's exit. "Hey, Charlie, what's going on?"

"I know you're having dinner with the fam. I'm sorry to interrupt."

"Don't be. What is it?" Allison asked as she stood outside.

"I pulled the DMV report on Andrew Chumbley, like we talked about."

"You're still at the office?" Allison asked.

"No. I'm home. Listen, I found a parking violation on the kid's record. It was only days before the other boy went missing. He was cited for loitering near a house. This house happened to be very near the school where the abducted boy attended."

Allison nodded. "Okay. Listen, I'll drop by your house once I'm finished here. Will that work?"

"Yeah. We'll go over it then. See you later. Oh, how's it going anyway?"

"Leo was just about to give us some news. I wonder what it could be?" She asked sarcastically.

"Probably wants alimony from you."

Allison laughed. "I have to go. See you soon." She ended the call and returned inside to the table. "I'm so sorry about that guys. Leo, you were about to give us some news?"

Leo dabbed the corners of his mouth and pulled up straight in his chair. "I've asked Jennifer to marry me and she said yes."

Allison couldn't be sure, but she thought her jaw must've hit her plate. She peered at Nolan as he seemed to choke down a piece of bread. "That's wonderful news, Leo. Congratulations. I'm happy for you both." What she refused to admit was that her chest felt like someone had driven a molten-hot screwdriver right through it. Yes, it had been more than five years, but she hadn't gone out on more than five dates, tops. And here he was preparing to remarry. Sure, Leo and Jennifer had lived together, and Allison had only just gotten used to that idea. Now this. She peered at Nolan again. "Nolan? Isn't that good news?"

He set down his knife and fork, placed his napkin on the table, and stood up. "I have to use the restroom."

When he disappeared, Leo's shoulders dropped. "Damn it."

"Give him some time. It's a lot to take in," Allison replied. "He'll get over it, just like he did when Jennifer moved in with you."

"And you? You really think this is good news?" He asked.

"I just want you to be happy, Leo. I know you want that for me too."

"I do. I do want you to be happy and you seem so happy in this job. This incredible new career you've started for yourself. You should be so proud. I am."

"Thank you." Her nose tingled and her eyes stung, but she cleared her throat and pushed back her emotions. "We were married for twenty years, Leo. You couldn't be faithful to me. What makes you think you'll be faithful to her?"

"That's not fair, Alli. That's not fair at all." He shook his head. "I'm a different man now and you know that."

She nodded. "Yes. I suppose you are. I'm sorry."

"And don't forget, it was you who ended it."

"Because you cheated." She checked her tone as it started to rise.

"And you couldn't forgive me. No matter what I did. No matter how hard I tried to make it up to you. You looked at me differently, like I was a stranger. You asked me to leave and I did. That didn't mean that I stopped loving you. It meant you gave up on us."

"Don't you dare suggest it was me who gave up. I was faithful our entire marriage."

Leo nodded. "Yes, you were the perfect one. You made that clear for a long time." He sighed. "I didn't want my news to go down like this. I'll pay the bill up front. You and Nolan finish your meal." He stood from his chair to leave.

She was angry. Not for the fact that he was remarrying. She didn't love him anymore and that didn't matter. She was angry because Nolan was hurt. "Well, too bad Micah isn't here for your big news. Maybe she'd stop thinking all this was my fault once and for all."

Leo stopped and turned back to her. He spotted Nolan return from the restroom but said nothing more and walked away.

Nolan sat down. "Are you okay, Mom?"

Allison reached for his hand. "I'm fine, baby. You?"

He shrugged. "I know I shouldn't be surprised. It's just that I wasn't expecting it. That's all. Dad's done a lot for me. I don't hate him."

"Of course you don't. Neither do I. Once we get over the initial shock, things will return to normal."

"What do you think Micah will say?" he asked.

"I have no idea. But I'm not sure I want to be in the same room when she finds out."

LUCY PULLED TO A STOP IN FRONT OF THE PUBLIC PARK. THE call had sounded urgent and while she hadn't come to a decision where Nolan Hart was concerned, he needed her right now.

She stepped out of the car and spotted him sitting on a swing nearby. "Hey. You look a little big for that."

"Hey. Thanks for coming," Nolan replied. "I know it's getting kind of late."

"It's fine." She sat in the swing next to him. "I didn't think I'd hear from you again so soon."

"Some things went down at dinner tonight." He used his heels to move the swing gently back and forth.

"You had dinner with your parents. I remember Allison mentioning that earlier. It didn't go well?"

"Nope."

"You want to tell me what happened?" Lucy pushed her hair from her face and turned to him.

"My dad said he was getting remarried."

"Oh. You don't care much for his girlfriend?"

"No. She's all right, I guess. It's not that. I just." He stopped swinging and held her gaze. "I know it's stupid, but I guess I thought maybe someday they'd get back together." Nolan sighed. "I sound like a child, I know."

"No, you don't. You sound like a kid from divorced parents. I don't know what that's like. I'm sorry."

"You lost your mom and then your dad. This is nothing compared to that."

"Don't do that," she began. "Don't minimize your pain. You're pissed off and you should be. How's your mom doing with the news?"

"I don't know. She wouldn't tell me the truth anyway. She never would admit how much it hurt her when he left. Mom never tried to make Dad look bad. Never said one bad thing about him. She won't start now."

"She's a good mom. You're lucky to have her."

He peered at her again. "I know I am."

"What do you want to do, Nolan?" Lucy asked with a warm smile.

"Kiss you."

She peered back at him. "You're only saying that because of how you're feeling right now."

"That's where you're wrong. Lucy, I know what I said at lunch today. I don't want to pressure you, but when all this went down, you were the first person I wanted to talk to. Not my friends, not my mom. You."

"I'm here for you, Nolan, because I do care about you. But it's not fair to put me on the spot like this. As much as I want to kiss you back, you have to let me figure things out."

He nodded. "You're right. I'm sorry. I'm just glad you came."

———

THE PORCH LIGHT FLICKERED ON AND THE DOOR OPENED. Charlie stood on the other side wearing pajama shorts and a long t-shirt.

"Well, hell," Allison said.

"Yeah. Come inside." Charlie closed the door behind Allison. "How's Nolan taking the news?"

"Not great. He and I finished dinner and didn't say a word. Then he said he wanted to stop by his friend's house before going home. What was I going to do, tell him no? I had already planned on coming here, so I guess it worked out."

"Well, I don't have a social life, so you can bet I'll be home."

Charlie smiled. "Do you want something to drink? A tequila shot?"

Allison laughed. "No. I wouldn't mind a coffee, actually."

"Coffee?" Charlie started into the kitchen. "This must be bad." She placed a pod into the machine and waited for it to brew the cup. "Here you are. Let's go sit down and chat."

Allison followed her to the living room and took a seat on the side chair before taking a sip of her coffee. "I shouldn't have been surprised. He's lived with her for over a year."

"It doesn't matter if you expect it, it still comes as a shock. I should know."

"Right," Allison nodded. "You've already been down this road. Here I am playing catch-up."

"Yeah, I've been down this road. Trust me, it'll get better. The boys didn't like it either and they were still pretty young, but you get over it."

"Well, I'm glad I have you to console me."

"Anytime. So, let me show you what I found on Andrew Chumbley." Charlie patted the sofa cushion beside her. "Come park it over here." She opened her laptop. "This is Andrew Chumbley's DMV record. Looks clean, right?"

"It does. Just like Bryant's background check. Nothing," Allison replied.

Charlie pointed to the screen. "Take a look here. Back in January, he was the subject of a citizen complaint. Apparently, a resident in the neighborhood near where he lives called the police and had them check out his car that had been sitting in the same location for several hours, with him inside."

"That's curious. Why would that be on a DMV record and not, say, a police report?" Allison asked.

"We'd have to check with Shane but, it looks like he was issued a parking violation. A police report was never filed."

"Why was he sitting in one spot for several hours?" Allison asked.

"I don't know." Charlie looked to her. "It could be worth our time to talk to the person who filed the complaint."

"It could be the one thing that connects the son to Ian Nygard, in a roundabout way. Enough that Bryant would take it seriously." Allison considered the idea. "Let's do it. We'll leave in the morning."

"Good. Then that brings me to one other thing." Charlie pulled up her Facebook account and logged in. "Alan messaged me a little while ago."

"And you didn't lead with that?"

Charlie grinned. "One problem at a time, huh? Anyway, take a look."

Allison peered at the message. "He says he had a good time with you and hopes to see you again."

"Yep. I figured I'd give him enough time to make the drive home and then respond. I sent him a message back that I'd love to meet up with him again the next time he's here in Tampa."

"And what did he say to that?"

"This is where things start getting interesting." Charlie scrolled over the messages to get to the most current one. "I have a feeling the detective in Kissimmee may have contacted Alan already."

"What makes you say that?"

"Well, take a look at this and you tell me," Charlie replied.

Allison leaned closer and pushed the reading glasses further up on her nose. "Oh. He wants you two to go away for a weekend?"

"I know, right? Keep reading."

Allison returned to the screen and read aloud. "Work's getting crazy. I could use the break. Would this coming weekend be too soon?" She pulled back. "First of all, 'work's getting crazy'? He's an eBay coin trader. How crazy can that be?"

"That's kind of what I thought," Charlie added.

"Why didn't you say anything sooner?" Allison asked.

"I just got this right after you called. I knew you were coming over, so I thought it best you see it for yourself. Here's what I think. I think the detective called him and said, 'hey, you need to come back here and answer a few more questions.'"

"Has to be," Allison said. "And it scared him. He could just be incredibly forward and asked to spend a weekend with you after seeing you twice, but he doesn't strike me as that type of man."

"I'm pretty sure he's not. This is bold for most men let alone Alan Chumbley." Charlie held her gaze. "What should we do about this, Alli? I know what I said, and I still believe he's innocent, but he could be looking for a way to get out of something."

"If he's afraid of the police, I'm not sure what we can do, Charlie. It doesn't look good, though."

"I think I've learned enough to understand his personality to an extent. I could say that it's all very sudden and ask him if he needs some kind of help with work. I could get answers, Alli. He's vulnerable." She looked down for a moment. "I can use it against him."

Allison noticed her hesitation. "I know you think he's a good guy, Charlie. I can see you don't want to hurt him."

Charlie returned her gaze. "I need to accept this for what it is. An investigation into a missing boy. Look at all we've been through lately? We've risked our lives. We've uncovered terrible crimes. This is who we are now. I want Tabitha Barnes to get closure."

"And what if all this ends up doing is destroying a man's life?" Allison added. "What if we're wrong?"

"There's only one way to find out."

———

THE MESSAGE HAD BEEN SENT AND NOW THEY WAITED ON Alan Chumbley's reply. Allison returned home and noticed Nolan's car was in the driveway. Relief at his return swept over her.

However, as she entered and noticed him in the living on his Xbox, it was clear he was still bothered by what happened. "Hi. I'm glad you're home."

He glanced at her. "Been home for a while. I thought you would've been here too."

"I stopped by to see Charlie. I guess I needed a friend to talk to, same as you." She set down her keys on the foyer table and walked into the living room. "You hanging in there, kiddo?"

Nolan shrugged. "You?"

She shrugged. "You want some ice cream?"

His eyes brightened a little. "Yeah. Sure."

Allison walked into the kitchen and dished out two large helpings of chocolate ice cream topped with whipped cream and chocolate syrup. She returned with the bowls in her hands. "Here you go."

"Oh, a sundae. Thanks, Mom." He smiled for a moment but returned his attention to the video game. "I'm almost finished."

"It's okay. I don't mind watching you play." Allison folded her legs onto the couch and tucked into the sundae.

21

What could Alan Chumbley say to Charlie Sweeten that wouldn't reveal more than he wanted her to know? Her reply reached him late last night, but he had yet to respond to her question. The call from Detective Santora alerting him that a warrant had been issued to gather his financial records sent him into a tailspin and he felt paralyzed.

The police had learned why he lied. It was the only logical explanation for the sudden turn of events. It still seemed like a giant leap to go from that to assuming he abducted a child from the fair three months ago. Gary was of the belief that was where all of this was headed. The idea was absurd, and Alan had no understanding of what brought them to that conclusion.

He picked up his phone and made the call. "Gary. It's me. I think it's time we sit down and talk about what's happening."

"Now?" Gary asked.

"Meet me at the coffee shop on Palm View Avenue in twenty minutes." Alan ended the call. It was as stern as he's ever been with his friend. Their relationship developed after his wife died and Alan thought Gary could be trusted. But in light of what he now faced, Alan wasn't so sure. One thing was certain, going to prison for something he didn't do wasn't an option.

Alan walked to the kitchen sink and dumped the rest of his coffee before walking into the living room. His son was still asleep and there was no point in waking him. This didn't concern him, and he didn't want the boy to worry. Alan tried to remember his son was an adult, but he couldn't let this fall on his shoulders. It was Alan's mess to clean up and that was what he intended to do.

The sun had already warmed the air while the dew point was still low enough to be comfortable. Alan backed out of the driveway of his bungalow-style home and headed to the coffee shop a few miles away.

Gary was supposed to know what he was doing. He said it was the only way and Alan listened. Now it appeared that his trusted friend was attempting to save his own skin, leaving Alan hanging out to dry.

The coffee shop was ahead, and Alan pulled to a stop in front of it. Inside the café, he smelled the aroma of freshly brewed coffee and breakfast breads. Gary raised his hand to garner his attention. Alan approached him. "Morning." He pulled out a chair and sat down.

"I hope you had a good reason for getting me out of my pajamas this early on a Sunday," Gary replied.

Alan's exacting stare landed on his friend. "I need to know what you said to the police."

"I told you what I said."

"Did you leave something out because the police got a warrant for my financial records. They don't pull warrants for nothing," Alan continued.

"Oh, shit. No, man. They asked about the fair, like I already said. And then about Tampa."

"They know what we've been doing. They know about the counterfeit certs. Reilly must've said something."

"Maybe so, but that's got nothing to do with that missing kid. That detective is trying to pin it on you."

Alan rubbed his thumb against his palm nervously. "None of this makes sense. I don't know why they think I had anything to do with that missing child from the fair. This all goes back to Tampa, but I don't know how."

Gary peered at him. "All I can tell you is that when I talked to Detective Santora, he asked me about the fair, then asked if I was in Tampa last March."

"What did you say?"

"I said I wasn't in Tampa."

Alan pulled back. "That's it then. We both lied about being there and they found out. What else did you say?"

"Nothing, man. I didn't say anything because there was nothing else to say. I don't know how any of this came up. They think it was you, man. They think you killed some kid."

"In Tampa, at that mall where we met with Reilly, a boy had gone missing. I don't know where you or Andrew were at the time, but I stood only feet away from the mother who was talking to the police. I had the collection in my hand."

Gary nodded. "Son of a bitch. I remember now. Some kid disappeared. So what? They think you took him and the kid from the fair?"

"Considering I lied about being at that mall out of fear they'd talk to Reilly, they must think it's more than a coincidence that I was at the same location where two kids went missing. Now, I'm a suspect. They're going to ask me if you were with me that day, too. It's only a matter of time before we're in the same boat. That's why they got a warrant. That's how they think they'll get me to talk." Alan peered at Gary. "If I come clean, your name will come up."

"Are you threatening me, Alan? Look, I don't know anything about kids getting kidnapped, okay?"

Alan pulled off his glasses and rubbed his eyes. "I never should've listened to you. You said when we were at the expo last year that this was the way to get back at Ed and make some money. You knew what I'd been through financially. I was still paying off my wife's medical bills."

"I was shit-faced that night. We all were. Besides, what in the hell does any of it have to do with some kids who disappeared?"

"I wasn't drunk that night. You and Andrew were."

"Yeah, well, we were all sober the next day when we went to the mall. Alan, just tell the detective the truth. It ain't half as bad as murdering a couple of kids. You need to clear this up. If you become their only suspect, you'll go down for it."

———

ALAN ARRIVED AT THE STATION AND STARED AT THE entrance, preparing for his defense. *"Yes, officer, I was at the mall, but let me tell you why..."* he thought.

Gary was right about coming clean and the fact that it was far better than being accused of taking children. He had felt awful that day when he stood there, listening to that poor mother describe her son. The boy had only been four or five, he recalled. So, maybe explaining what had happened and why he had lied would clear him of being considered a suspect. Yes, it seemed an odd coincidence he'd been at the fairgrounds that night too, but coincidences happened. He was innocent, and he needed to be firm about that.

Alan stepped out of his car and walked inside with his chin up. "Good morning. I'm here to see Detective Santora."

"I'll have him come up for you." The officer picked up the phone and called back.

Alan stepped away from the desk and surveyed the nearly empty lobby and the desks situated a few feet away.

"Mr. Chumbley, I was surprised to get your call this morning." Detective Santora offered his hand.

Alan took it. "Since you informed me of the warrant, I realized I needed to clear up a few things."

"Well, then, come on back."

Alan followed the detective to an office.

"I hope you don't mind but after we spoke, I went ahead and asked Detective Bryant from the Tampa Police department to join us," Santora said.

Alan's ease slipped away as he spotted the detective. "No problem at all. Detective Bryant." He offered his hand. "Pleased to meet you."

"Likewise," Bryant replied.

"Okay, Mr. Chumbley, why don't you have a seat here and we'll get down to business?" Santora took a seat at his desk while Bryant leaned against the windowsill behind him. "First of all, I want to say that I appreciate your willingness to offer clarification. There seems to be a whole lot of moving parts here and last thing we want is confusion."

Alan glanced at Bryant. "Before we begin, may I ask why the Tampa police is represented here today?"

"I've been heading up the search for a missing five-year-old boy who disappeared from a Tampa mall last year. You happened to have been at that mall at that same time," Bryant said.

"I am aware. And, while I was hesitant to come forward with details as to why I denied being at the mall, I'd like to come clean now."

"Please do, Mr. Chumbley," Santora replied.

"It's a fairly long and complicated story," Chumbley began. "But to get to the heart of the matter, I'll say this. I was at the mall back in March. I was there when that boy went missing. In fact, I recall seeing you there, Detective Bryant, speaking to the victim's mother."

"Uh-huh," Bryant replied.

"And the reason you withheld this information, Mr. Chumbley?" Santora asked.

"Because I was afraid."

"Afraid of what?" he pressed on.

"I'm not proud of it, but I was involved in forging documents regarding the certifications of coins."

"What do you mean, exactly?" Santora asked.

"Valuations. Certifications. That's how insurance companies place values on coin collections. I was at the Tampa mall that day because a former business associate of mine, well, let's just say there was a dispute. I took what was mine and that was when I saw what had happened with that boy."

"Do you have any proof of this?" Santora asked.

"Apart from the collection I took? Another friend of mine, Gary Lucado, he was there and so was my son. They can vouch for me. I promise you both, I had nothing to do with either of those missing children. I swear to you. I have kids. I could never..."

"Mr. Chumbley, do you have a collection of buffalo nickels?" Bryant asked.

Alan cocked his head. "Well, yes. Nothing of great value."

"How many, would you say, do you have in your possession?" he pressed on.

"I'd have to go back and count, but off the top of my head, I'd say roughly 20. I had a few and then added to my collection when I bought them from a friend of mine."

"Would that friend happen to have been Gary Lucado?" Bryant asked.

"Yes. May I ask how you knew that?"

Bryant glanced to Santora.

"Mr. Chumbley, I spoke with your friend the other day while you were at the Tampa Expo. He said he couldn't vouch for your whereabouts during the fair. Is there anything you'd like to clarify there?"

Alan's face turned white. "I was there. I'm not sure what else I can say. Plenty of people saw me there too." He shifted in his seat. "Detectives, if you both think I had anything to do with those…"

"There's something else you should know," Santora interjected. "And in fact, is the primary reason we were issued that warrant for your financial records."

"Yes, well, I was hoping that my being here would alleviate any financial questions you might have. You see, I did what I did because I was in terrible debt."

"You say you took back what was yours," Bryant continued. "Your former associate had no problem with this? He didn't file a report or a complaint?"

"He didn't file a report because he participated in the scheme initially. Then he wanted out," Chumbley replied.

"Let's get back to the fairgrounds and why we obtained a warrant," Santora continued. "What you need to understand, Mr. Chumbley, is that also discovered at the site of the fairgrounds and the mall were buffalo nickels."

He shot a look to each of the detectives. "Okay. So you think because I have a collection of them that must mean the ones you found belonged to me. I hate to say this, but they aren't that difficult to find."

"You do have a point. But if you look at it from our perspective, Detective Bryant's and mine, finding two such nickels and discovering there were two men at the scene of those abductions, one who happens to be a coin collector and the other who had several of these nickels, makes for rather strong evidence. Circumstantial, I'll grant you, but strong enough to get a judge to grant us a search warrant for not only your finances but now your property too."

Alan's mouth turned dry. His breath grew shallow. "I don't understand. I'm telling you, I didn't do this. There are tens of thousands of those nickels still in circulation. There's no way to prove they're mine."

Detective Santora nodded and turned to Bryant. "What do you think, Detective? Is he right?"

Bryant folded his arms and cast his gaze to the ceiling. "Technically, yes." He turned to Chumbley. "However, as Santora here alluded to, given what we have, it wouldn't be hard to turn your life upside down to look for more proof."

Chumbley's upper lip glistened with beads of sweat. "What can I do to prove I'm innocent?"

"Now we're getting down to business," Santora said. "You want to prove it? Tell us more about your friend, Gary Lucado."

22

They let him go—for now. Alan told them everything he knew about Gary Lucado, which was to say—not that much. They'd only been friends for the past three or four years and he had been unaware of Gary's domestic battery charge. This brought their friendship into question. Alan had been vulnerable when Gary came along after his wife passed. His son had been too. Concern now arose at the knowledge that Andrew and Gary had grown so close.

Faking the certifications had been Gary's idea, too. Alan went along with it knowing it was wrong but doing it because he needed the money. As he emerged from the police station, Alan allowed himself to play the victim, relinquishing accountability onto Gary, who it seemed had brought all of this on. Maybe it had been Gary who took those children because it appeared that Alan hadn't known Gary Lucado at all.

The police had succeeded in turning Alan's life upside down. What they hadn't made clear was whether Alan was still in their crosshairs, given his cooperation. However, he hadn't given them proof of anything because he had none to give. Alan wasn't finished with the police. Not by a longshot. Now the time had come that he was going to have to reveal the truth to his son.

As he drove away from the station, he made a call to Charlie. The one bright spot in all this. If anyone could improve his state of mind, it was her. "Oh, I'm so glad you answered my call."

"It's nice to hear from you, Alan. Is everything all right?" Charlie asked.

"Sure, of course. I saw your Facebook message early this morning." He paused. "Can I see you?"

"What, now?" she asked.

"I know it's short notice, but yes, if you have the time." He detected the long pause on the other end. "Charlie?"

"Yes, I'm here. Of course. Of course, I can meet you. But I'm right in the middle of something now. Can we meet in a couple of hours? Say around 1 o'clock?"

Alan sighed. "Yeah, sure."

"Alan, is everything okay?" Charlie asked.

"Yeah, of course. Everything's fine. 1 o'clock will be great."

"Should we meet somewhere in the middle, so you don't have to drive as far?"

"I'd like that. Yes. I'll find a place now and text it to you," he replied.

"Great. You just tell me where and I'll see you at 1." Charlie ended the call and peered at Allison, who continued to drive. "How much longer before we arrive at the woman's house?"

"We're almost there. He wants to meet you, huh?"

Charlie nodded. "You should've heard his voice. Bryant and Santora must've done a number on him. He sounded really shaken up."

Allison made the turn into the neighborhood. "We're coming

up on the house now. We'll talk to her and then you can meet him, although I'm not thrilled with the idea, given his apparent state."

"I can't back down now. We're too close. He's fragile. If he knows what happened to those kids, I have no doubt that he'll talk. Alli, I have to do this."

"If he didn't say anything to the police, which I assume he didn't because Bryant would've called, what makes you think he'll say anything to you?"

"Because he trusts me," Charlie said.

"Yeah, I'm starting to pick up on that." Allison pulled to a stop in front of the house. "This is the place."

"Do we know if she's home?" Charlie asked.

"I'm taking a chance that on a Sunday morning, she is." Allison stepped out of the car.

Charlie followed as they walked to the front door of the small two-story that appeared to have been recently built. She noticed a tricycle in the front yard. "She must have young kids."

Allison nodded. "All the more reason to make a call to the cops when there's someone just hanging out in their car on your street." She approached the door and knocked.

A woman who looked to be in her early thirties opened the door. "Can I help you?"

"Ms. Montenegro?"

"Yes?"

"My name is Allison Hart. I'm a private investigator and this is my partner, Charlie wells."

"What's this about?" she asked.

"I wanted to ask you a couple of questions regarding a call you made to the Kissimmee police department earlier this year. I believe it was in January."

"Yes, I made a call. There was a man just sitting in some old faded red SUV parked right over there." She pointed to the other side of the street. "I kept watching him, wondering if he was ever going to leave. I have two young kids, a boy and a girl, and I'm a single mom. I wasn't taking any chances."

"I can understand that," Allison replied. "I have children too. They're grown now."

"So you get it," Ms. Montenegro added. "Anyway, the cops came out, told him to leave and he did. I never saw him again."

"The car belonged to a young man about 25 years old," Allison began. "Had you seen him before that day?"

She shook her head. "Nope. Never. I don't know who he was or what he was doing here."

Charlie held up a picture of him. "I know it's been a while, but does this look like him?"

She examined the photo. "Hair's a little longer, but maybe. Honestly, I can't be sure. Why are you here asking about him now? It's been months."

"I know, but please bear with us," Allison began. "Do your children attend Orange Grove Elementary?"

She knitted her brow. "Yes."

"And back in January, I don't suppose you took your children to the school's fair they put on?"

Ms. Montenegro swallowed hard and peered at Allison. "We did go to that, actually. The kids loved it, until... Why are you asking me this?" She paused for a moment. "The boy who went missing that night. We've all been torn up about that. Was that man there that night? The one who sat in his car across from my house. Is that why you're here?"

"That's what we're trying to figure out, Ms. Montenegro. We're tracking down leads right now," Charlie added.

"I don't understand. Why aren't the Kissimmee police here asking me these questions?"

"We're working in conjunction with the local authorities,"

Allison said. "And there was a similar case in Tampa, one I'm working on with the victim's mother. We think there is a strong possibility it also involves that young man."

"My children." A tear ran down her cheek. "Were they a target of this creep?"

A boy ran up to her and grabbed hold of her leg, peering at Allison and Charlie.

Allison nodded to Charlie. "Show her the coin."

She retrieved a buffalo nickel from her pants pocket. "Ms. Montenegro, could you do me a favor and ask your son if he's ever seen one of these coins before?"

"Why?" She asked.

"We think the abductor used these unique coins to lure the children. If he approached your son, this might jog his memory."

Her lips quivered as she took the coin from Charlie. "Reese, honey, have you ever seen one of these funny nickels before?" She held it so the boy could see.

He took it from her. "It has a cow on it," he replied.

"That's a buffalo," Allison replied.

"I saw one before." He looked up at his mother.

"When, baby? When did you see something like this?"

"At the school fair."

"Did somebody show this to you?" Ms. Montenegro asked.

"A man. He was behind me in line at the Ferris wheel. It was my turn and I had to get on."

The mother nodded and tried to hold back her emotions, but her eyes welled. She looked at Allison. "Ian Nygard. He's the boy who was taken that night. My God. It could've been..."

"I know. I'm sorry to put you through this, but you have no idea how much you've helped." Allison nodded. "Thank you for your time."

"Wait. This man from the car," she continued. "Did he do it?"

"We're here to find that out." Allison reached for Charlie's arm. "We should go."

They returned to Allison's car when Charlie began, "I didn't think it could be Alan's son. I was sure it had something to do with Gary Lucado. I'm not so sure anymore."

Allison keyed the ignition and pulled away. "The son was here, he was at the fair, and he was at the mall. That's one hell of a coincidence."

"And when you throw in Gary Lucado." Charlie sighed. "Cripes, Alli, the only thing that does make sense is that the two of them worked together to take those children."

Allison glanced at her. "You might be the only person who can get Alan Chumbley to tell you what he knows because I'll tell you what, he knows something."

———

CHARLIE HAD JUST ENOUGH TIME TO GET HOME AND CHANGE before she was out the door again. Now, as the restaurant came into view, she prepared to get to the bottom of what had transpired with Ms. Montenegro. The restaurant was a local joint tucked into a strip mall between Tampa and Kissimmee. She parked her car and quickly checked her appearance in the rearview mirror. Reading the truth that she wore on her face right now would be all too easy for Alan. A dead giveaway that she knew what was going on, whether he did or not. Charlie inhaled a deep breath. "Calm down. Relax." A moment later, composed, she walked inside the restaurant.

"Hi there. How many?" The older woman behind the podium with white-blonde hair smiled.

Charlie cast her gaze into the dining area and spotted Alan. "Actually, the person I'm meeting is already here."

"Then enjoy your meal."

Charlie headed toward the two-person booth pressed against a wall painted dark green. "Hi, Alan."

"Charlie. Thank you so much for coming." He stepped out of the booth and kissed her cheek. "You're a sight for sore eyes."

"Well, it's only been a day, but thank you." Charlie slipped into the booth. "I'm happy to see you too. You sounded on edge when we spoke."

"Good afternoon. What can I get for you two today?" The waitress seemed to sneak up to their table as if from nowhere.

"I'll have a Diet Coke," Charlie replied.

"Great. And what can I get for you, sir?"

"A regular Coke. Thanks," Alan replied.

"Okay. I'll be right back with your drinks."

After the waitress disappeared, Charlie began, "So, Alan, tell me what's on your mind. I can see you're worried about something. You asked me to spend the weekend with you. From what I know about you so far, that seemed a little out of character."

Alan chuckled. "Maybe you know me well enough already. Look, I know we really only just met, but I feel like I can tell you anything."

"Of course you can." A pang of guilt shot through her knowing this was nothing but a ruse.

"You see..."

"Here you are." The waitress set down their drinks. "You two ready to order?"

Charlie closed her eyes, mildly irritated at the quick service. "I'll have the plain cheeseburger and fries. Thanks."

"Actually, that sounds good. I'll have the same," Alan replied.

"That's easy enough." She collected the menus. "I'll get that up as soon as I can."

Charlie smiled as she waited for her to leave. "Alan, you were saying."

"Well, I'm just so embarrassed," he began.

She reached out for his hand. "Don't be. You can tell me anything."

His cheeks flushed as he tightened his grip. "It's a long story, so I won't bore you with the details but suffice it to say, it appears that I've had a bit of a run-in with law enforcement."

"Is that so?" Charlie convincingly feigned surprise.

"Sounds scary, I know. What it boils down to is that I'm afraid. I have to be honest with you, Charlie, I'm not the strait-laced man you might think I am. I've done things I'm not proud of. And while it now appears as though those things have caught up to me, something else, something much worse now seems to have landed in my lap as well." He inhaled a breath and looked away for a moment. "You remember me telling you that the police believed my good friend had done something awful?"

"I do. And did he?" she asked.

"I honestly don't know the answer to that. I didn't think so, but the more the police tell me about what happened, the more I think, well, maybe. The thing is, I think they're going to use my indiscretions of the past to coerce me into helping them prove their case."

Charlie felt the truth was coming. The lump in her throat was choking her, her nerves frayed at his every word, but she had to stay calm. "What are you going to do?"

"Initially, I wanted to run. That was why I asked you to go away with me. I needed time to think all of this through. Unfortunately, in light of these developments, running might make me look guilty of something I didn't do. Charlie, they have a search warrant for my finances and my home. I'm at the end of my rope."

"Alan, what do the police think that you know?"

"They think I know that Gary kidnapped and murdered two children." His eyes reddened. "And if I don't help get them proof, I'm afraid they'll put me in jail for fraud, or worse."

———

As late afternoon arrived, Charlie returned to the office, pacing with nervous energy. "I'm telling you, he doesn't know anything."

Allison was perched on the edge of her desk while Shane and Lucy appeared as anxious as she had. "How did you leave things with him, Charlie?"

"I said I had to pick up my kids and needed to get home. I didn't say a word about Andrew, but it's clear Alan thinks this all rests with Gary Lucado."

"He doesn't suspect anything?" Shane asked. "He doesn't suspect you're working against him?"

"No. Not at all." Charlie finally dropped onto her chair. "Which makes me feel even worse. And now we know what his son had done, and I couldn't say a thing about it. Whatever's going on between his friend and his son, I can assure you Alan Chumbley knows nothing about."

"Are you being objective about that?" Allison asked.

"Of course I am and I take offense to the question," Charlie snapped. "Alli, I'm not trying to protect him. I agreed to meet him because he asked, and we need answers more than anything right now. By the way, what does Bryant say about all this? He was the one who grilled Alan this morning. What's he think?"

"I wanted to wait until you returned to hear what happened and now that we know about Andrew Chumbley, too." Allison turned to Shane. "I wonder if there's a way Bryant could get

Detective Santora to put a tail on both Lucado and Chumbley's son. With what we know now about Andrew, it should be the next logical step."

"There's nothing more I can learn from Alan," Charlie interrupted. "He's in the dark about all of it. He said Bryant and Santora were insisting he help them prove their case against Lucado, but I don't think he can."

"They'll put a wire on him," Shane said. "That's how they'll get what they need. Tailing the POIs, that makes sense, but putting a mic on Alan Chumbley might be quicker."

"I'm sorry. I wish I had gotten more information," Charlie added.

"Charlie, you've been great," Allison said. "You eliminated Alan Chumbley as a suspect."

"Don't be so certain, Allison," Shane added. "I know we all want the lonely coin collector to be innocent, and in all likelihood, he is. But understand this, the two main suspects now are his friend and his son. The son who lives with him. Look, Charlie, I get you want this guy to be innocent. Hell, I think we all do at this point. But let's not overlook that he's still connected to these people. And we don't know to what extent."

"What are you saying?" Charlie asked. "That Alan is protecting his friend? He doesn't even have the slightest clue what his son might have done."

"Assuming he doesn't, Bryant will use that to his advantage. And when he does, Alan Chumbley will have a choice to make," Shane replied.

Charlie crossed her arms and appeared defiant. "And what choice would that be?"

"He'll have to decide who to believe, his best friend, or his kid."

"And if both are the culprits?" Allison asked.

Shane scoffed. "Then I'll feel damn sorry for that man because he'll have to turn on both of them."

23

A task as mundane and undemanding as doing the laundry was almost too daunting for Allison in light of what the team had uncovered today. Sunday evening had arrived, and Nolan prepared to leave for training camp once again. Nevertheless, her focus remained on Bryant and Santora and how they would use what they found to get Alan Chumbley to turn on those he loved.

She pulled Nolan's clothes from the dryer and folded them neatly. Adding to the stress of the day was the guilt she felt for not having spent enough time with her son. With the clothes tucked under her arm, she walked into his bedroom. "This is the last of it."

Nolan shoved the clothes haphazardly into his duffle bag. "Thanks."

"Do you know when you'll get to come home again?" Allison asked.

"There's going to be a bye week next month around Easter. I'll have to check the schedule, but I should be able to come home then." He continued to toss toiletries into his bag. "You sure you'll have time to visit?"

"You know I will," Allison replied. "I'm sorry I haven't been around much this weekend. This case has just been..."

"I know. I'm starting to get it now—how this works."

"What do you mean?"

"I mean your job. I get it. I'm not mad. You're in the middle of an important investigation and I get that you can't just drop everything to spend time with me."

"You say you're not mad, but you sound mad. I don't blame you. I would be if I were in your shoes," Allison added.

Nolan turned squarely to her. "I'm not mad. A little disappointed maybe, but I think that has more to do with Dad than you."

"Your father seems happy. You should be happy for him."

"And what about your happiness, Mom? Doesn't that matter too?"

She smiled. "Yes, it matters very much, and I am happy. Nolan, I've started a whole new life for myself. I've hit a few bumps along the way. Maybe more than a few. But this is what makes me happy. I don't need a man in my life to make me feel complete. I can do that all on my own."

"I'm glad to hear that, Mom. You deserve to be happy." He zipped his bag. "I have to get going. We're up at 5am for practice tomorrow."

Allison followed him back into the living room and toward the foyer. "Did you manage to spend any more time with Lucy?"

He stopped and turned to her. "Why" Did she say anything to you?"

"No. She keeps to herself where that stuff is concerned. I do know she's been seeing Logan on occasion."

"She told me." He slung his bag over his shoulder. "She has a decision to make and I can't make it for her." Nolan kissed Allison's cheek and wrapped his arms around her, his tall frame almost engulfing her. "I love you, Mom. Be safe, okay?"

"I promise. I'll be fine. We all will. You do the same and call me once in a while, okay? Not just text. I like to hear your voice."

"I will." Nolan reached for the handle and pulled open the door. "Bye."

On the other side of the door were Detectives Bryant and Sully. "Oh, hello," Nolan said.

"I was just about to press the doorbell," Shane said. "You heading out, Nolan?"

"Yes, sir. Got to get back to training." He turned to his mother a final time before squeezing past the men. "See you later."

"I hope it's not too late to stop by," Bryant said. "Sorry for the interruption."

"It's fine. Come in." Allison let them in and stood in the doorway as Nolan backed out. She waved a final time before closing the door. "I guess we have some things to discuss." Allison headed into the kitchen. "Can I offer you a beer or water?"

"I'm fine, thanks," Bryant replied.

"I'll take some water, Allison. Thank you." Shane pulled up a stool at the kitchen island. "Now that Bryant's had a minute to consider what happened today, he thought it best to agree on a plan to follow up on Andrew Chumbley and Gary Lucado."

"We have a lot that appears to be coming to a head and I don't want to let anything slip through the cracks," Bryant replied.

"I agree." Allison set down a bottle of water in front of Shane and opened one for herself. "Tabitha Barnes is coming into the office in the morning. She's going to need to be updated too."

Bryant nodded. "Here's the deal. I'm meeting with Detective Santora tonight. I'll relay the information you all gathered today regarding Chumbley's son. I think it'll be enough for his department to expand the warrant on the property to include anything they might find on the son."

"What do you think his son is going to do?" Allison asked. "If he's responsible, even if only partly, I don't see him sticking around until the police put him in cuffs."

"That's why the search will take place as early as possible. We know the kid works second shift most nights, meaning he'll be coming home in the wee hours and will likely still be asleep when his team arrives."

"And what about Chumbley's friend, Gary Lucado?" She pressed on. "All we have on him right now is the fact that we know he has a small collection of the coins and he was also at the crime scenes. That's it. And that's hardly enough to get a warrant unless I'm missing something."

"I plan to keep watch on Lucado," Shane began. "There's a strong chance word will reach him when the cops search the Chumbley home. I don't want to risk him flying the coop."

"That brings me to another point," Bryant added. "Charlie's been taking the lead on getting closer to Chumbley. Given what we have to date, it might be time to cut that cord. People start thinking they're about to go down for something, they start to get nervous and take it out on folks. I don't want her in the way if that happens with our buddy, Alan Chumbley. He might seem like a mild-mannered person, but when put in a scary situation, you never know how someone might react. You need to tell Charlie the game's over. She's gotta cut him off."

Allison nodded. "Okay. You're right. She's done enough to help get us there. You and the Kissimmee police can take it across the finish line."

FOR THE FIRST TIME SINCE OPENING THIS INVESTIGATION, Allison believed they had a real shot at getting to the truth and putting away the person or persons responsible for taken Hayden Barnes. However, the odds that Tabitha Barnes would see her son alive again were nothing short of abysmal. She was sure there was a part of Tabitha who already knew this, but that wouldn't make it any easier when Allison would have to spell it out. The best she could offer was closure. That closure could come in the next 36 to 48 hours. Then, Tabitha and her ex-husband could move on with their lives in whatever form that took.

Charlie put on a pot of coffee. Lucy set out a tray of bagels in an effort to make all of this seem somehow normal. Detective Bryant was already in Kissimmee regarding the warrant, while Shane went with him to offer Santora assistance in trailing Gary Lucado. The snowball was growing and there was no telling how big it would get or how many people it would envelop.

Tabitha walked inside the office. "Good morning."

"Hi, there. Please, come in." Allison offered a warm embrace. "Can I get you a coffee or something to eat?"

"I'll take a coffee." Tabitha sat down at Allison's desk. "I can see by the look on everyone's faces, you have news for me."

Allison nodded. "We do need to bring you up to speed on a few things. Tabitha, we're not out of the woods yet, but we have made some significant progress on two potential suspects."

"Two?"

Lucy handed her the mug.

"Thanks, Lucy." After a sip, she cleared her throat and turned back to Allison. "Okay. Who are they?"

"First of all, none of this would have been possible had you not been brave enough to come forward again," Allison said.

"Alli's right," Charlie walked over to the desk. "What you recalled while you were under anesthesia. Your memory resurfacing regarding the man at the mall. Those details were crucial in getting us to this point."

"Then please, tell me where we stand and how we catch the bastards who took my son."

———

Detective Bryant walked into the Kissimmee station with Shane behind him. "I've got a pretty solid relationship with Santora. He doesn't know you, so let me do the talking."

"Sure thing," Shane replied.

They hadn't walked far when Bryant spotted Detective Santora standing nearby.

"Good morning. We have a lot to mull over. Let's get started." Santora led the way to his office. "I was able to expand the warrant based on what you and I discussed late last night."

Bryant walked beside him. "That is very good news. Oh, I should introduce you. This is Detective Shane Sullivan. He and I have been working alongside one another and I figured he could lend a helping hand."

"We can always use an extra set of hands. Detective Sullivan, it's nice to meet you," Santora replied.

"Same here."

Santora reached his office. "Right through here, fellas." He returned to his desk. "Aside from the property search warrant, I was just informed that the IRS will turn over Alan Chumbley's tax filings in a matter of days. That should help us build a good solid case against him."

"Leverage. Good. That's going to be important to get what we want from him," Bryant said. "Here's what we know, the woman who called in the complaint against Andrew Chumbley back in January has agreed to sign a sworn statement indicating her son had, in fact, been approached by the younger Chumbley the very night your Ian Nygard went missing."

"Excellent. I must ask, though, Sullivan, how did you find this complaint?"

"I didn't. That was the work of the private investigators hired by our victim's mother. It was on his DMV records. The complaint resulted in a minor parking violation and never ended up on any criminal records. In fact, the kid doesn't have a criminal record at all," Shane replied.

"There is still the matter of Gary Lucado," Bryant said. "And the reason I asked Sully to join us. I think the time has come to keep watch of Mr. Lucado. Once you and your people search the Chumbley home, there's no way to ascertain how that man will react. We need to have eyes on him."

Santora appeared to consider the plan. "Are we operating under the assumption both of these fellas are working together? But Alan Chumbley, himself, may not be aware?"

"That's the theory we're running on," Bryant said. "Until we can find out more about each of them, I don't see how we can separate one from the other. We're here to see if you're on board with running the operation in this manner. We're also open to any ideas you might have, Detective. I don't want you to think we're trying to take the lead on this."

"Not at all. I would like to update the family of the missing boy from the fairgrounds before we move forward. I can make that happen ASAP."

"Of course." Bryant held his gaze. "There's always the possibility the family will consider this move to be a step in the right direction of finding their son. On our end, we're trying to temper the idea that our investigation will lead to us finding the boy alive. It's been a year."

"No doubt," Santora replied. "I'm sure I'll be in the same boat.

We all know the stats. Our window closed about a week after that kid disappeared. I'll present it to the family in such terms as to also mitigate their hope for a positive outcome. I will say this, it might be best to put a tail on Gary Lucado ahead of the execution of the warrant, which I would expect to happen here in the next hour or so."

"I'll get on it," Shane replied.

———

ALLISON WALKED TABITHA BARNES TO HER CAR. "I CAN'T pretend to know how all of this has been for you. But I want you to know that we are getting close."

Tabitha opened her car door. "I know. I feel it. And I appreciate you doing all of this. I know Detective Bryant has been doing his part too. Were it not for you three, though, I'm not sure we would be this close."

"He's a good man and a good detective. As we speak, he's preparing everyone to pull the trigger to see this to its long-overdue conclusion."

Tabitha appeared relieved. "I know what you said earlier—about coming to terms with the inevitable knowledge my son isn't coming home—I do understand that. I think I've known for a long time. For me, this is about letting him rest now. Allison, I know he didn't come to me in that dream. I'm not some crazy person. But I also know that those memories came forward because my son is watching out for me. So, I accept the truth. Now I want to be done with this. Erik needs this too. Despite our having separated, he's a man who is lost. We both are."

Allison pulled her into an embrace. "You are stronger than anyone I've ever known, Tabitha Barnes."

She waited for Tabitha to drive away before returning to the office. Inside, Lucy and Charlie were huddled together. "What's going on?"

"Our resident technical expert appears to have come across another brilliant idea," Charlie said.

"I'm no technical expert," Lucy replied.

"Compared to us you are. Go on, tell Alli the idea."

"I was thinking about how you met with that parent who had been at the fair that night. The same one who issued the complaint about Chumbley's son."

"Yeah." Allison returned to her desk.

"I thought... I wonder if she took pictures or videos of her kids riding the rides at that fair. Then I thought, I'll bet she has other parent-friends of her kids who probably also took video or pictures at the fair."

Allison nodded. "And you think Ms. Montenegro might be able to track down said parents and see if all of these people can send us their cell phone video."

"What are the odds we'll see either Lucado or Andrew Chumbley on one of them?" Lucy asked.

"If I was willing to place a wager," Allison began, "I'd say we have at least a 50% chance someone captured either of them at the fair. Of course, we already know Lucado was there. We don't know for sure if Andrew Chumbley was, despite the incident with Montenegro's son. I doubt after this long, the boy would be able to positively ID Andrew. That would strengthen the case against them if we saw them together at that school fair."

"Do you think Ms. Montenegro would agree to help us track down additional video?" Lucy asked.

"To find the person who took one of her kid's friends. I'd say she'd jump on the chance." Allison picked up her phone. "I'll make a quick call to Shane. He's at the Kissimmee station."

When he answered, she began, "It's me. I hope I'm not catching you at a bad time, but I need to ask you something."

"We're finished meeting with Santora. In fact, I'm headed over to track Lucado's movements now. See if we can start piecing together if or how he could be involved. What did you need?"

"Lucy came up with the idea to take a look at videos the parents at the fairgrounds might have taken on the night Ian Nygard disappeared. However, there's a chance Santora already gathered that evidence. Can you ask him about that?" The line was quiet for a moment. "Shane? Are you still there?"

"I am, yeah. Sorry. I was just thinking. I'll bet he does have that and as with the mall footage, didn't think to look for Lucado or Andrew Chumbley. Let me make a call to him."

"We'll wait to hear back from you. Thanks, Shane." Allison set down her phone. "Shane's going to check in to see if they've already gone this route."

"Of course," Lucy began. "He's probably right. I'm sure that detective already gathered as much evidence as he could."

"That's probably true. However, we have more information than they did at the time," Allison said. "And, he's not the original detective. They may not have seen the boy, but our two prime suspects could be on there, possibly seen working together. It's a good plan."

24

Lucy had become the de facto technical wizard of the ACL team. Allison and Charlie could accept that their ages might've been part of the reason the ideas hadn't come from them. Lucy Boyce, daughter of the hard-edged Tommy Boyce, had all the smarts and the techno-savvy skills to implement ideas that would bring them that much closer to getting to the truth.

Word had gotten back to the women that photos and videos of the area were copied and viewed by the original detective assigned to the case, who had since passed. Santora hadn't reviewed the evidence for himself yet, meaning it was about to have some fresh eyes on it.

"Ladies." Detective Santora approached. "Detective Bryant said you were coming. I appreciate you driving down. As you know, time is of the essence, so let's get you started because I have warrants to serve. Follow me."

They followed Santora to the small Forensics department, which consisted of three officers sitting at desks surrounded by high-tech equipment.

"I'll leave you with Officer Nichols. He'll get you started on the video gathered from the night of," Santora said.

"How long will you be?" Allison asked.

"I don't know. It depends on what we find. You do what you need to do here, and we'll meet up on the other side. Hopefully, we'll both find something." Santora walked away.

"Ma'am? The videos you're looking for are here." Officer Nichols rolled back in his chair. "Let me know if you need me for anything else."

"This is all of it?" Lucy asked.

"Yes, ma'am."

Lucy pulled up a chair. "Great. Let's see what you have."

———

SHANE PULLED ONTO THE STREET WHERE GARY LUCADO resided. In a matter of minutes, the police would converge on Alan Chumbley's home. Word would undoubtedly make its way to Lucado, most likely via the son, his apparent partner. How would Lucado behave? More importantly, would he lead Shane to the answers he needed?

With the windows cracked open, Shane killed the engine and kept his eyes on Lucado's house. It approached 10am and Detective Santora, along with Bryant, was just about to arrive at Chumbley's house.

He unbuckled his seat belt and stretched his back before he picked up his phone to scroll through social media. However, when a call arrived, the caller was unexpected. A tone of concern laced his words. "Hey. What's up?" He peered through the windshield at Lucado's house.

"I got it."

Shane went slack-jawed. "Wait a minute, Baylor. You're telling me you got it? You're sure?"

"Hell yeah, I'm sure. You think I'd be calling you spinning lies?"

"No. No, I'm sorry, I'm just. I'm just right in the middle of something right now. I'm not even in the city."

"Where the hell are you?" Baylor asked.

"Kissimmee. You remember that case I was telling you about? It's all coming to a head now."

"Shit. Man, I need you here, brother."

"How did you get it?" Shane asked.

"Well, my friend, that was all your doing. Isabella Gonzales, the ex-girlfriend we tracked down after you got the envelope," Baylor said.

"Yeah. Reddick's girl from New Mexico. You got her to talk this time?" Shane asked.

"Didn't have to. She got arrested last night. Guess who was her first call?"

Shane grinned. "She called you?"

"You know it. I'm working on getting her out now in exchange for her testimony against Reddick. She says she has enough on him to prove he was on the take and that Martin Hernandez knew it. Get this, Hernandez had a little thing for her. Said she deserved better than a crooked cop."

"What, she deserved a drug dealer instead?" Shane replied. "Man, I can't believe this." He peered again at Lucado's house. "I can't get out of here for probably a few hours, at the earliest. We got a lead on the man who abducted two kids. I gotta stick this out."

"Here's the deal then. All that evidence we've been working on, when you're done, get it out of the safe deposit box, yeah? Get it ready because once I get her back here to Tampa, things are going to move fast. Like balls to the wall, fast, you feel me? If not, Reddick will get wind and all bets are off if that happens. You might as well drive the hell out the state."

"Yeah, no, I get it. As soon as I can, I'll get down to the bank and get the proof. Man, I can't believe it. All the bullshit and it ends up coming down to some ex who's willing to squeal."

"And someone who gave us her name. You must have a guardian angel, brother. We got Reddick dead to rights. Listen, I gotta go. I'm pulling all sorts of strings and asking favors to get her here. Call me when you have what we need."

"I will." Shane ended the call. From the corner of his eye, he spotted Lucado's front door open. "Shit." He sprung to attention and let his eyes follow Lucado, who was on his cell phone. "Who are you talking to? Your buddy, Chumbley or his kid?" He watched him step into his older model Ford F-150. "It's on now." Shane placed his hand on his key, ready to fire up the engine.

Gary Lucado roared out of his driveway and headed toward Shane. He tucked down into his seat until the truck passed. When the truck was in his rearview, he keyed the ignition and pulled away, careful to keep his distance. His mind raced with the call from Baylor at the forefront. However, he didn't have the luxury to appreciate the culmination of many months of work. Right now, he needed to know where Gary Lucado was headed.

The truck was in his sights and he followed, keeping one car in between them. He was no expert in this sort of thing, thanks, in part, to his working mostly counterfeit crimes. But he hearkened back to his training at the Academy.

Shane couldn't afford to screw this up. He now had Bryant in his corner but recalled his initial dismay at Shane's nose being inserted where it hadn't belonged. Not to mention his future lieutenant who reminded him his bump upstairs could depend on what happened with FBI Agent Dave Reddick.

"Stop. Focus on what you're doing," he said to himself.

Gary Lucado was his priority. The rest of it would have to be pushed aside. Baylor had a handle on things.

Lucado headed north while Shane followed. "Where the hell are you going, man? Come on. Give me something I can use."

It took four more miles, but Lucado finally pulled into the parking lot of a grocery store. He drove around back where the trucks unloaded their shipments. Shane watched as Lucado turned the corner of the building. "I can't go back there." He knew he'd be spotted in an instant. "Shit."

———

GARY LUCADO JUMPED OUT OF HIS TRUCK AND MARCHED TO the back door near the loading bays. Two workers stood nearby smoking cigarettes. "You two know Andrew Chumbley?"

"Yeah," one of the men replied.

"I need to see him."

The other man flicked away his cigarette. "I'm done anyway. I'll tell him he's got company."

Gary waited while the worker retreated inside. He paced in small steps around the entry until Andrew emerged.

"What are you doing here?"

"You think I wouldn't find out?" Gary asked. "You think I don't know what you've done."

Andrew appeared taken aback. "What the hell are you talking about? Why are you here?"

Gary stepped closer. "Your dad's getting his house turned over by the cops right now. He just called me. You want to tell me why that is?"

"Something about what you two did with Ed Reilly. That's all

I know," he replied. "I swear it. That's what Dad said last night. You should've seen him. He was freaked out."

"Why are you still here and not at home?" Gary pressed on.

"I took another shift. Look, what the hell is this about, man? Dad says he didn't do anything wrong, so I figured the cops wouldn't find anything. What's the big deal?"

Gary smirked. "He didn't do anything wrong, huh? And what about you?"

———

As Shane waited in the grocery store parking lot, trying to come up with a plan, it finally came to him. Lucado had never met him. In fact, neither Chumbley nor anyone associated with Chumbley had crossed paths with him. He drove an unmarked car and could drive past the loading docks. No one would pay any attention to him. It was his only choice to see who Lucado had gone to meet.

Shane drove toward the back of the building. When it came into view, he slowed. Gary Lucado stood in front of someone, but Shane couldn't see just yet. He rolled forward, trying to look as though he'd made a wrong turn somewhere and needed a way out.

It was when he reached the masonry wall at the end of the building that he finally turned around his car. Still, no one looked or cared that he was there. As he pulled forward again, he got a better look. "Son of a bitch."

Gary Lucado loomed over the younger Chumbley as though he was scolding him. The two were engaged in heavy conversation that looked to be on the verge of coming to blows. Lucado shot a look to him and followed Shane with his eyes until he drove away from the loading area.

His nerves on end, Shane pulled to a stop and grabbed his

phone. "Allison, it's me." He surveyed the parking lot to be sure no one approached. Or rather, to be sure Lucado and the kid didn't approach. "Listen, Lucado shot out of his place and headed to a grocery store. He's meeting up with Chumbley's kid now."

"Detective Santora served the warrant. They're at Chumbley's house," Allison replied. "We're still here at the station combing through the video evidence. We haven't seen either Andrew or Gary Lucado yet, but it sounds like you might have better luck depending on what he does next."

"I'll stay on him. Give Bryant a heads-up for me. Something's going on between those two, Allison. Lucado looked pissed. Let me know if you come up with anything."

———

ALLISON RETURNED HER ATTENTION TO THE VIDEO AS SHE SAT next to Lucy. "Still nothing?"

"No," Lucy replied. "What did Shane say?"

"Gary Lucado and Andrew Chumbley are looking mighty guilty right now. Shane said Lucado took off from his place and met up with Chumbley's son at a grocery store. He said it looked like they were having words."

"That's where the kid works," Charlie said. "But I thought he worked the night shift. In fact, I was sure that was why Detective Santora went this morning—to make sure his son was there too."

"Well, he's not. Shane's going to keep at it and see if Lucado tries to make a run for it."

Charlie's phone vibrated in her purse. She looked at Allison with concern before digging it out of her bag. "It's Alan. Just a text."

"What does it say?" Allison asked.

Charlie viewed the message. "He says the cops are searching

his house. He's scared. Alli, he knows it's because they think his son is involved." Her phone rang this time. "It's him."

"Don't, Charlie. Let it go to voicemail," Allison said.

"I have to talk to him." Charlie walked into the corridor and answered. "Hey, I just saw your text."

"I'm terrified, Charlie. They're telling me that they think Andrew's in on this. It's just not possible. I don't understand any of it."

"Hey, hey, it's okay," Charlie said. "Take a breath. Where are you?"

"At my house. They're turning it completely upside down. I wish you were here."

"Me, too. I'm so sorry you have to go through this, Alan." Charlie was genuine. She hated how afraid he sounded. Her heart broke for him. "Is there anything I can do?"

"No. When they're done, can I see you? I just need to see you, Charlie. Please. I could use a shoulder."

Charlie glanced back toward the room where Allison and Lucy searched for proof against Alan's son and his friend.

"Charlie? Are you still there?" he asked.

"I'm here. Yes, I can meet you when it's over. You just call me, and I'll head straight out, okay?"

He sighed with noted relief. "Oh, thank you. I must sound so desperate."

"You don't. You just need a friend," Charlie said. "I'll wait for your call. And Alan, everything will be fine. I need you to trust me on that."

———

ALAN CHUMBLEY STOOD IN THE HALL OF HIS MODEST HOME; his face masked in horror. Drawers pulled out, papers dropped on the floor, pictures removed from the walls. His home looked like it had been hit by a hurricane and they weren't finished yet.

He approached Detectives Santora and Bryant. "I don't understand. I thought this was about the bank records. I'll give you whatever you want. I didn't do anything wrong."

"As I mentioned on the outset, this warrant covers anything we find that might pertain to the missing boy, Ian Nygard," Santora replied. "That said, our offer still stands, Mr. Chumbley. You scratch our backs, we'll scratch yours."

"I already told you I had nothing to do with that or the other boy in Tampa. You said yourself you thought it was Gary Lucado. Why are you turning my house upside down?" Chumbley pulled down his glasses and rubbed his eyes as they welled. "This is all a mistake. You think I'm someone that I'm not."

"I'm a patient man, Mr. Chumbley," Santora began. "I'll wait for you to come around to our way of thinking. But in the meantime, I'd appreciate it if you just let us do our jobs."

"I thought your son lived with you?" Bryant asked him.

"He does, but he's at work," Chumbley replied.

Bryant raised a brow. "Interesting."

"Why is that interesting?" Chumbley asked. "He works at a grocery store, usually the night shift, but they asked him to stay longer because someone called in sick. He texted early this morning."

"Did you tell him about the warrant, Alan?" Bryant asked.

"I didn't want him to be afraid when you all burst into here like I was some kind of criminal. What I did, I take full responsibility for. This doesn't involve my son."

"You sure about that?" Bryant walked away and pulled his phone from his pocket to make a call. "Sully, it's Bryant. Where are you?"

Alan Chumbley turned away from the detective and

witnessed the continued destruction of his home. He walked down the hall and noticed his personal items had been tossed around. Andrew's bedroom was just ahead, and Alan peered inside. They hadn't been in here yet. The yellow copy of the parking ticket still rested on the nightstand where he had left it days earlier. It appeared obvious his son had still chosen to ignore it. Alan walked toward the nightstand and peered at it again. "January 26th." He continued to read it. "Loitering on a private street." Alan noted the address. Footsteps of officers approaching sounded in the hall, so Alan tucked the ticket into his pocket.

"Mr. Chumbley, we're going to need you to stay outside while we do our jobs," one of the officers said.

"Of course." Alan walked past them and into the front yard.

———

"Bryant, yeah, I'm following Lucado. He met with Chumbley's kid at a grocery store. Looked like the kid worked there. They were having an argument."

"Did they leave together?" Bryant asked.

Shane still followed Lucado in his car. "No. I waited in the parking lot and Lucado flew out of there pretty damn fast. I have no idea where he's headed now. What's going on there?"

"The kid was supposed to be off work, but apparently one of his coworkers called in sick and being the good worker that he is, decided to stay and help out."

"How's that for timing?" Shane replied. "Did he know about the warrant?"

"Pops spilled the beans, apparently," Bryant added. "Keep a tail on him. He wouldn't have gone to meet the kid without a reason. Keep me posted."

25

Detective Bryant walked through the hall and made his way outside of Alan Chumbley's home. Detective Santora stood outside speaking to a member of his team when Bryant interrupted. "Can I have a word?"

The two stepped aside and Bryant began, "We got nothing so far. How much longer are we going to keep at it?"

"I trusted you and your people to steer me in the right direction. Now I have half a dozen of my people here turning over this man's house and for what?" Santora asked.

Bryant turned away and peered into the home once again. "We aren't walking away with nothing. We just didn't find anything we could use at present to make an arrest. Look, we have Chumbley over a barrel. Either his kid is in on it, or his buddy, or both. What we need to do is look at getting him to turn on them, just like we talked about. I think he's sufficiently scared now. We can work with that."

"What about the son? We all thought he would be here," Santora continued.

Bryant nodded. "The kid stayed at work. Funny how it turned out like that. Here's the real kicker. Sully's still tailing Gary Lucado, who happened to stop by the kid's place of business to have it out with him. Took off from there and now we're waiting to see where he goes."

Santora pressed his hands against the white porch column and gazed into the front yard. "Let's see if we can talk some sense into the elder Chumbley, then."

———

WHILE LUCADO CONTINUED NORTH, SHANE MAINTAINED HIS pursuit. It was looking less and less likely he might be attempting to get out of town. He'd had no luggage and hadn't stopped at a bank or ATM to get money. In fact, he appeared to drive on as if nothing was happening. Maybe he knew he was being followed. If that was the case, Shane could find himself running in circles while Chumbley's house continued to be flipped by the Kissimmee police department.

"Oh, shit. The kid," Shane said. "This is nothing but a diversion. Lucado knows I'm here. Damn it. How could I have been so stupid?" He slammed his palm against the steering wheel. Shane dropped back and turned around. He called Bryant again.

"You better be calling with something, Sully," Bryant replied.

"Lucado was a distraction. I'm sure of it. This guy isn't going anywhere. He wanted to pull me away from Andrew Chumbley. Bryant, someone has to get back to that store and follow the kid."

"Are you sure about this?" Bryant walked onto the path of the front yard. "We're about to talk to Chumbley and see just how much he knows about his son."

"I thought following Lucado was the right move, but he hasn't made any hint that he's leaving town or going anywhere for that matter."

"Goddamn it." Bryant inhaled a breath. "How long will it take you to get back to that grocery store?"

"Fifteen, maybe twenty minutes," Shane replied. "If the kid is still there, I'll wait it out."

"And if not?" Bryant asked.

"Then Lucado would've accomplished his goal."

———

CHARLIE PONDERED A RESPONSE WHILE LUCY CONTINUED TO study the videos from the fairgrounds. She needed an excuse to leave when Alan called again, which would undoubtedly be soon.

Allison glanced at her while they stood behind Lucy. "Hey, you okay?"

"Uh, yeah. Fine. Just thinking about everything."

"You're thinking about Alan, aren't you? The call you took?" she pressed on.

"I wish I'd never contacted him, Alli."

"At the time, it was our only way of following a lead. But you have to let it go, Charlie. This isn't on you."

"It isn't on him either. It's his friend or his son or who knows?" Charlie shook her head. "Alli, he's going to call me when it's over. When the cops leave. He just wants to talk to me. That's all."

"Charlie, I thought we agreed to cut him off? There's nothing more you and I can do apart from what we're doing right now. Let the police work on Alan and get him to cooperate. I know you feel guilty..."

"Yeah, I do. What's the harm, huh? Who's to say that after all this, he won't open up to me? Maybe he'll tell me that he suspected his friend all along and tell me why. Alli, please."

Allison's phone buzzed in her pocket and she answered. "Detective Bryant. How are things looking over there?"

"Everything we're going to get is being loaded onto a truck now," he replied. "It doesn't look too promising, that I can tell you. Chumbley's son isn't here either, which wasn't supposed to happen. None of this has gone to plan and I've got Santora breathing down my neck for answers."

"And Shane is still keeping track of Gary Lucado?" she asked.

"He's going back to the store where the son works to see if he's still there. He's convinced Lucado sent him on a wild goose chase to give the kid time to take off," Bryant replied.

"I wish I could say we were having better luck here. Lucy has examined every frame of video and so far, we haven't seen Gary Lucado or Alan's son on any of it."

"Figures." He inhaled a deep breath. "We're calling it, Allison. Alan Chumbley practically wet his pants when we showed up. Santora and I are going to use it to get him to talk about his son and Lucado. But we're going to let him stew for a while. And frankly, we have nothing we can legally bring him in for, so we're banking on the idea that he'll cooperate because he's scared. There's still the off chance we'll find something in his finances, but at this point, I'm not holding my breath."

"Will Alan Chumbley be able to leave his home?" she asked.

"Yes. Why?" Bryant asked.

"He wants to meet with Charlie. You're right, he's freaking out and wants her shoulder to lean on."

"Now?"

"When you leave his house, I assume," Allison replied. "What do you think?"

"Hell, I don't know. You could just wait it out until we convince him the people he cares about will face life in prison.

That might get him to talk," he began. "But I know you ladies are going to do what you think will help your client, so it's your decision. Allison, listen, I have to go and help these guys wrap this up. It's your call, but if it were me, I'd cut him off."

Allison returned her phone to her back pocket.

"What did he say?" Charlie asked.

Allison peered at Lucy. "How much more do you have to look at?"

"Not much. Maybe thirty minutes or so, at the most. I'm not sure we're going to see what we want to see, Allison."

She nodded. "I'm beginning to notice that."

Charlie grabbed her shoulder. "Alli, what's the plan?"

"Tell him something came up and that you can't meet. Detective Bryant is right. It's in their hands."

———

Charlie was on her way back to the office while Lucy and Allison finished reviewing the video. She had planned to meet with Alan, but that plan had been squashed. It was clear Detective Bryant was frustrated at the end result. He'd believed they were on the right track and yet nothing had come of it. Not yet, anyway. Andrew Chumbley's behavior along with Gary Lucado did leave a bad taste in their mouth and they were all pursuing that now. But it was a far cry from bringing murder charges.

There had to be more that Alan knew and wasn't saying. Charlie figured he was being a protective father, but had he really known what his friend and maybe his son had done? Was he so naïve?

Charlie wasn't ready to give up. If the shoe was on the other foot, she would do her damnedest to convince Alli to quit, just as

Alli had tried to convince her. But Charlie couldn't do it, partly because she knew Alan was innocent. Maybe the other part of that was because she had feelings for him regardless of being warned against exploring those feelings. The end result was that Charlie was going to do what she believed needed to be done.

She was playing it safe. The same restaurant they'd eaten at only a day earlier. A nice, public, safe place. She arrived at the restaurant as it approached noon and noticed Alan sitting in a booth. "Oh my gosh. How are you?"

"Charlie." He stood. "It's so good to see you. You have no idea what this day has been like for me."

She allowed him to pull her into a gentle but brief embrace before sitting down. "I just can't believe this. It's so surreal. You must be on your last nerves."

"They think I'll help them." Alan rubbed his forehead. "I just thank God my son wasn't there to witness it."

"Where was he?" Charlie asked.

"By the grace of God, someone at his work called in sick and he volunteered to cover for him."

"And he didn't know the police were coming?" she asked.

"He did and he seemed okay. He tried to convince me it was all a scare tactic and that there was nothing for me to worry about. Well, I'll tell you, Charlie, if they were looking to scare me, they did a good job."

She reached for his hand. "Oh, Alan, I'm so sorry. I can't imagine how you must feel right now."

"They obviously didn't find whatever it was they were looking for because they left, and I wasn't arrested." He smiled half-heartedly. "So that's a bonus."

"What are you going to do now?"

"I'll do my best to put the house back in order before my son gets home. And now, all of a sudden, Gary isn't answering his phone. I feel like I'm out here on my own."

Charlie offered a warm smile. "You're not on your own. I'm here. I know I can't do much to help you with whatever's going on, but I'm here for you, Alan."

"You have no idea how good it is to hear you say that."

It was time. Charlie needed to come clean now in an effort to help him out of this mess. "Alan, there's something I need to tell you." She swallowed down the nervous lump in her throat. "I'm so glad that I met you. I think you're the kindest, gentlest man I've ever known. And what you're going through right now..."

"It's okay, Charlie. I've done nothing wrong. I'll find a way out of this. You believe me, right?"

"Of course I do. This is just their ham-handed attempt to bend you to their will. It has more to do with your friend than you."

"Well, who knows?" he replied.

"Do you have any idea how this all happened?" she asked.

"It started with a lie. It was my fault. I said I wasn't in a particular place when I actually was."

"Why would you lie?" she asked.

"I was afraid. I knew I'd done something—illegal."

"And your friend, Gary, was he involved in it too?" Charlie continued.

"Yes, but by no means should that have come down to this. I don't know how all of this transpired from that one lie." He peered at her. "What did you want to tell me, Charlie?"

She cocked her head. "You know what, it's not important. Let's enjoy lunch and try to take your mind off what's going on, even if just for a little while."

"You sure?"

"I'm sure."

———

"I'M SO SORRY, ALLISON. I REALLY THOUGHT WE MIGHT FIND something on here," Lucy said.

"We both did. Hey, we had to take a shot, right?" she replied.

"What are we going to do now? What are we going to tell Tabitha?"

"The truth. Look, we still have a line on Andrew Chumbley and Gary Lucado. Bryant is working closely with Shane. This isn't over. We were just trying to make it easier to build a case. That doesn't mean we don't already have one," Allison replied.

"Should we tell Charlie it's done?" Lucy asked.

"She's back at the office. I'll give her a call when we leave."

Lucy nodded and turned to the officer who waited with them. "Thank you for letting us take over for a while. I'm sorry if we wasted your time."

"You didn't waste my time, miss. This is part of the job. You win some. You lose some," the officer replied.

"We need to update Bryant first. He's in with Detective Santora." Allison started toward the door and held it open for Lucy.

They walked through the wide halls of the station and made their way to Santora's office. Bryant was inside and the two appeared to be in deep conversation.

"Sorry to interrupt." Allison walked in. "We're finished. We didn't find anything new."

Bryant lowered his shoulders. "Damn. Lucy, it was a good idea. Don't think it wasn't."

"Thank you. I just wish it had turned into something beneficial."

"Well, that ain't on you, kid. I hadn't had the chance to dip my toe in those waters yet and you jumped on it," Santora replied. "That said, I wouldn't say today was a complete loss. Things could still turn around on this."

Allison checked the time. "We're going to head back to our office. Any word back from Sully?"

26

The faded red Nissan Pathfinder belonging to Andrew Chumbley was still in the parking lot of the grocery store. Shane already knew the make and model thanks to ACL's work. What he didn't know was what this kid intended on doing. It was agreed that the Kissimmee police would keep an eye on Lucado's place to see if and when he returned. He hadn't as of yet.

It was almost 1 o'clock in the afternoon and Shane sat in the parking lot waiting for Andrew Chumbley to make a move.

A figure emerged from the rear of the building. A short but athletic man with sandy blonde shoulder-length hair appeared. Shane's eyes sharpened. It was the younger Chumbley. He kept his sights on the kid as he headed toward his Pathfinder. When he slipped behind the wheel, it looked as though he'd picked up his phone.

Shane retrieved his own to relay the news. "Bryant, it's Sully. Listen, the kid is getting ready to leave the store."

"Stay on him," Bryant replied. "Santora still has a car at Lucado's place but he hasn't returned."

"He's on a call right now. My guess is that he's talking to Lucado and planning their exit strategy. I'll keep you posted on his location." Shane ended the call. "All right, kid. Where are you heading to?" A moment later, the SUV headed south through the parking lot and toward the main road. "I'm right behind you."

———

CHARLIE NOTICED THE AFTERNOON SUN PEEKING THROUGH the window of the booth. She wiped the corners of her mouth and smiled at Alan.

He returned the gesture. "I really needed this, Charlie. I feel so much better."

"I'm glad." Charlie's phone buzzed in her purse and she reached for it, keeping it out of Alan's sight to read the message.

"Is everything okay?" he asked.

"Yes. It's my youngest. I don't mean to be rude, but I need to text him back."

"Of course."

The text had come from Allison who had expected her to be at the office. Charlie typed her reply that was not going to go over well. It wasn't part of the plan, but it was done. She returned her attention to Alan. "Are you ready to go?"

"If we must." He stood and waited for her to join him. "I do have a house to put back in order before my son realizes the extend of my trouble with the law. I would like to walk you to your car if that's okay."

"I was about to ask you to anyway." Charlie headed toward the exit. As they walked into the parking lot, she inhaled a deep breath to calm her nerves. The time for the truth was now. When they reached her car, she began, "Well, this is it."

He cocked his head. "All good things must come to an end."

"I suppose so. Look, Alan, I need to tell you that the reason we met...the reason I reached out to you..." she hesitated.

"What is it, Charlie?" he pressed on.

"All of this stuff that's going on. Alan, those children who disappeared. The one in Tampa and the one from the school fair... it wasn't a coincidence that we met."

His face masked in confusion. "I don't understand. What are you trying to say to me?"

"I want you to know that I believe you're innocent and that I know you didn't abduct those children."

"How do you know that's why the police came to my house? I never told you the reason." Alan's face twisted from confusion to something that verged on anger.

"I work for a private investigator. Alan, we were hired by the parent of one of those missing children to help her find whoever took her son."

"And you think it was me?" His voice turned cold.

"No. That's what I'm trying to tell you. We have evidence to prove it couldn't have been you. But all of this—it's my fault. You're in this mess because of the work my team has been doing. Alan, the police believe your son and maybe your friend, Gary, are the ones responsible for abducting both children. The one in Tampa last year and the one from the school fair back in January."

"You're telling me our friendship was planned? That you befriended me to find out if I was some sort of killer and now you think my son is?" He recoiled with disbelief.

"Alan." Charlie struggled to find the words. "The firm I work for... we had reason to believe..."

"You did this? You brought the police to my home? Do you have any idea what you've done?" He pushed his hands into his pockets before pulling out the yellow copy of the parking violation.

"Look, I know you're upset, but please let me explain." Charlie eyed the ticket in his hand. "What is that?"

"Proof."

"Proof of what?" she asked.

"I found it in my son's room. The date, the location. It hadn't occurred to me why they believed I took those children or was involved in some way with their disappearance. Then it began to fall into place. Funny how all this started around the time I met you. I kept thinking to myself, how could they think I did such a thing? How could the police have known so much about me?"

"Alan, I..."

"When I was told my son had become a person of interest, well, that changed everything. This ticket—it didn't look good. I got an inkling when the police seemed hell-bent on making me tell them things I didn't know. And now with what you're telling me, it's all become very clear. You learned an awful lot about me, Charlie."

"It didn't take long to figure it out," she said. "We realized you had nothing to do with it, but we couldn't say the same thing about Gary Lucado, or your son."

Alan's breaths grew louder and deeper. His chest heaved with mounting rage. "You're a mother, Charlie, and I'm sure you would do anything to protect your sons. I already lost my wife. I won't lose my son, too." He gripped her arm and squeezed.

"Alan, you're hurting me. Please. There's a reason for all of this. You can help us prove your son is innocent. If we work together..."

Alan pulled her close. "Charlie, I really wish you would've

just kept your mouth shut." His eyes welled and he pulled a gun from his waist before pushing it into her hip. "Now get in the car."

———

ALLISON PRESSED THE END CALL BUTTON. "SHE'S STILL NOT answering. It's been an hour since she texted and now, she's not answering me at all."

Lucy wore concern. "What should we do? Maybe she was able to get him to cooperate."

"I think we would've heard from her by now if that was the case," Allison replied. "We're going to have to go to the restaurant." She started into the corridor at the Kissimmee police station. "We'll tell Bryant what's going on."

They arrived at Detective Santora's office where he and Bryant finished unloading the evidence taken from Chumbley's home.

"Can I talk to you for a minute, Detective Bryant?" Allison asked.

He followed her and Lucy into the hall. "What's going on? I thought you two were headed back to your office?"

"We were, but when I checked in on Charlie, she told us she went ahead and met with Alan Chumbley at a nearby restaurant."

"Damn it." He pushed his hand through his hair. "Didn't you tell her we needed to cut him off and to let us handle things from here?"

"I did, but she thought she could get him to open up and end this sooner," Allison said. "Charlie was trying to do the right thing and we all believed the father was innocent in this."

"But now you say she's not answering her phone and it's been an hour?"

Allison lowered her gaze for a moment. "Yeah. Lucy and I were going to drive to the restaurant now and make sure everything's okay. I'm sure she's fine. She's in a public place."

"I'm going with you." Bryant returned to Santora's office. "Hey, I got a situation brewing. I need to head out."

"Anything I can do?" Santora asked.

"Not yet, but I'll let you know as soon as I get some clarification." Bryant returned to Lucy and Allison. "Let's go. Now."

———

The restaurant was ahead, and Allison drove into a spot near the front. Bryant pulled alongside them. She rolled down her window and turned to him. "I'll try her again." She held the phone to her ear but again, the call went to voicemail. "Come on, Charlie." She looked at Lucy. "I should go inside and try to get her attention. It's not like Alan Chumbley knows who I am. It's the safest bet to keep from blowing her cover."

"Assuming she hasn't already told him who she really is," Lucy said.

"Right." Allison unbuckled her seatbelt. "I'll be back in a minute." As she opened her car door, she peered into Bryant's vehicle. "I'm going to see if I can get her attention inside."

He nodded.

Allison approached the entrance and walked inside the restaurant. It was 2:30 in the afternoon and the restaurant appeared to be slow.

The host at the podium spotted her. "Hello. How many?"

"I'm actually just looking for a friend. Is it all right if I go back?"

"Absolutely. Go right ahead," she replied.

Allison walked into the dining area and surveyed the tables and booths. She walked toward the restrooms. Nothing. She started toward the bar. Nothing. Allison picked up her phone again. "Where are you, Charlie?" Her eyes closed when her voicemail picked up for the third time.

Allison hurried through the restaurant again, still eyeing for Charlie, but not seeing her or Alan Chumbley. She pushed through the front door and back into the parking lot.

Lucy spotted her approach. "Did you get her attention?"

Allison leaned into the driver's side window. "She's not there."

Bryant must've figured something had gone awry as he quickly moved in. "Where is she?"

Allison shook her head. "I need to find her car. It has to be here." She quickly walked through the parking lot leaving Lucy and Detective Bryant behind.

"Where are you, Charlie?" Allison's voice cracked with nerves. "Don't do this to me." She jogged through the lot and couldn't find the car anywhere. On her return, she was panic-stricken. "I don't see it. Charlie's car is gone." Her hands shook as she retrieved her phone again. "Come on, Charlie, answer your damn phone." At the sound of the voicemail message, Allison lowered her head.

"What are we going to do?" Lucy's voice trembled. "Where is she, Allison? Where's Charlie?"

———

SHANE CARRIED ON FOLLOWING ANDREW CHUMBLEY AS HE headed northwest. It had been about 45 minutes and he still hadn't known where the kid was going. No word had come regarding Gary Lucado, so he continued on his pursuit. He started to wonder if the kid was going to leave the state, given the length of time he'd been driving.

Shane peered at his phone as a call came in. He pressed the Bluetooth. "Allison. What's going on? Are you guys back at the office?"

"Charlie's gone."

His face turned blank. "What do you mean she's gone? Allison, what happened?"

Her voice was full of nerves as she continued. "Charlie went to meet with Alan Chumbley on her own. She thought she could convince him to cooperate."

"No." Shane closed his eyes.

"When she wasn't answering her phone, we drove to the restaurant where she was supposed to meet him. Her car is gone."

"Where's Bryant?"

"He's calling Santora to get his people lined up to help find her. Where are you, Shane?"

"I'm following Andrew. Allison, I have to stay the course."

"I know. We'll find Charlie. Do what you have to do. I'll call you later. I have to go."

The line went dead. Shane's knuckles turned white as he tightened his grip on the steering wheel. His foot pressed down harder on the gas pedal as he drew closer to Andrew's car. He wanted to ram right into it, but he had to fall back. He couldn't risk the kid spotting him. "What the hell are you and your dad up to?"

———

Bryant ended the call with Santora and walked to Allison as she stood beside her Honda with Lucy. "Any luck contacting her?"

"No. It's still going straight to voicemail. I just talked to Shane. He's following Andrew."

"That might be our saving grace." He placed his hands on his hips and turned his eyes to the restaurant. "Okay, here's what we're going to do. Let's go inside and ask the wait staff. Find out if any of them remember seeing her or Chumbley and when they might've left."

Allison nodded. "Okay. Lucy, let's go."

They followed Bryant back inside the restaurant. He approached the hostess with his badge in hand. "Hi. I'm wondering if you might recall seeing a woman about yay high." He held his hand to his shoulder. "Short black hair. She was with a man. Slim, wore glasses."

The older woman behind the podium furrowed her brow. "Yes, I remember them. Let me get the server who was assigned to their table." She walked into the dining area and quickly returned with the waitress. "Maddy, they're looking for the short woman with black hair and the thin-looking man who wore glasses. They were at your table, right?"

"Yeah. They left about forty, forty-five minutes ago, maybe. Why?"

"Did the woman appear distressed in any way?" Allison asked.

"No. I don't think so," Maddy replied.

Allison checked the time and turned to Bryant. "That means they left only 30 minutes before we arrived."

"It's enough of a head start and we have no idea where they were going," Bryant said.

"Is everything all right? Should we do something?" the hostess asked.

"No, thank you. You've both been very helpful." Bryant headed toward the exit.

Allison pushed through the doors behind Bryant. "Forty-five

minutes. I don't get it. I don't understand. Why would she go with him?"

Bryant stopped and turned to her. "And not tell you? I don't know, but it's not looking good."

Her eyes welled and she placed her hand on her forehead. "Charlie, where are you?"

"We'll find her, Allison." Bryant looked to both her and Lucy. "Whatever it takes, we'll find Charlie. For now, we'll head back to the station and see how far Santora is on assembling a team. We may want to consider a BOLO on her car." He looked at Allison. "You said Charlie had been communicating with Chumbley through social media?"

"Yes."

"Okay, then we need to see those conversations," Bryant replied.

"I don't know her password."

"I do," Lucy jumped in. "She needed some help with adding friends and liking posts to make the account look legit. She asked me to help her with that."

"Oh, thank God," Allison replied.

"Let's not waste any more time standing out here. We'll go now and start looking at what those two were talking about while I get with Santora." Bryant ushered Allison back to her car. "You're okay to drive?"

"I'm fine."

"Meet you all there in ten." Bryant returned to his car.

Allison started the engine and headed out of the parking lot. She could find no words to offer Lucy any comfort, or comfort for herself, for that matter.

Lucy peered at her. "I know you blame yourself, Allison."

She glanced back, knowingly.

"You blamed yourself for what happened to my dad, too. Or at least, you felt guilty about it, which was why you tried to help me," Lucy added.

"I'm supposed to keep my team safe."

"Says who? We're all in this together. Like you said, we're a team. Meaning we all can think for ourselves. Charlie was going to search for answers whether you wanted her to or not. We just have to focus on finding her."

Allison pulled into the parking lot of the station and they walked inside. Detective Bryant had beaten her by a minute or two and stood with Detective Santora.

Santora peered at Allison. "I'm sorry about your friend. Come on back. I'll give you a laptop you can work on and we'll get a BOLO issued for Charlie's car."

They followed him to a small conference room where a table rested in the middle along with several chairs.

"Make yourselves comfortable. I'll be right back with a computer." Santora walked out of the room.

"While Lucy is finding out what those two talked about, I'll work with Santora to see if we can track her phone through GPS."

Detective Santora returned with a computer. "Okay, have at it."

Lucy opened the computer and logged into Charlie's fake Facebook account. She pulled up the Messenger app and scrolled through their communications. "I'm in."

Allison walked behind her and peered over her shoulder. "I know they've been texting on her phone too, but since we don't have that, I hope we'll find something here."

"Allison, we're going to Forensics and see what they can do about getting a location on Charlie," Bryant said. "We'll reconvene just as soon as one of us picks up anything." Bryant tapped Santora on the shoulder and the two walked into the hall.

"Hey, Allison, take a look at this." Lucy pointed to the screen. "Two days ago, Alan asked Charlie to go away for a weekend."

"Oh, that's right." She leaned closer to view the chat thread. "He told her he wanted to get away for a while because of all this stuff happening around him."

Lucy scrolled farther down. "Charlie didn't reply until the next day. Something about asking if he needed help." She read the message verbatim.

"I remember now," Allison began. "Lucy, keep looking. Does he offer any more details on where he wanted to take her?"

Lucy continued to view the messages. "Wait! He has a cabin." She whipped back toward Allison. "He has a cabin. That was where he wanted to take her."

"We need to find that cabin. Now." Allison dashed out of the room in search of Bryant who had gone to the Forensics department.

Lucy jogged to catch up to her.

"Detective Bryant, we know where he took her," Allison said.

"Where?"

"Lucy found a message that Chumbley asked her to go away for the weekend. He said he had a cabin," Allison began. "That's where she is. It has to be."

Bryant nodded. "Okay. If he owns a cabin, we'll be able to pull up the tax records and get an address. We're still working on triangulating her signal, but nothing yet." He turned to Officer Nichols. "Can you pull up the tax records for Alan Chumbley?"

"Sure thing." The officer keyed in several commands and waited for only a moment for the information to appear. "Says he owns a property here in town. Detective, it looks like he owns just the one."

"No, that can't be. Check again," Allison said.

"Ma'am, this is it. This is the extent of the property tax records for him."

"Check the records for Gary Lucado," Lucy added.

Allison nodded. "Of course."

"On it." The officer typed again and this time, Gary Lucado's records appeared. "He does own two properties. One here and one in Land O'Lakes."

Allison spun around to Bryant. "That's where they are."

Santora nodded. "Go. But I'm sending back up with you."

27

It was the longest 90 minutes of Shane's life, but Andrew Chumbley revealed his destination. Shane dropped back as they meandered through the streets of cabins that rested on large plots of land. He was in Land O'Lakes. "So this is where you plan on holing up?"

Many of the homes were large and newly built, but as he drove farther back, modest cabin-style homes appeared that had been around for some time. Several backed up to marshy lakes and were nestled in heavily wooded areas. A perfect place for laying low while the cops got closer to the truth.

Shane spotted Andrew pull onto a long crushed-rock driveway. He stopped several houses back and parked behind an old truck in front of someone else's home. It was time to go on foot from here.

He stepped out of the car and checked his weapon before his cell phone buzzed. Shane answered immediately when he saw Allison's name on the caller ID. "Tell me you found her." He spoke in a whisper.

"She's headed to a cabin in Land O'Lakes. Gary Lucado owns it and Lucy found messages on Facebook pointing us to it," Allison replied. "Where are you? Where's Andrew Chumbley?"

"A cabin in Land O'Lakes? That's where he's taking her? Right now? That's where he's taking her?" He asked, still keeping his voice down.

"Yes. Shane, what's wrong? Why are you whispering?"

"Allison, I'm here. I followed Andrew Chumbley and he just parked at a cabin up the street."

"Oh my God. Is Charlie there? Do you see her car? Shane, they're in her car."

"I think it's just the kid. I was getting ready to approach on foot," he replied. Allison could be heard mumbling in the background as though she was speaking to someone else. It took a moment before she returned to the call.

"Shane, don't get near him. I'm with Bryant now. We have back up and we're headed there as we speak. He says not to approach him."

"Shit. Why not? I can finish this now, Allison." He heard her put the call on speaker.

"Because I don't want Alan Chumbley rolling up there with Charlie and seeing your car or any cop car for that matter. He'll turn around and we'll lose him. You gotta hold off until we get there, man," Bryant said.

"How far out are you?" Shane asked.

"An hour."

"Damn it. I can't wait that long. What if the dad gets here before you?" Shane pressed on.

"That's what I'm counting on. I'll bet a dime to a dollar he doesn't know his son is there. We got a shot to bring them both in, but not if you go in there. You're on your own and it's not safe."

Shane knew he was right. "What the hell am I supposed to do then?"

"Do your best to keep an eye on him. Make sure he doesn't leave, or if he does, follow him again. Whatever you do, do not lose that kid, you hear me, Sully?"

"Fine. I'll wait it out, but I'm moving in. I need to be able to see if and when Charlie arrives. I'll stay out of sight."

"You'd better. We'll text when we're nearby."

———

CHARLIE GLANCED AT ALAN FROM THE DRIVER'S SEAT AS SHE continued to a place unknown to her. There was a rule about not allowing a kidnapper to move to a different location when faced with abduction, but when the gun was pushed into her hip, resisting wasn't an option. "Why did you have a gun, Alan?"

He peered at her from the passenger seat. "After the police left my house, after I understood what it was they thought my son had done, I was terrified. Then realizing that the timing of our meeting and my mounting troubles, well, it no longer seemed like a coincidence. I had to know the truth and that was why I asked you to meet me. The gun? I wasn't sure what your answer would be. I thought I might need it. Turned out, I should've been afraid of you all along."

She blinked away the tears that welled. "I'm sorry I lied to you. I was only looking for the truth and then I got to know you."

"You claimed to be someone you're not. I'm in this situation because of you. Charlie, you have no idea the lengths I'll go to protect my family."

Charlie kept her eyes on the road. "Did you do it? Did you take those kids?"

He scoffed. "I don't know how all of this even came about,

273

Charlie. Why would you point the police in my direction? What did I do to make you think I was a killer?"

"The victim's mother—the one who lives in Tampa—she recalled new details from the day her son disappeared. Through a series of hits and misses, the evidence led us to you."

"Then you all must not be very good at your jobs. You said you didn't believe I did it and now you're here asking me if I did," Alan said.

"When someone forces you into a car at gunpoint, opinions change." She glanced at him. "Alan, the mother remembered seeing you at the mall. That was how we figured you were innocent."

"Turn here." Alan pointed ahead.

"Where are we going?" she asked.

"Someplace that will let me think this through and figure out what I'm supposed to do to get out of this mess."

———

ANDREW CHUMBLEY PULLED HIS PATHFINDER INTO THE garage and closed the door, glancing around as if to be certain he was alone. He had wanted to go to his dad, but Gary insisted it was better not to. Now he was here, and he had no idea what to do.

He walked to the front entrance and unlocked the door. Inside, sunlight spilled into the open living space. The paneled walls and wood beams across the vaulted ceiling revealed the warmth of the cabin. It was comforting, as if he was only here for a quick visit as he had been many times before. Andrew had spent the past few years coming here most weekends, ever since his dad befriended Gary Lucado.

Andrew dropped to the side chair and stared through the

window that overlooked the lake. He was stuck here, knowing there was no escape.

———

CHARLIE HAD VISITED THIS AREA WHEN SHE WAS STILL married. She and her ex-husband would bring the kids and rent one of the cabins on a lake. But as she arrived and followed Alan's instructions to head to the cabin at the end of the gravel road, she realized how secluded it really was here.

"Turn onto that driveway there," Alan said.

She pulled near the garage door before shifting the gear into park. "What now?"

"We're going to stay here until I can figure this out." Alan raised the gun. "I'll walk around and open your door. Don't try to get out."

"I won't." A part of Charlie believed Alan would never hurt anyone, let alone her, but Bryant had been right. Alan had been faced with a situation he couldn't get out of and turned into someone she hadn't recognized.

Alan opened her door. "Get out. Once we get inside, I'll be able to clear my head."

Charlie didn't speak as she stepped out and stood beside him. He made his way to the front door with her by his side and opened it.

Andrew jumped from the chair and swung around to the door. "Dad! What are you doing here?" He spotted the gun. "Why do you have a gun?"

Alan gasped in surprise as he pulled Charlie close. "Andrew." He instinctively lowered the weapon.

Charlie tried to twist from his grip. "Your dad is here because of what you did. You and Gary Lucado."

"Don't, Charlie. Don't talk to him." Alan moved closer with Charlie by his side. "Did Gary tell you to come here?"

Andrew nodded. "He said I needed to stay out of sight for a while."

"Why would he say that to you?" He held his son's gaze. "Was it you after all?"

Andrew stepped back. "What are you talking about?"

"Did you take those children?" Alan demanded.

"No. I don't know what you're talking about. Dad, come on, what is all this?"

"Were you working with Gary Lucado?" Charlie added. "If you can help your dad out of this mess, you should."

"I said don't talk to him." Alan pulled her toward the sofa. "Sit down."

"Is it true, son? Was this Gary's doing and you helped him? Did you hurt those children?"

Charlie watched in horror as it dawned on her that Alan had no real idea what his son was capable of doing. Her concern now was that Alan appeared to be on the end of a fraying rope and he was the one with the gun.

"Dad, I can explain." Andrew shoved his hands in his pockets.

"Explain? Explain that you abducted two children? Why, Andrew? Why would you hurt children?"

"I didn't hurt them, okay? Gary was the one who took them. He talked to them. He convinced them to follow. I don't know. I wasn't there."

"But you knew?" Alan asked.

Andrew nodded.

It made sense to Charlie now. Gary Lucado was the man with no hair that Tabitha recalled. She must've seen him in passing or maybe it really was her boy who led her down this path. Charlie was never one to believe in such things, but right now, it seemed to be the only explanation. "Did you help pick them out?"

Alan whipped around to her with his gun aimed at her head. "Please don't make me do something I don't want to do, Charlie. I told you to stop talking."

"You're innocent, Alan, just like I always knew you were. You can end this," she pressed on.

Alan closed his eyes and clenched his jaw. "Stop talking." He turned back to Andrew. "Is she right? Did you help him find these kids? Are there more?"

"No. No more. I swear to you, Dad. Something's wrong with Gary and I thought that if I didn't help him, he'd hurt you. I couldn't lose you after losing Mom. I just couldn't take that chance."

Charlie wanted to scream out and find out why he didn't just go to the police. Something about this wasn't right. Andrew had to be lying. He was putting all of it on Lucado. She closed her eyes while her chin quivered from the building fear. "Where are the children?"

———

SHANE SQUATTED BEHIND A LARGE SHRUB IN THE ADJACENT yard near the driveway and watched Alan direct Charlie inside the home. It took all of his strength not to burst in there and put an end to this, but he saw the gun. The risk was too great that Charlie would be hurt if he made a rash move. He had sent a text to Allison letting her know Charlie was there and the reply just came in.

"We're ten minutes away. Bryant says to sit tight. We have backup."

"Damn it. She could be dead in ten minutes." Shane's

emotions were driving him right now and that was never the way to go. But if something happened to Charlie and he stood by and did nothing, he'd never forgive himself. Allison would never forgive him either. "Ten minutes. Just wait ten minutes."

Shane moved as close as he could to the house without the risk of detection. He listened for raised voices but heard nothing. "Get your ass here, Bryant," he whispered.

Then, as if Bryant had heard Shane cursing his name, a car sounded in the distance. Shane stepped back, trying to look down the road and then he spotted them. With his eyes raised to the heavens, he mouthed, "Thank you."

———

BRYANT PICKED UP THE RADIO. "FELLAS, PARK IT WHERE you're at. We'll take it on foot from here. I don't want Chumbley getting spooked by cars racing up to his house." He unbuckled his seatbelt and turned back to Allison. "I know that if I tell you to stay put, you'll tell me to shove it up my ass, so I won't bother. But I will tell you this, stay close and listen to every word I say, you hear me?"

"Yes."

"Good. Now we know that Shane's up there a ways, so we'll need to split up. I'll have Santora's guys go around back. You and me, we'll go find Shane and get the lay of the land. He's scoped out the place. Let's see if he might know where they are inside that cabin."

Allison nodded.

"You sure you want to come with me?" He asked.

"I'm sure. She needs to know I'm here for her."

"Fine. But I'm telling you now, Allison, stay close and do whatever I tell you to do." Bryant jogged toward the two officers behind them and instructed them to take the rear entrance. He returned to Allison. "Let's go."

Allison stayed close to Bryant as they approached the front of the home. The rear of the property was unfenced and Santora's team headed back. Shane must've seen them as he peeked out from behind a tall shrub about 100 feet from the front of the cabin.

"You saw her?" Allison immediately asked Shane. "You know she's okay?"

"She's okay. There's been no indication of movement inside. No arguing. I have no idea what's been happening in there over the past several minutes." Shane turned to Bryant. "What's the plan?"

"I have two men heading around to the back entrance now. Santora's men. You and I will take the lead and move inside."

"Alan Chumbley is armed," Shane added. "He had a gun pointed at her when they walked in."

"Oh no." Allison covered her mouth.

"Hey, we'll get her out. The kid is in there and I don't think Chumbley senior is going to do anything stupid," Shane said.

"He kidnapped Charlie. That's high on my list of stupid things to do," Allison replied.

"We need to make this happen now." Bryant retrieved his sidearm. "Let's get her out of there."

———

CHARLIE REMAINED ON THE SOFA WHILE THE FATHER AND son appeared at an impasse. "It's not too late to stop this, Alan. I can say I came here voluntarily. You can end this now. They will come looking."

"Where's Gary now?" Alan asked his son. "Halfway to Mexico?"

"I don't know. He told me to come here and that was it. Dad, please, you have to believe me."

"How did you two do it? The boy from the mall in Tampa and the one from the school fair? Where did you take them?" Alan raised his gun to Andrew. "Don't lie to me, son."

Andrew's eyes grew wide as he raised his hands in defense. "I'm telling you, Dad. It was Gary. All of it was his idea."

"Then tell me what happened."

Charlie watched Andrew's expression. "He's lying, Alan. He was just as much a part of it as Gary. He's trying to come up with a story you'll believe."

Andrew shot her a look. "You're going to believe her? What is she like your girlfriend or something? Did you forget about Mom already?" He wiped away a tear that looked forced. "I didn't want to do it, Dad. I swear it. These kids, they were happy. I saw them with their parents. They had everything I used to have until Mom died. Why did they deserve a mom and not me? It wasn't fair."

Alan's hand trembled as he tried to keep the weapon aimed at his son. "What are you talking about?"

"You're so blind, Dad. You never talk about her. You hardly acknowledge that she existed."

"That's not true. I loved your mother," Alan replied.

"You pulled away from me and Alana. Why do you think she went out of state for college? She wanted to get away from you." Andrew's face reddened as his eyes welled. "Everyone thinks you're this meek little coin collector guy. But look at what you did with Gary? You're a crook."

"You don't know anything, son," Alan replied.

"I know about what you and Gary did at the mall with that other collector. I know you were forging certificates and making money off them. Did you know that Gary went back and threatened the man? Did you know that? I did. That was why he never pressed charges." Andrew turned to Charlie. "Whatever you think you know about him, think again."

"You're trying to blame me now? Maybe I did let myself get caught up with the wrong man, but that doesn't make me a killer," Alan said. "What you did..."

The front door crashed open and splintered along the frame. Charlie jumped at the sound. Alan spun toward the door.

"Police!" Bryant charged through the opened door with his weapon aimed and ready to fire. "Alan Chumbley, let her go. It's over."

Charlie turned to him with pleading eyes. "Please, Alan. There's no point in this anymore. Don't die for something you didn't do. What about your daughter, Alana? Forget about protecting your son or your friend. She needs her father."

Shane stood next to Bryant with his gun pointed to Andrew. "Whatever your boy did, you don't want it to end this way."

Alan turned back to Charlie and held her gaze. "You're right. I don't want it to end this way. I didn't want any of this. I couldn't save my wife. I resorted to fraud. I couldn't even raise my son to be a decent human being. Instead, I raised a monster." He put the gun to his temple.

Andrew lurched forward. "Dad, no!"

"No!" Charlie shouted.

"Put down the gun, Alan," Bryant demanded. "You don't want to do this in front of your son."

"Dad, please don't. I'll tell the cops everything. Just don't..."

The crack of the bullet rang out and Alan Chumbley collapsed to the ground.

Santora's men rushed inside, bursting through the rear entrance.

"It's okay," Bryant said. "He's down." He marched toward

Andrew. "You're under arrest for the kidnapping and murder of Hayden Barnes and Ian Nygard."

———

Allison waited outside the front of the home as Bryant had instructed, but when the shot rang out, she ran inside. "Charlie?"

"Alli, you're here." Charlie threw her arms around her. "He killed himself. Alan killed himself."

Allison squeezed her tight. "It's okay, Charlie. You're going to be okay. You're safe."

"I didn't think it would end like this," Charlie said, still holding onto her.

"I know you didn't. None of us could've known."

Shane approached them. "Let's head back to the station and make sure Lucy knows you're all safe."

Charlie pulled away from Allison and turned to Bryant. "What about Gary Lucado?"

"Santora will put out a BOLO on his truck. They'll find him. In the meantime, I need to stay here and secure the scene." He looked at the officers. "You fellas mind taking that one to the station?"

"Don't mind at all," one of the officers replied as he yanked on Andrew's arm.

Allison peered at Alan Chumbley's lifeless body only feet away. She turned to Charlie. "Come on, hon. Let's go."

28

I nside the Kissimmee police station, Lucy awaited their
return. It had been over an hour since Allison called to say
they were coming back. Dusk spilled into the lobby when
finally, relief welled in Lucy's chest at the sight of their arrival.
"Oh, thank God you're safe." She ran to Charlie and hugged her.

Charlie heard her sobs. "Hey, now. It's okay. I'm fine."

"I wanted to come and help..."

"I know. Alli told me. You did help, Lucy. You knew how to
get into my Facebook account. You were the one who found me."

"What happened? Where's Alan Chumbley?" Lucy asked.

Charlie cast down her gaze. "He took his own life. I don't think
he could accept what his son and best friend had done. Detective
Bryant is securing the scene and won't be back for a while."

"Santora sent along a team of officers. They have Andrew in
custody and should be here any minute. They left shortly after we
did." Allison inhaled a deep breath. "We still don't know what
happened to the missing boys."

Santora appeared from the hall as he made his way toward the

ACL team. "Charlie, I'm glad you're safe. Everyone was beside themselves with worry." He held her gaze. "Do you want to go to the hospital to get checked out?"

"No, thank you. I'm fine," she replied.

He nodded and turned his attention to Allison. "Once Andrew Chumbley arrives, we'll book him into custody."

"What about Gary Lucado?" she asked.

"Everyone's out looking for him. Don't worry, we'll catch up to him." He placed his hands on his thick waist. "In the meantime, I don't think there's anything more you ladies can do. But I will tell you, I'm humbled by your tenacity."

"We had help. Detectives Sullivan and Bryant make for good allies," Allison replied.

"Fair enough."

"Detective Santora," Charlie began. "We need to know what happened to Hayden Barnes and where he is now."

"Oh, I am well aware of that and I have a feeling the younger Chumbley will be cooperative."

"He's insisting it was Lucado's doing. That he only helped to protect his father," she added.

"I'd expect a desperate man to say such a thing. I assure you, Charlie, we will get to the bottom of this. Now, as I said, I think you all have done more than your fair share. You should head on back to Tampa. I'll be in touch just as soon as we get word on Lucado's whereabouts."

———

THE CORONER FINISHED LOADING THE BODY OF ALAN Chumbley into the truck while Detective Bryant cleared the rooms. He considered the idea that the bodies of the two children could be somewhere on the property and that may have been why

Lucado insisted Andrew come here. It felt like a set up to him and he needed answers before going back to the Kissimmee station.

"If there's nothing else, we're ready to go," the driver said.

"Go. I got it from here." Bryant waited for the truck to pull away before walking around to the back of the property. The sun was setting, and its rays shimmered on the lake's surface. He spotted the dock and as he turned back, a shed came into view.

It was secured with a padlock, so Bryant used the butt of his gun to break it open. Inside, a waft of warm and stale air hit him. He pulled the string on the light. The shed was all but empty. A tackle box, a few fishing rods. That was it. "Damn."

As he started back toward the cabin, Bryant noticed mounds of dirt along the side of the house. They appeared relatively fresh with only small weeds having emerged from the top. With his foot, he kicked away some of the material. Looked like he was going to need a shovel.

Once again, he searched the property only this time, in search of gardening tools. He made his way into the garage and spotted a shovel resting against a wall. "Here we go."

On his return to the mounds, Bryant dug, and it didn't take long for the odor to be exposed. His nose turned up at the smell. "For the love of God." When he squatted down, he knew what the smell was—death. He exposed the carcass of an animal and given its state of disfigurement and decay, the best he could figure was that it had been a cat. A mutilated cat.

He started into the next mound, uncovering a similarly disturbing scene. It didn't take long for him to figure out the four mounds contained the remains of mutilated animals. It took several more minutes before he exposed them completely and photographed each one. "Son of a bitch." Boot prints appeared nearby, and he photographed those too.

Bryant thought he knew who killed those children. He was

sure Lucado had attempted to frame the kid to take the rap. But with Charlie indicating the son had all but confessed, and now seeing this, odds were, these animals were the work of the younger Chumbley. It was almost textbook. It was as if Andrew Chumbley had seen this act depicted on some movie and decided to try it out, to take out his aggressions. Now, Bryant had no idea what to believe.

———

DETECTIVE BRYANT, THE LEAD INVESTIGATOR IN THE disappearance of five-year-old Hayden Barnes, stood next to his counterpart inside the interrogation room.

"It's only a matter of time before we catch up to your buddy, Lucado. You can deny your involvement all you want, but we have a witness who says you confessed. That's enough to put you away," Detective Santora said. "Do yourself a favor and tell us what you did with the bodies."

"I didn't do anything," Andrew began. "My dad just killed himself right in front of me."

"Because he couldn't bring himself to believe you murdered two children," Bryant added. "What a shame the only innocent person in all this, apart from the children, is dead and it's because of you." He paced inside the small room. "I hear your mom passed away a few years ago too. I wonder if she knew the kind of man you'd become and figured she was better off dead as well."

"Shut up. You don't know anything about my mom," Andrew snapped back.

"Then you got those dead animals," Bryant continued.

"What? What are you talking about?"

Bryant tossed the images onto the table. "Found these at the cabin. I'll bet when they go back to your house, they'll find the boots to match those prints."

"Well, that's how it starts, isn't it?" Santora began. "You should think carefully, Andrew. The cards are stacked against you. Let me ask you this, how did you lure little Ian? There were a lot of people at the fair. How did you get that young boy to go with you?"

Bryant snapped his fingers. "You know what? I'll bet it was those coins. What were they? Buffalo nickels or something like that?"

"I don't know what you're talking about. I didn't lure anyone," Andrew replied.

"Then you got the citation on your vehicle right near the school," Bryant added. "What were you doing there that day, huh? Scoping out your next victim? Look, it's going to be a very long night if you don't cooperate. We'll have to tell the judge you didn't help at all. That won't bode well for you when this goes to trial. Young, sporty-looking kid like you." Bryant eyed him. "They'll eat you alive in prison."

Andrew eyed them as he bit his lower lip. His leg bounced under the table in a nervous twitch.

An officer opened the door of the room. "Detective Santora, there's someone here I think you need to talk to."

Santora walked out. "Who is it?" He carried on into the halls of the station.

The officer didn't respond because as they made their way into the lobby, his question was answered."

"I don't know what that kid is telling you, but I had nothing to do with taking those children."

Santora nodded. "Mr. Lucado. You're a tough man to track down."

"Seeing three cop cars in my driveway made me think I wasn't going to have much choice but to clarify my position."

———

THE RIDE BACK TO THE ACL OFFICE WAS QUIET AS IT appeared Charlie was more distressed by what happened than she let on. Allison was just happy to have her back safely. "Detective Santora offered to have one of his officers drive your car back here in the morning." She peered at Charlie. "It'll be safe at the station overnight."

Charlie kept her gaze straight ahead as Allison parked in front of the office. "I'm not worried about my car."

"No, I'm sure you're not. I just thought..."

Charlie turned toward her from the passenger seat. "I was careless, Alli. I had it in my head that Alan Chumbley couldn't hurt a fly."

"He was faced with a terrible knowledge," Lucy said from the backseat. "You couldn't have known how he would react."

"It's my job to know, Lucy. You would've thought I'd have learned my lesson after dealing with drug runners and corrupt mayors." She closed her eyes. "What would my boys have done if something had happened to me?"

Allison placed her hand on Charlie's thigh. "But nothing did."

"You know, I think your dad was right, Lucy. I think this line of work changes you." Charlie stepped out of the car and while Allison stepped out to join her, she continued, "I'm not going home until I know they found Gary Lucado."

"Okay." Allison nodded. "Then I'll stay with you."

"Me too," Lucy added.

They made their way upstairs and Allison unlocked the door. "I'll let Shane know we're back. I think he said he was heading to the downtown station when Bryant had things under control." At her desk, Allison sent him a text message. "Are you guys hungry?"

Charlie shook her head and dropped onto her chair.

"I don't feel up to eating right now." Lucy returned to her desk.

"Sure." Allison's phone buzzed with a returned message. Upon reading it, her eyes widened, and she looked to Charlie. "They have Lucado. Shane said he returned to his house where they took him into custody."

Charlie jumped from her chair. "Did he say what happened to the boys?"

His message just says that Bryant and Santora are talking to him now. He says he'll keep us posted. This is good news, Charlie."

Charlie revealed a hint of a smile. "Yeah. Best news I've heard all day."

———

GARY LUCADO SLUMPED LOW IN THE CHAIR IN ANOTHER interrogation room, appearing merely inconvenienced by the situation. "Look, do you plan on charging me with something because I'm getting the feeling I don't want to talk anymore without a lawyer present."

"Andrew Chumbley says you're the ringleader. That it was all your idea and you took the kids," Bryant said. "So tell me where they are and things will go much smoother for you, otherwise, no deal. Chumbley went to your cabin. Is that where you took them? Or we can just wait until the cops are finished turning the place over. I found the dead animals. Not much of a stretch to think the kids' bodies are there too."

"Yeah, it's my place, but I let Alan use it whenever, you know.

And his kid. Look, that boy has issues, you know what I'm saying? I tried to help him. Tried to keep him out of trouble for Alan's sake, but damn, he's messed up in the head. Something went off in him after his mom died. I saw the animals, yeah. In fact, I confronted Andrew about them. He promised to go back and dispose of them and said he'd get some help. I trusted that was what he was going to do. I'm not some monster, Detective. I was only trying to help the kid."

"If he was so messed up, why didn't you tell your friend, Alan?" Bryant asked.

"Have you met Alan Chumbley? The guy was so scared of his own shadow, it would've sent him over the edge. I figured Andrew would snap out of it, you know? Then all this shit come up about Alan abducting some kids," Lucado replied. "Didn't make any damn sense at all. All's I knew was that you all were trying to pin it on Alan. I tried to help him out of some money problems, that's it."

"That was the deal, right?" Bryant asked. "You took a cut of the profits from his fraudulent certifications? Santora's people had a chance to look into Alan's finances. Your name shows up a whole lot."

"So? Doesn't make me a killer," Lucado replied.

"No, but it makes you someone who would do what he could to keep the gravy train going. Hiding the truth about your partner's son?" Bryant walked around the table. "What about those buffalo nickels?"

"What?"

"Did you know that we found buffalo nickels at both crime scenes?" he continued.

Lucado raised his hands. "Wait. Hold on. Yeah, I had some worthless buffalo nickels, but I gave them to Andrew. We were up playing cards long after Alan went to bed one night and I used them to gamble with. Kid cleaned me out. You found buffalo nickels, they weren't mine. Sounds like you all are reaching."

Bryant stood up and walked out of the room. He knocked on the door where Santora still questioned Andrew Chumbley. When Santora opened it, Bryant began. "A word."

The two convened in the hall. Bryant crossed his arms and widened his stance. "They're pointing the finger at each other. Are you getting any further with the kid?"

Santora shook his head. "No. Like you said, he's laying the blame on Lucado."

"And we don't have a lick of hard evidence either one of these guys did the crime," Bryant added. "Charlie heard him confess, but any lawyer could say Andrew did that to stop his father from taking his own life."

"That won't be nearly enough." Santora appeared to think on the matter. "Why don't you come in with me for a minute. Let Lucado stew. I want to try something."

"I'm game." Bryant followed Santora back into the interrogation room and let Santora take the lead.

"You know, kid," Santora began. "I am sorry about what happened to your dad. But as it turns out, your father wasn't the man we thought he was. Turns out, he was a stone-cold killer."

The 25-year-old sat back in the chair and brushed away a rogue tear as if it hadn't mattered.

Bryant caught onto the game pretty quickly. "We know you were at the crime scenes with your father and Gary Lucado. We have witnesses. We also know that the abductor used the buffalo coins to get their attention. Something new they'd never seen before."

The kid shrugged.

"Your pops put a bullet in his brain. I have to assume he had a part in all of it. I'm thinking maybe he was the killer after all, and you're just an innocent in all this," Santora continued. "That's what the media will say. Guess you don't mind folks around here thinking he was a killer."

The kid's face shifted, and he swallowed hard. "What do you want from me?"

"The truth, Andrew. You want it to go down this way or are you going to be a man?" Santora asked. "Your buddy, Lucado, he's got a pretty solid alibi. That just leaves you and your dad."

Bryant threw onto the table a photo of Alan Chumbley lying on the floor with blood pooled around his head. "You did this to your dad."

The kid stared at the picture. His bottom lip quivered, and his eyes reddened. "I want a lawyer."

Bryant glanced at Santora. "Yeah. That's what we thought."

———

THE ACL TEAM ARRIVED AT THE DOWNTOWN TAMPA stationhouse to meet with Detective Bryant. Tabitha and Erik Barnes were being brought in by one of the officers and they were ready to deliver the news.

"Thanks for coming down this morning," Bryant said. "How are you holding up, Charlie?"

"Doing better, thanks."

"Good. I'm glad to hear it. It was quite an ordeal you went through."

"I have you to thank for my safety," she replied.

"At the end of the day, I don't believe Alan Chumbley would've hurt you. But you took quite a risk."

"I know I did. What can I say? My feminine wiles were at their peak. I couldn't squander the opportunity," she replied.

Allison grinned because it was a good sign that Charlie drew on her wit for a quick retort. It was what she had come to expect and hoped it would always be there. She relied on it.

"Detective?" An officer walked into Bryant's office. "Tabitha and Erik Barnes are here." He stepped aside to let them in. "Go ahead."

"Thank you." Tabitha walked inside with her soon to be ex-husband. She immediately looked to the women. "Thank you. All of you. Thank you for believing me."

"These ladies did a hell of a job exposing the truth," Bryant began. "Please sit down. I want to start by telling you that however your memories of that day were brought forward, I'm glad as hell they were. I didn't know what to think of all of it at first, but Allison and her team knew right away what needed to be done. I'm grateful." He inhaled a breath. "Andrew Chumbley was the man who took your son."

Erik grabbed Tabitha's hand as they sat across from the detective.

"He worked real hard at pointing the finger at someone else, but we got to the bottom of it. The boy wasn't able to handle the death of his mother a few years' back. He spiraled down, doing things that should've raised red flags. Finally got himself to the point of blaming other kids for having happy homes. Like they somehow didn't deserve it because he didn't have his mom anymore." Bryant glanced at Allison and turned back. "The bald-headed man you recalled? He was in the store with you and your son.

"He was the man I bumped into. I remember now," Tabitha said.

"Turned out, Lucado was only talking to the boy and nothing more," Bryant added.

"I don't understand," she continued.

"Well, when Gary Lucado walked away from your son after

that brief encounter, your son's attention was drawn to another, and that was Andrew Chumbley. Chumbley waited for Lucado to leave and coaxed your boy into showing him some toys in another section of the store. Then we figured he offered up one of his coins to keep him interested."

"Hayden knew not to go with strangers, Detective. We already taught him that," Erik replied.

"I'm sure you did, Erik. But kids at that age, hell, at most ages, they don't fully comprehend the dangers that lurk."

"You say this man, Andrew Chumbley took our son. Where? Where is he?" Tabitha asked.

"I'm afraid not far from the mall." Bryant looked at Allison as if this was the part he dreaded the most. When he turned back to the Barnes', he gathered his strength. "There's a pond behind that old mall, oh, I'd say about a few hundred feet away."

"Yes. I remember you looked there first thing." Tabitha pressed her hand against her mouth. "Did you find him in there?"

"There's a dive team out there now. We'll know soon, but that is what the suspect told us. There was another abduction a few months ago, over in Kissimmee. He confessed to that one too. So far as we know, those were his only victims. Mr. and Mrs. Barnes, the man who murdered your son will spend the rest of his life in prison. I'm sure that's little in the way of consolation, but...."

"It will help us move on." Tabitha peered at Erik. "We needed to know for sure and now we do."

———

To say that the past couple of weeks had been trying for the team at ACL would have been the understatement of the year. It had been their most difficult case yet in terms of how close it had hit home. It had changed all of them. Made them wiser, less trusting, and probably a little more cynical than they were before. That was more so for Lucy, the youngest member of the team. Then again, she'd been around this stuff since she was in diapers. Allison believed she was probably the most resilient of them all.

"What I don't get is why they didn't find Hayden in that pond the first time," Charlie asked as the three headed downstairs to see Shane.

"I asked Bryant that very question when he called me last night to deliver the news," Allison replied. "He said they had searched it that day and then the next day too when they brought in divers."

"And they didn't find him?" Lucy asked, trailing the other two on the steps.

"No. There had been a heavy storm a few days earlier that made for a lot of runoff into the pond. I guess it kicked up sediment and made the water just too murky. By the time it cleared, they'd already moved the investigation into another direction."

"I'm sure that'll haunt Bryant for some time to come," Charlie replied.

"I have no doubt." Allison reached the bottom steps and headed to Shane's desk.

He gazed up at them. "You guys are finished up there? How did the parents take it?"

"About as good as could be expected," Allison replied. "I think they're relieved it's finally over and they can bury their son."

Shane nodded. "I imagine so." He peered at Allison. "Can I talk to you for a minute—alone?"

Charlie raised her hands in surrender. "Don't mind us. We'll get out of your hair. Lucy, let's go grab a soda from the kitchen."

After they disappeared, Allison sat down. "What is it?"

"After all that happened yesterday, when I got back here later in the evening, I met with Baylor. Allison, we got what we needed."

She sat fully upright. "Reddick?"

He nodded. "His ex flipped on him. Baylor brought her in and got a statement. I pulled the evidence we had gathered first thing this morning. We kept it in a safe deposit box."

"That was smart. What happens now?"

"We met with an agent Baylor knew from way back at the FBI field office here. That was at about 6 o'clock this morning."

"Can you trust him?" Allison asked.

"I was hesitant, but Baylor insisted it was our best shot. Better to keep it out of this department anyway. I have a feeling whoever was on Reddick's side might've suspected what we were up to and used their connections here to issue warnings."

"Doesn't that make you concerned about Lieutenant Duran who's supposed to be your new boss?"

"I'll keep my guard up," he added. "Once the truth comes to light, I'm pretty sure Duran and anyone else who thought Reddick was being railroaded will distance themselves from him. He won't have any friends left after this. This whole situation has been a risk, but I did the right thing. I did my job and I have you to thank."

"I didn't do anything. In fact, I washed my hands of it."

"And I understand why you did. Allison, you're not a cop. It wasn't your job to police the FBI. Hell, it wasn't really my job either, but I am a cop."

"What do you think this will mean for your move upstairs?" she asked.

"Like I said, I'll have to see how it plays out, but Duran would be risking a lot if after he already promised me the position, he walked it back. But who knows? We'll find out."

"I'm proud of what you did, Shane." Allison smiled. "All

you've done for me, for the agency, and now this?" She hesitated, "Shane, I..."

"What?" he asked.

"Just... thank you for everything." She cleared her throat. "We were thinking about going out for dinner tonight to release some of the stress of the case, to try to move on from it. I'd like you to be there. You helped and I know the girls would want you there too." Allison turned back and spotted Charlie and Lucy headed her way. "Shane's going to join us tonight."

Charlie rolled her eyes. "Again? Fine. You know you hang out with us so much, we should make you an honorary member. We should get you a badge that says, 'Junior Investigator.' That settles it. I'm ordering it today."

There it was again, Allison thought. Charlie was coming back. It would take a while for all of them to get past this one, but in time, she knew they would.

"Better order it for yourself too, little one," Shane replied.

Charlie smiled. "That's more like it."

"Hey, Lucy, if you want to bring Logan, that'd be fine too," Allison said.

She cast down her gaze. "I'm not seeing him anymore. We weren't right for each other."

"Oh. Okay." Allison regarded her for a moment, but decided it was better to let it go. "Then it'll just be the four of us."

"What? I don't get to bring a date?" Shane winked at Charlie.

She nodded in reply. "Nice one, Sully."

"Just be there at 7, okay?" Allison chuckled. "Let's get out of here, and let the man do his job."

They headed toward the exit.

Shane watched them walk away until Bryant captured his attention.

"Sully?"

"Hey, you wrapped things up?" Shane asked him.

"Just about." Bryant moved in. "I hear you and Baylor caught a big break, huh?"

Shane peered at him with uncertainty but said nothing.

Bryant patted him on the back. "Glad it all worked out for you, Sully. Isabella's better off anyhow." He turned away and started up the stairs.

Shane's mouth fell agape, unable to find the words. He eventually smiled. "Huh."

———

ALLISON WAS JUST ABOUT AT THE DOOR WHEN SHE STOPPED and turned back to see Shane at his desk.

"What? Did you forget something?" Charlie asked as she walked beside her.

"No. Sorry, it's nothing," Allison replied.

"Nothing, huh?" Charlie pushed back her shoulders and continued. "I knew you'd come around eventually. He's a good guy, Alli."

Charlie might've been right this time. Leo had moved on. Maybe it was time for Allison to move on too.

THE END

ABOUT THE AUTHOR

Robin Mahle has published more than 30 crime fiction novels, many, of which, topped the Amazon charts in the US, Canada, and the UK. And most recently, she has delved into the world of psychological thrillers.

Also a screenwriter, she has adapted some of her works into teleplays, which have gone on to place in film festivals nationwide.

From detectives to federal agents, and from killers to corruption, her page-turning tales grab hold and refuse to let go. Throw in tense action and thrilling twists, and it becomes clear why her readers come back for more.

Robin lives in Coastal Virginia with her husband and two children.

If you enjoyed Ms. Mahle's work, please share your experience by leaving a review on <u>Amazon.</u>

ALSO BY ROBIN MAHLE

The Kate Reid FBI Thriller Series (17 books)

The Chef (stand-alone psych thriller)

The Man in My Attic (stand-alone psych thriller)

The Compound (standalone psych thriller)

The Remy Fontaine Fugitive Hunter Thrillers (4 books)

The Det. Rebecca Ellis Thrillers (5 books)

The Allison Hart PI Thrillers (5 Books)

The Lacy Merrick Thrillers (4 books)

**Visit robinmahle.com and sign up to receive Robin's Newsletter so you can stay up to date on her new releases, events, contests and even exclusive new material!

www.ingramcontent.com/pod-product-compliance
Lightning Source LLC
Chambersburg PA
CBHW061130200626
46817CB00016B/597